spontaneous

also by aaron starmer:

Meme

spontaneous

aaron starmer

PENGUIN BOOKS

PENGUIN BOOKS
An imprint of Penguin Random House LLC, New York

First published in the United States of America by Dutton Books,
an imprint of Penguin Random House LLC, 2016
Published by Penguin Books, an imprint of Penguin Random House LLC, 2020

Visit us online at penguinrandomhouse.com.

LIBRARY OF CONGRESS CATALOGING-IN-PUBLICATION DATA IS AVAILABLE.

Printed in the United States of America

Penguin Books ISBN 9780147517708

1 3 5 7 9 10 8 6 4 2

Edited by Julie Strauss-Gabel
Design by Theresa Evangelista
Text set in Chronicle Text

To the ones who feel like it could all come apart at any moment . . .

and to the ones who comfort us and keep us together

spontaneous

Call the death by any name Your Highness will,
attribute it to whom you will,
or say it might have been prevented how you will.
It is the same death eternally—inborn, inbred,
engendered in the corrupted humours of the vicious body itself,
and that only—Spontaneous Combustion,
and none other of all the deaths that can be died.

charles dickens

Bleak House

how it started

When Katelyn Ogden blew up in third period pre-calc, the janitor probably figured he'd only have to scrub guts off one whiteboard this year. Makes sense. In the past, kids didn't randomly explode. Not in pre-calc, not at prom, not even in chem lab, where explosions aren't exactly unheard of. Not one kid. Not one explosion. Ah, the good old days.

Katelyn Ogden was a lot of things, but she wasn't particularly explosive, in any sense of the word. She was wispy, with a pixie cut and a breathy voice. She was a sundress of a person—cute, airy, inoffensive. I didn't know her well, but I knew her well enough to curse her adorable existence on more than one occasion. I'm not proud of it, but it's true. Doesn't mean I wanted her to go out the way she did, or that I wanted her to go out at all, for that matter. Our thoughts aren't always our feelings; and when they are, they rarely last.

On the morning that Katelyn, well, *went out,* I was sitting two seats behind her. It was September, the first full week of school, an absolute stunner of a day. The windows were open and the faraway drone of a John Deere mixed with the nearby drone of Mr. Mellick philosophizing on factorials. Worried I had coffee breath, I was bent over in my seat, digging through my purse for mints. My POV was therefore limited, and the only parts of Katelyn I saw explode were her legs. Actually, it's hard to say what I saw. Her legs were there and then they weren't.

Wa-bam!

The classroom quaked and my face was suddenly warm and wet. It's a disgusting way to say it, but it's the simplest way to say it: Katelyn was a balloon full of fleshy bits. And she popped.

You can't feel much of anything in a moment like that. You certainly can't analyze the situation. At least not while it's happening. Later, the image will play over and over in your head, like some demon GIF, like some creeper who slips into your bed every single night, taps you on the shoulder, and says, "Remember me, the worst fucking moment of your life up to this point?" Later, you'll feel and do a lot of things, but when it's actually happening, all you can feel is confusion and all you do is react.

I bolted upright and my head hit my desk. Mr. Mellick dove behind his chair like a soldier into the trenches. My red-faced classmates sat there in shock for a few moments. Blood dripped down the windows and walls. Then came the screaming and the obligatory rush for the door.

The next hour was insane. Hunched running, hands up, sirens blaring, kids in the parking lot hugging. News trucks, helicopters,

SWAT teams, cars skidding out in the grass because the roads were clogged. No one even realized what had happened. "Bomb! Blood! Run for the fucking hills!" That was the extent of it. There was no literal smoke, but when the figurative stuff cleared, we could be sure of only two things.

Katelyn Ogden blew up. Everyone else was fine.

Except we weren't. Not by a long shot.

let's be clear

This is not about Katelyn Ogden. She was important—all of them were—but she was also a signpost, a starting point on a path of self-discovery. I realize how corny and conceited that sounds, but the focus of this should be on me and what you ultimately think of me. Do you like me? Do you trust me? Will you still be interested in me after I say what I have to say?

Yes, yes. I know, I know. "It's not important what people think of you, it's who you are that counts." Well, don't buy into that crap. Perception trumps reality. Always and forever. Simply consider what people thought of Katelyn. Mr. Mellick once told Katelyn that she "would make an excellent anchorwoman," which was a coded way of saying that she spoke well and, though it wasn't clear if she was part black or part Asian or part Hispanic, she was pretty in a nonthreatening, vaguely ethnic way.

In reality, Katelyn Ogden was Turkish. Not part anything. Plain old Turkish. Her family's original name was Özden, but they changed it somewhere along the line. Her dad was born right here in New Jersey, and so was her mom, but they both had full Turkish blood that went back to the early Ottoman Empire, which, as far as empires go, was a pretty badass one. Their armies were among the first to employ guns and cannons, so they knew a thing or two about things that go boom.

Katelyn's dad was an engineer and her mom was a lawyer and they drove a Tahoe with one of those stick-figure-family stickers on the back window. Two parents, one kid, two dogs. I'm not entirely sure what the etiquette is, but I guess you keep the kid sticker on your window even ... after. The Ogdens did, in any case.

I learned all the familial details at the memorial service, which was closed casket, for obvious reasons, and which was held in State Street Theater, also for obvious reasons. Everyone in school *had* to attend. It wasn't required by law, but absences would be noted. Not by the authorities necessarily, but by the kids who were quick to label their peers *misogynistic assholes* or *heartless bitches*. I know because I was one of those label-happy kids. Again, I'm not necessarily proud of that fact, but I certainly can't deny it.

The memorial service was quite a production, considering that it was put together in only a few days. Katelyn's friend Skye Sanchez projected a slideshow whose sole purpose was to remind us how ridiculously effervescent Katelyn was. There was a loving eulogy delivered by a choked-up aunt. A choir sang Katelyn's favorite song, which is a gorgeous song. The lyrics were a bit sexy for the occasion, but who cares, right? It was her favorite and if they can't play your favorite song at your memorial service then when the hell can they play it? Plus, it was all about saying good-bye at the wrong moment, and at least that was appropriate for the occasion.

There's a line in it that goes, "your hair upon the pillow like a sleepy golden storm..." Katelyn's hair was short and dark, the furthest thing from sleepy and golden, but that didn't matter to Jed Hayes, who had a crush on her going all the way back to middle school. That hair-upon-the-pillow line made him blubber so loud that everyone in the balcony felt obligated to nod condolences at the poor guy. His empathy seemed off the charts, but if we're being honest with ourselves—and we really should be—then we have to accept that Jed wasn't crying because he truly loved Katelyn. It was because her storm of hair never hit his pillow. Sure, it's a selfish thing to cry about, but we all cry about selfish things at funerals. We all cry about "if only."

- If only Katelyn had made it through to next year, then she would have gone to Brown. She was going to apply early decision and was guaranteed to get in. No question that's partly why her SAT tutor, Mrs. Carbone, was sobbing. All those hours, all those vocab flash cards, and for what? Mrs. Carbone still couldn't claim an Ivy Leaguer as a past student.

- If only Katelyn had scammed a bit more cash off her parents, then she would have bought more weed. It was well-known among us seniors that Katelyn usually had a few joints hidden in emptied-out mascara tubes that she stashed in the glove box of her Volvo. It was also well-known that she was quickly becoming the drug-dealing Dalton twins' best customer. Such a loss was surely why the Daltons were a bit weepy. Capitalism isn't an emotionless endeavor.

- If only Katelyn had the chance to accept his invitation to the prom, then she would have ended up with her hair upon Jed Hayes's pillow. It was within the realm of possibility. He wasn't a bad-looking guy and she was open-minded. You couldn't begrudge the kid his tears.

That's merely the beginning of the list. The theater was jam-packed with selfish people wallowing in "if only." Meanwhile, outside the theater, other selfish people had moved on and were already wallowing in "but why?"

As you might guess, when a girl blows up in pre-calc and that girl is Turkish, "but why?" is fraught with certain preconceived notions. It can't be "just one of those things." It has to be a "terrorist thing." That was what the cable-news folks were harrumphing, and the long-fingernailed women working the checkout at Target were gabbing, and the potbellied picketers standing outside the theater were hollering.

Never mind the fact that no one else was hurt when Katelyn exploded. We were all examined. Blood was taken. Questions were asked. Mr. Mellick's class was considered healthy, if not in mind, then in body. We were considered innocent.

Never mind the fact that there wasn't a trace of anything remotely explosive found in the classroom. The police did a full sweep of it, the school, Katelyn's house, the nearest park, and a halal restaurant two towns over. They didn't find a thing. FBI was there too, swabbing everything with Q-tips. Collective shrugs all around.

Never mind "if only." A girl with so much potential doesn't suicide-bomb it all away. She just doesn't. Sure, she smoked weed, and if the rumors were true, she was slacking off in pre-calc and fighting with her mom, but that's not because senior year was her year to blow things up. It was her year to blow things off, perhaps her last chance in life to say fuck it.

It was a lot of people's last chance to say fuck it, as it turned out.

how you feel

To describe how you feel after a girl explodes in your pre-calc class is a tad tricky. I imagine it's similar to how you feel when any tragedy comes hurtling into your life. You're scared. You're fragile. You flinch. All the time. You may have never even thought about what holds life together. Until, of course, it comes apart.

Same with our bodies. You can imagine cancer and other horrible things wreaking havoc on our doughy shells, but you don't ever expect our doughy shells to, quite literally, disintegrate. So when the unimaginable happens, when the cosmos tears into your very notion of what's possible, it's not that you become jaded; it's that you become unsure. Unsure that you'll ever be sure about anything ever again.

You get what I'm saying, right? No? Well, you will.

For now, maybe it's easier to speak about practicalities, to describe what exactly happens after a girl explodes in your pre-calc class. You get the rest of the day off from school, and the rest of the week too. You talk to the cops on three separate occasions, and Sheriff Tibble looks at you weird when you don't whimper as much as the guy they interviewed before you. You are asked to attend private therapy sessions with a velvet-voiced woman named Linda and, if you want, group therapy sessions with a leather-voiced man named Vince and some of the other kids who witnessed the spontaneous combustion.

That's what they were calling it in the first few weeks: spontaneous combustion. I had never heard of such a thing, but there was a precedent for it—for people catching fire, or exploding, with little-to-no explanation. Now, unless you've been living in the jungles of New Guinea for the last year, you already know all this, but if you want a refresher on the history of spontaneous combustion, head on over to Wikipedia. Skip the section on "The Covington Curse" if you want the rest of this story to be spoiler-free.

From Linda, I learned that it was normal to feel completely lost when a girl spontaneously combusts in your pre-calc class. Because in those first few weeks I'd find myself crying all of sudden, and then making really inappropriate jokes the next moment, and then going about the rest of the day like it was all no big deal.

"When something traumatic happens, you fire your entire emotional arsenal," Linda told me. "A war is going on inside of you, and I'm here to help you reload and make more targeted attacks. I'm here to help the good guys win."

At the group sessions, Vince didn't peddle battlefront metaphors. He hardly spoke at all. He simply repeated his mantra: "Talk it out, kids. Talk it out."

So that's what we did. Half of us "kids" from third period

pre-calc met in the media room every Tuesday and Thursday at four, and we shared our stories of insomnia and chasing away bloody visions with food and booze and all sorts of stuff that therapists can't say shit about to your parents because they have a legal obligation to keep secrets.

Nutty as she was, Linda helped. So did Vince. So did the rest of my blood-obsessed peers, even the ones who occasionally called me insensitive on account of my sense of humor.

"Sorry, but my cell is blowing . . . spontaneously combusting," I announced during a Thursday session when my phone kept vibrating with texts. It had been only six weeks since we'd all worn Katelyn on our lapels. In other words, too soon.

"I realize that jokes are a form of coping," Claire Hanlon hissed at me. "But tweet them or something. We don't need to hear them here."

"Sorry but I don't tweet," I told her.

That said, I did fancy myself a writer. Long form, though. I had even started a novel that summer. I titled it *All the Feels*. I think it was young adult fiction, what some might call paranormal romance. I didn't care, as long as I could sell the movie rights. Which didn't seem like an impossibility. The story was definitely relatable. It was about a teenage boy who was afraid of his own emotions. In my experience, that summed up not only teenage boys, but teenagers in general. Case in point:

"This is a healing space and that makes it a joke-free zone," Claire went on. "I don't want to relive that moment and you're liable to give me a flashback."

"I like Mara's jokes," Brian Chen responded. "They help me

remember it's okay to smile. I don't know if I'd still be coming to these things if it wasn't for Mara."

"Thank you, Bri," I said, and at that point I began to realize that we were a bit of a cliché. Stories about troubled teenagers often feature support groups where smart-ass comments fly and feelings get hurt, where friends and enemies are forged over one-liners and tears. But here's the thing. Even if we were a bit of a cliché, we were only a cliché for a bit. Because almost immediately after announcing his dedication to my humor, Brian Chen blew up.

sorry

I did that on purpose. I didn't give you much of a chance to know Brian and then I was all, like, "Oh yeah, side note, that dude exploded too." I understand your frustrations. Because he seemed like a nice guy, right? He was. Undoubtedly. One of the nicest guys around. He didn't deserve his fate.

That's the thing. When awful fates snatch people away, sometimes it happens to someone you know a little and sometimes it happens to someone you know a lot, and in order to shield yourself from the emotional shrapnel, it's better to know those someones a little. So I was trying to do you a solid, by getting the gory details out of the way from the get-go. Unfortunately, you won't always have that luxury. Because to understand my story, you're going to have to get to know at least a few people, including a few who blow up.

A bit about Brian, because he deserves a bit. He was half Korean and half Chinese. I'm not sure which half was which,

which is racist I guess. I don't doubt that Brian knew that Carlyle is an English name while McNulty is an Irish name, but all these months later and I still can't be bothered to find out if Chen is Korean or Chinese in origin. I know. I'm a total dick. As I said, I'm not necessarily proud of it.

Thing is, I liked Brian. I even kissed him once. On the eighth grade trip to Washington, DC, we were in the back of the bus and he rested his head on my shoulder. We weren't good friends or anything, but it was one of those moments. Hot bus. Long drive. All of us tired and woozy.

When no one was looking, I kissed him on the lips. No tongue, but I held it for a couple of seconds. It was more than a peck. I did it because I thought it would feel nice. His lips seemed so soft. And it did feel nice. And soft. But Brian pretended to be asleep, even though it was obvious he was awake. My elbow was touching his chest and I felt his heart speed up. So I also pretended to be asleep, because that's what you do when you kiss a guy and he pretends to be asleep. You follow suit, or you end up embarrassing yourself even more.

We went on with our lives after that. Went to the Smithsonian Air and Space Museum, the Washington Monument, the Pentagon. Then we went home. We didn't talk about what I did. Which was fine by me. Brian didn't spread rumors or try to take advantage of the situation. Like I said, one of the nicest guys around. He still smiled at me in the hall, used my name when he saw me.

"Good to see you, Mara."

"How'd that bio test turn out, Mara?"

"Can I offer you a baby carrot, Mara?"

Brian liked baby carrots. Loved them, actually. Ate them all the time. Raw. Unadorned. No dip or peanut butter or anything to make them taste less carroty. He kept a bag of them in his backpack and munched his way through life. I don't know if it was an addiction or a discipline, but either way you kind of had to respect it.

What you didn't have to respect was that he wore the same pair of filthy neon-blue sneakers everywhere, even to dances and Katelyn's memorial service. He called them his "laser loafers," a term that didn't catch on, as he'd obviously hoped it would. He'd gone viral once and figured he could harness that magic again. It doesn't work that way, though.

Viral, you ask? The boy went viral? In a manner of speaking, yes. Because Brian Chen was the proud creator of Covington High's favorite catchphrase: "Wrap it up, short stuff!"

It was dumb luck, really. He had first said it during a group presentation in English class when the five-foot-two-inch Will Duncan kept blabbing on and on about how sad it was that Sylvia Plath "offed herself by sticking her head in the oven because she was actually pretty hot, in addition to being crazy talented."

"Wrap it up, short stuff!" Brian blurted out to shut his pal up and everybody lost their shit. By the end of the week, "Wrap it up, short stuff!" was something we said to long-winded people. Then we started hollering it at my parents' deli to the guys who literally wrapped up the sandwiches. Then we started using it as shorthand for "please use a condom or else you're gonna end up with a baby or a disease, basically something that will ruin your life."

I know. Wrap it up, short stuff.

So, yeah, Brian Chen was a nice guy. A carroty guy with soft lips, filthy sneakers, and a catchphrase. Now you know him, and I hope you understand that when I make jokes about him and the other people who were here and gone in an instant, it's because of a billion things that are wrong with me. But it's not because they deserve it.

what was wrong with us

Here's what happens when a guy blows up during your group therapy session that's supposed to make you feel better about people blowing up. The group therapy session is officially canceled. You do not feel better.

What also happens is all nine remaining members of the group therapy session are escorted to the police station in an armored vehicle. With Katelyn, they let us shower before the cops got involved, but no such luck with Brian. It was too much of a coincidence. Same group of people, same *wa-bam*.

This wasn't terrorism. Or, to be more accurate, Brian wasn't a suicide bomber. Around here, nobody thinks an East Asian person would be a terrorist. Which is silly, really, because East Asia has plenty of terrorists. Back in the nineties, there were a bunch of Japanese terrorists who filled a subway station with poison gas and killed a shit-ton of people. No Turk has pulled off something that audacious, as far as I know. It's definitely racist to think that Katelyn was a terrorist and Brian wasn't.

But that's what people thought. Or they thought someone else in our class was behind both incidents. So the cops shuffled us precalc, group-therapy saps into a conference room where we sat, bloody and stunned, under awful fluorescent bulbs that flickered every few seconds.

"Gahhh!" Becky Groves screamed as soon as the cops left us alone. They had gathered in the hall to talk to some FBI agents. To strategize, I guess.

"Let 'em cool their heels a bit," they were probably saying as they blew on their coffee. "Get their stories straight and then, blammo, we'll work the old McKenzie Doubleback on these perps."

Yes, yes, I know, I know. There's no such thing as the "McKenzie Doubleback," but I'm sure they have names for their interrogation techniques.

Anyway, once Becky Groves was done screaming—which was a few seconds later because she's Becky Groves and she has the lungs of a water buffalo—Claire Hanlon said, "So who did it?"

"Really?" I replied.

"Really!" Claire snapped. "The police know this can't be a coincidence . . . and I know this can't be a coincidence . . . and I know I didn't do it . . . and so it has to be one of you." An aneurysm seemed imminent the way Claire was panting out the words.

"How?" Malik Deely asked.

"However . . . people like you . . . do these sorts of things," Claire said.

You don't use the term "people like you" around people like

Malik (that is, black people), but he had a cool-enough head to let logic beat out emotion.

"Seriously?" he said. "Seriously? There was no bomb. The guy's chair was completely intact. Becky was sitting right next to him and she's fine."

"Gahhh!" Becky screamed again, this time with her eyes squeezed shut and her hands clawing at her frizzy red hair.

"Physically fine, I mean," Malik said. "We all are. Something inside these kids just . . . *went off.*"

Greyson Hobbs, Maria Hermanez, Gabe Carlton, Yuki Dolan, and Chris Welch were all in the room too, but they weren't saying anything. Their perplexed eyes kept darting back and forth as we spoke. It was like they were foreign tourists who'd stumbled into a courtroom. They weren't trying to figure out who was innocent or guilty. All they wanted to know was "How the hell did we end up in this place? Which way is the way back to Disney World?"

When the door opened, those perplexed eyes all darted to Special Agent Carla Rosetti of the FBI. I would learn later that she wasn't necessarily the best and brightest, but at that moment, compared to our schlumpy local boys-in-blue, she looked like the real goddamn deal.

She stood in the doorway decked out in a white shirt, dark blazer, dark pants, and dark pumps. Standard FBI attire, I assumed, though a bit baggier than what the chicks on TV rocked. The clothes were obviously chain-store bought, but from a nice chain store. Ann Taylor or something. Even without the outfit, her name was Carla Rosetti and how could she not be an ass-kicking federal agent with a name like that?

"Your parents are here to collect you," Special Agent Carla Rosetti said as she stepped into the room. "But first you will be surrendering your clothing. There are showers and sweat suits. You'll wash down, dress up, and go home. You'll be hearing from us tomorrow morning."

"No. *You* will be hearing from *my lawyer*. *Tonight*," Claire said. "I have rights, you know?"

"I never said you didn't," Special Agent Carla Rosetti remarked. "I simply asked you to give me my evidence, evidence I obtained a warrant to collect. The alternative is to walk out the door and face some serious criminal charges, which I'm sure will delight your parents, especially after you've covered the interiors of their Audis with bloodstains. Kids have been getting changed for gym class for time immemorial. This is no more a violation of your rights than that. I'll blow a whistle and force you to play dodgeball if that'll make you feel more comfortable, though I'm not constitutionally obliged to."

Special Agent Carla *Fucking* Rosetti.

in case you were wondering

Showers in police stations can burn the sun off a sunbeam, and sweat suits from police stations have pit stains the size of pancakes, but you don't complain about those things, considering that you've lived through two spontaneous combustions. You simply go home washed and dressed in gray cotton and when your parents ask you what you need, you tell them you need to be alone, and they respect that, for the time being. Then you flop down on your bed with your laptop and you see the story invading every corner of the internet.

ANOTHER EXPLOSION ROCKS SCHOOL

MORE TERROR AT COVINGTON HIGH

WE RANK THE TOP TEN SPONTANEOUS
COMBUSTIONS IN HISTORY

So you close your laptop and turn to your phone, which is blow-ing . . . spontaneously combusting. There are a ton from your friend Tess, but the last text that comes in is from a number you don't recognize.

It says:

> You were there for both of them. That must have been invigorating.

Not scary. Not sad. Not difficult.

Invigorating.

You should be creeped out, but you're not. Because it's the first time that someone gets it right. Both explosions were exactly that. Invigorating. A terrible thing to admit, but it's in those moments of admitting and accepting your own terribleness that you realize other people can be terrible too. And if they can be terrible too, then maybe they can be vulnerable too, caring too, and all the things that you are and hope to be.

You fall in love, which is the stupidest thing you can ever do.

other stupid things
that were done

Since I had no new information about the explosions, the morning meeting with Special Agent Carla Rosetti and her suspiciously quiet partner, Special Agent Demetri Meadows, was as unproductive as the ones I had with the cops. The big difference this time was that my mom and dad weren't there. A lawyer named Harold Frolic was my counsel instead.

Frolic was a business attorney who helped my parents with any legal issues concerning their deli, Covington Kitchen. As delis go, it was an exceptionally profitable one, with a signature sandwich called the Oinker, which was a hoagie stuffed with different cuts and preparations of pig—prosciutto, pancetta, pork loin, and pork shoulder—and topped with Muenster cheese, pickles, and a garlicky sauce. The sauce was made from a secret recipe and my parents bottled and sold the stuff at local grocery stores under the name Oinker Oil. The plan was to go national with it someday and Frolic was helping them with that process. In the meantime, he was also helping me by saying, "You don't have to answer that," to every question Rosetti posed.

"But she *should* answer that," Rosetti would invariably reply or, "It would help with the investigation. Doesn't she want the investigation to succeed?" Her partner, Demetri Meadows, simply sat there, feet up on the table, staring me down, occasionally petting the graying stubble on his cheek like he was stroking a fucking cat.

Frolic was unflappable, though. The only thing he let me talk about was what I saw, which again, wasn't much. Brian Chen popped. He was there, then gone. Then there was blood. Exactly like with Katelyn.

"You ever have beef with Brian Chen?" Rosetti asked me. "A reason to want him dead?"

Have beef. That's funny. Who says that? Special Agent Carla Rosetti, that's who. I wanted to answer, "I kissed him on a bus once and he pretended to be asleep instead of kissing me back. I was tempted to push him out the emergency exit, because that's a messed-up way to treat a dame. So sure, I had beef, but that was a long, long time ago. I got over the beef."

Frolic didn't let me get a word out, though. "Don't answer that," he said for the millionth time. And then, "Are we done here?"

Meadows stroked his cheek as Rosetti shrugged and said, "Appears you two are."

Frolic looked like he wanted to gather up a bunch of papers and stuff them in his suitcase before storming out of the station, but he didn't have any papers or a suitcase. He took notes on an iPad and wore a shoulder bag. So there was a tense moment where we all just stood there. Until, of course, Rosetti stepped back from the table and, quite literally, showed us the door. I regretted not shaking her hand on the way out. I was sure of my innocence, but I liked her, so skipping the gesture of respect was kind of a dick move.

My parents met us in the parking lot and Frolic high-fived my dad like I imagine guys do at strip clubs. Then we divided up into two cars and caravanned to the Moonlight Diner, where Frolic ate a burger and blabbed on and on about my rights. I listened to maybe ten percent of what he said (Constitution *this* and permanent record *that*), because I spent most of the time with my phone in my lap, staring at that text from the night before.

Invigorating. Invigorating. Invigorating. What do you say to that? I considered a few responses.

Who's this and how'd you get my number?

Invigorating how? Explain yourself, mystery texter!

I. Lurve. You.

What I finally settled on was:

Fuck you sicko.

About ten seconds later, there was a reply:

You don't mean that.

Then the volley of texts began.

Me: Hmmm . . . so you can read minds?

Mystery texter: I know you feel things.

Me: Perv.

Mystery texter: Come on. You have a soul. You
have ideas.

Me: Flattery will get you NOWHERE.

Mystery texter: I only want to talk to you.

Me: Then what?

Mystery texter: IDK.

Me: You a dude?

Mystery texter: More or less.

Me: You breathtakingly ugly?

Mystery texter: Not physically.

Me: OK. Here's the dealio. You found my number. Now
find my house. Ring the bell. Get past my
parents. Prove you really want to talk to me.
If you don't show up, then I won't ever know
who you are and shit won't have to be awkward.
Up to the challenge?

Mystery texter: Challenge accepted.

"At least do us the courtesy of occasional eye contact as we discuss your future," Dad said.

My eyes moved up from my lap, skipped his scowl, and moved on to Mom's disappointed/sympathetic face. She mouthed, *We fuckin' love you.* Which wasn't weird because Mom swears a fair bit. Yeah, I know. Apples falling far from trees and all of that.

"I was checking the weather," I said.

Dad motioned with his head to the window across from our booth. "Not a cloud in the sky."

"I'm sorry," I said. "I'm getting weird texts."

Like everyone, I sometimes lie to my parents. I can never sustain it, though. I always end up telling them the truth. The more truth your parents know, the fewer things they suspect. No joke. If you're a kid who constantly lies to your parents then, *news flash*, they know you lie and they probably think you're a complete degenerate.

"Weird texts, as in threats?" Mom asked.

"No," I said. "Some curious guy."

Frolic took a bite of his burger and said, "Forward them all directly to me." He used a voice that was supposed to sound wise and lawyerly, but considering he had a gob of ketchup on his cheek, it sounded a bit more like a skeevy old man asking a teenager to share her private correspondence with him.

"They're not of the . . . legal variety," I said.

"Almost anything can and will be exploited by the FBI if they count you as a suspect," Frolic said.

"She's not a suspect. She's not a suspect." Dad said it twice because he thinks if you say something twice, the more likely it is that it will be true.

"Well," Frolic replied, "I'll be seeing to it that the world knows and understands that soon enough. You have my word."

I had to say it, so I said it. "And you have ketchup on your face."

as you might have guessed

Mystery Texter didn't show up at my house that day or the next. School was shuttered for the entire week, and all its homecoming festivities were put on hold, so the guy certainly had his opportunities to pop in. It's not like he even had funerals to attend. The Chen family didn't have the money that the Ogden family had and rumors were that they'd only be inviting close friends and family to Brian's memorial service. Fine by me. More crying wasn't going to help a thing.

The support group was canceled because Vince called it quits. He sent us all an email saying he would be pursuing other interests. Presumably, not hanging out with kids made of nitroglycerin. Who could blame him? My parents tried to book some immediate extra sessions with Linda for me, but she wasn't returning their calls. Either she was throwing in the towel as well, or she was too busy fielding requests from new patients. It's tough enough when one kid in your school blows up, even if you don't really know her.

When a second kid blows up . . . well, I don't care if you've never even heard of him. You take it personally.

"Kids blow up now. And I'm a kid. Therapy please."

Every news organization in the world had arrived. Perched on a gorge and overlooking town, the Hotel Covington's parking lot was a hive of vans with giant retractable antennae. You couldn't go anywhere without someone shoving a microphone in your face. On the other hand, you couldn't stay home and zone out behind the TV or mess around on the internet because Covington High was all anyone could talk or write about. You couldn't even watch things on mute, because people were making explosion gestures with their hands. This included newscasters, which is a bit unprofessional and undignified if you ask me.

To keep my mind off things, I spent a lot of time with Tess McNulty. She hated terms like "bestie" and "BFF," but Tess and I were two people who knew how to best distract each other, so I think we qualified. We'd been inseparable since elementary school and, at the age of nine, had decided to grow old together.

We were spending a few weeks down the shore at my grandparents' place after Tess's dad took off on her and her mother. One evening, the two of us were riding our bikes past these gorgeous Victorian houses along the beachfront, and we spied two old ladies sitting in beach chairs at the edge of a porch. They were wearing kimonos, holding hands, and smoking a hookah while dipping their toes in the sand. Which was obviously adorable.

"Let's be those old ladies, always and forever," we pledged with the sunset as our witness.

Ten years later and the pledge remained intact. Only now we

were getting around in cars. Since I never drove and she always did, Tess was the captain. And since she rarely partook in mind-altering substances and I often did, I was the wacky sidekick.

In the first few days following the demise of Brian Chen, we must have logged five hundred miles on her Civic. She had a play-list called Drive, Fucker, Drive!, which consisted mostly of songs with loads of swears. Hip-hop, obviously, but also some punk and even some country of the shit-kicking variety. We played it full blast with the windows down and drove west into the hills and farmlands near Pennsylvania, where the autumn colors were pop-ping. We turned off the GPS and took roads we didn't know.

This was something we'd done before, and almost always the plan was to get into adventures. Though our adventures usually consisted of getting dirty looks from old men as we pulled into ru-ral gas stations. It's illegal to pump your own gas in New Jersey, so Tess and I would sit in the car with the stereo still on, singing along to songs about being "higher than a motherfucker," and the geezers would stand there shaking their heads and mumbling un-der their breaths until we drove off in a fit of giggles.

Of course, Tess was never higher than a motherfucker. She was responsible like that. Me, not so much. For instance, the Dal-ton twins had sold me some shrooms a few months before. At a farmer's market, appropriately enough. I'd only taken them once, during a camping trip to the Poconos. They freaked me out at first, but then the experience mellowed and I eventually became "one with nature" and decided I was willing to give them another shot. I'd stashed them in the base of my bedside lamp and had been saving them for an outdoor concert or some event where my ermahgerd-your-voice-is-full-of-rainbows! shtick would be tolerated.

During one of our drives away from memories of Katelyn and Brian, swear-singing with Tess wasn't helping me forget enough, so I insisted we stop by a Dunkin' Donuts. I bought a steaming-hot pumpkin latte and I dropped a double dose of shrooms in it.

"You're gonna make yourself sick," Tess said.

"The opposite," I said. "You brew them in liquid first to make sure you don't get sick. That's what Native Americans do."

"In pumpkin lattes?"

"Well, they had pumpkins at least. Thanksgiving. Pumpkin pie. Duh."

"Yeah. Duh."

Tess was right. Twenty minutes later I was puking along the side of the road somewhere in the Pinelands. Tess rubbed my back and I imagined her hand was a bear's paw—but not a scary bear's paw, a cuddly bear's paw, a cartoon bear's paw—and it was at that moment I realized that shit was about to get loopy.

"Someone loves me," I told her.

"I love you, baby," Tess said.

"I know that, but I mean a phantom. Someone who lives in space between the spaces."

"Jesus? Dumbledore?"

"Don't joke, Tess. You haven't got your real eyes on." I meant this last part literally, because instead of her regular brown eyes, she had glimmering diamonds in her head.

"Let's get you in the car. You can lie down in the back. I'll play something acoustic. Something soothing."

"Invigorating. Invigorating. Invigorating," I said.

"Soothing," Tess repeated in a voice that fit the word, and she guided me into the backseat.

"He reads my mind," I said with a gasp. "Do you think he has especially big ears, like satellites that can read brain waves?"

"I have no idea what you're talking about," Tess said.

As she pushed me on the chest and down into the seat, I handed her my phone, which was queued up to my texts. She took a second to read them and handed the phone back. "See. He loves me," I said.

Tess leaned in and kissed me on the cheek and I felt little happy ants on my skin. "Well, whoever he is, he isn't here. And I'm guessing he hasn't shown up at your door yet."

"Nope. He's a chicken. *Bock-bock-bock*," I clucked, and I wondered why people said chickens sounded like that because I wasn't sure what they really sounded like, but I knew it wasn't that. Definitely not that.

My feet were dangling outside, so Tess lifted and placed them on the seat and closed the door to keep them in place. It sounded like the air hatch on a rocket ship sealing shut. Noise, then silence. Then a few seconds later, noise again and Tess was at the controls, firing up the engine and launching us into space. Music burst from the stereo like bats from a cave and I felt every curve and bump of the road. I laughed hysterically as Tess sang along to some dopey old thing from the sixties or seventies.

"You just call out my name, and you know wherever I am,
I'll come running, to see you again . . ."

you've got a friend

Usually in these situations, we'd end up at Tess's house. Her mom was a single mom and the thing about single moms is they tend to tolerate teenage shenanigans. I can't remember how many times I've been drunk and draped over Tess's shoulder as she led me upstairs while Paula peered over the top of whatever novel she was reading and remarked, "Hope it was worth it, Mara."

That said, the other thing about single moms is they tend to date, and when that happens, they prefer not to have their seventeen-year-old daughter and her friend who's swatting at imaginary dragonflies show up just as they're pulling the cork from some chardonnay. On this particular night, Paula was on a date with a guy named Paul. It couldn't possibly work out, for obvious reasons, but she'd asked if Tess could sleep at my house anyway.

This meant that Tess had to smuggle me past *my* parents. Not mission impossible, but not exactly easy. It was a good thing that Tess was charming and Mom and Dad liked her. They called her Tessy—which I guess she didn't mind because she never objected—and they were always asking her about field hockey.

"Heard it was a close one, Tessy."

"How do your playoff chances look, Tessy?"

"Flex your goddamn muscles, Tessy! Flex!"

Okay. Maybe not the last one, but they loved that she was an athlete, even though she wasn't a star. Only started a few games that year. Didn't score a single goal. Still, Mom and Dad were jocks in the days of yore and I never was, so Tess might as well have worked for ESPN. She was the one they always talked jock to.

Most of the time, it was annoying, but now it was essential. Tess had to distract them as I tiptoed up to my room. The shrooms were wearing off, but I couldn't risk saying something embarrassing. And I couldn't lie. I already told you about my problem with lying.

I know what you're going to say. "Not telling equals lying!" Well, that's just bad math.

Example: Say you pleasure yourself. Not that I'm saying you do . . . Actually, yes. I am saying you do because everyone does. But even if you're the world's most honest person, do you run downstairs after every sweaty session and holler, "Mom! Dad! Guess what?"

Of course not. Same thing with shrooms, though in this case it was pleasuring the mind. Okay, that's going a bit too far, but I think you get the point.

As we pulled into the driveway, Tess gave me a pep talk. "All you have to do is make it to the stairs. You can do it, sweetie. I know you can. It's seven o'clock, so they'll be watching the news. I'll pop my head into the family room, tell them that we grabbed some Dunkin on the road and now you've got a stomach thing—"

"Yeah, good. Dunkin. Stomach thing. That's actually not a lie."

"Right. And then they can ask me about when practice is going to start up again and you can slip into some jammies and into bed and if they want to come check on you, you can pretend to be asleep."

"But I want to cuddle you." This was partly the shrooms talking, but it was also the way we were. Neither of us had sisters, so we spent a lot of time doing what we thought sisters did. Braiding each other's hair, cuddling, fighting. We hadn't fought in a few weeks, but I knew a fight was coming. Maybe mid-cuddle, probably in the morning.

"Get your shit together, kiddo," Tess was bound to tell me in her exasperated big-sister voice. And I would nod and she would scowl and we would both know that it doesn't matter because I always end up doing the same shit all over again.

For now, in the driveway, we weren't fighting. We were moving. "First things first," Tess said as she grabbed my shoulders and pointed me to the door. "Upstairs. Eyes on the prize."

"Aye-aye, cap'n," I said, and strode up the brick walkway. Though I was still noticing so much—the rustle of leaves that sounded like rain, the glint of evening sunlight on the silver knocker that reminded me of a sword—I must not have noticed some obvious stuff, such as the skateboard resting against the oak tree in the front yard. I pushed open the door without knowing what I was really walking into.

Now, here's something you've got to understand. No one *ever* hangs out in our living room. It's strictly a Christmas-Eve-and-the-grandparents-are-visiting corner of the house. So when I stepped inside and saw three people sitting on the living room couch together, I was tempted to turn tail and not look back. Figured I'd stumbled into the neighbor's place.

Dad's voice cast an anchor, though. "Speak of the devil!" he hollered.

My head pivoted, and then my gaze landed on the person sitting between my parents. A boy. In a suit. On our living room couch. He stood, and I spoke. "And the devil doesn't have a clue what the hell is going on."

Mom rose to her feet next and she presented the boy like he was a car for sale. "It's Dylan . . ."

"Hovemeyer, ma'am," Dylan said as he pulled down on his jacket to straighten out the wrinkles. There were a lot of wrinkles.

Now it was Dad who stood and remarked, "Hovemeyer? I've seen that name in the old cemetery by St. Francis."

"Our family goes back a ways," Dylan said with a nod. "And people tend to die."

I knew Dylan. Well, I didn't know him personally, but everyone at school *knew* him. He was the one you suspected. Of what? Well, name it.

"Hey, it's . . ." Tess had joined me in the doorway, her hand on my back.

"Dylan Hovemeyer," he said, stepping toward us with a hand outstretched. I wasn't sure which one of us the hand was intended for, but Tess was quicker on the draw. As she shook Dylan's right hand, I presented my left one and soon I was shaking his left one. A pulse of energy zipped between the three of us, back and forth, like people doing the wave at a stadium. "We all have econ together," he went on.

"Riiiight," Tess and I said at the same time, as if this were something we'd never thought about before, which was total BS. We'd discussed Dylan. We had theories about him.

Mom's face crinkled up as she said, "I assumed you were already friends."

"We're *becoming* friends," Dylan said, staring at me. "Fast friends."

The handshake à trois was still going strong and Tess gave me that what-now? look and I gave her that um-I'm-still-pretty-high look and so she took control, like always. She pulled her hand away and placed it on top of mine. It was the fuzzy hand again, the cuddly cartoon bear paw.

"You look great, Dylan," Tess said. "And we'd love to catch up, talk econ and all that, but Mara is feeling crazy sick."

I nodded, but I didn't pull my hand away. I liked it, sandwiched up and tangled in their fingers. It was melting like grilled cheese.

"Vomit-all-over-the-place sick," Tess added.

"Oh, honey," Dad said.

"Pumpkin latte," Tess informed him.

Mom's eyes narrowed because she knew I downed those things like they were water during months that ended in *BER*. So I added a key detail. "Probably something fungal too."

This made Mom cringe, but Dylan didn't budge. The words *vomit* and *fungal* can usually scare away even the most dedicated panty-sniffer, but it required Tess's field-hockey-honed arms to pry our fingers apart.

"Straight to bed for this one," she said, pulling me toward the stairs. "Sorry, Dylan. Again, you look ... dashing."

Dylan seemed to take it in stride, shrugging as if he were called dashing all the time, which I knew for a fact he was not.

"Mara—" Mom started to say, but soon Tess and I were at the stairs and her tone shifted from surprise to embarrassment. "I'm so sorry, Dylan. She's ... well, she's got a sensitive stomach."

"That's cool," Dylan said. "I did what I came here to do."

"And that is?" Dad's voice was suddenly suspicious. He wasn't an idiot. He could see through a wrinkled suit.

"I wanted to meet you two. And I wanted to shake Mara's hand. Thank you for being nice to me. Your home is a nice home."

By the time I reached my room, I had already heard the front door close. I looked out my window to the front lawn. Dylan was jogging across the grass, skateboard in hand. As soon as he reached the road, he tossed the board to the asphalt, hopped on, and escaped, suit and all, into the evening.

I opened the window so I could hear the squeaking wheels retreating into the distance as I collapsed on my bed. They sounded like sails being raised, a ship setting out to sea.

a trilogy

Before we dive back into things, I should probably tell you three stories about Dylan. Rumors, really, but rumors are as important as anything. Even if they're not true, they end up turning people into who they are.

Story Number One: His dad died under a pile of shit.

I should elaborate, I suppose. Dylan started attending our school halfway through sixth grade. Middle school is a tough time for any kid, but being a new kid smack dab in the middle of middle school is about as tough as it gets. If you show up on the first day of classes, it's not so bad. New teachers, new lockers. People are distracted. A few kids might say, "Hey, I don't remember that guy," but pretty soon you're integrated into the pubescent stew. Yet another dude dishing out or dodging wedgies.

Show up after Christmas break and things are way different. Then kids are, like, "Hey, what's this interloper's deal. His mom move him to Jersey after his parents got a divorce? He get kicked out of his last school for sexting the nurse? This douche-nozzle ain't one of us, that's for sure." Names are Googled, local news stories pop up, links are followed, until a tale emerges. The one for Dylan was that his dad died under a pile of shit.

I never looked it up to confirm, but I think Tracy Levy told me that Dylan was from some Podunk town in Pennsylvania and he lived on a farm with his parents and one morning his dad bought a bunch of manure (which is technically shit) and when the old man was unloading it—he hit the wrong button on the dump truck or whatever—it all came tumbling down on him and he suffocated beneath the pile. Dylan supposedly found him over an hour later and tried to dig him out with his bare hands, but it was too late.

Now, kids are cruel. We all know this. It's no surprise that the story spread quick and thick. Thanks in no small part to people like me, who love some good gossip. But as cruel as kids are, they aren't monsters. It wasn't like they teased Dylan about it. It merely branded him with a reputation.

Dylan came from a farm, which meant he was poor. His father died doing something stupid, which, if you're taking genetics into account, meant Dylan was stupid. On top of that, the stupid thing involved a pile of manure that Dylan pawed his way through, and now you've also got a kid who's dirty. And stinky.

So almost immediately, Dylan was known as a dumb and smelly hick who was probably scarred for life by what he came upon one afternoon out there in Pennsyltucky. Everyone felt bad for him, but no one wanted to be his friend. Myself included.

Story Number Two: He burned down the QuickChek.

Again, this requires a bit of elaboration. At the intersection of

Willoby and Monroe, there used to be a QuickChek convenience store. In the summer after seventh grade, Tess and I would ride there on our bikes and buy Mountain Dew, Twizzlers, and the latest issue of *Vogue*. We'd take it all down to a nearby creek, sit on the rocks, and use the Twizzlers as straws to drink the Mountain Dew while we'd tear pictures of models out of magazines and then fold them up into little paper boats that we'd race in the currents.

"Go Adriana! Go Svetlana! Go, go, go you glorious anorexic Romanians!"

Okay, fine. I'm fairly certainly we didn't use the words *glorious* or *anorexic* or *Romanian*, but we got pretty damn excited about it. What else was there to do? We couldn't drive. We didn't drink, yet. Boys were an interest, of course, but they were all inside killing zombies or watching people kill zombies and Tess and I really weren't that into zombies and . . .

Sorry. Zombies aren't the point. QuickChek is. So it turns out that thirteen-year-old girls buying the occasional fashion mag, caffeinated soda, and bag of strawberry licorice isn't enough to keep a convenience store in the black, and by the winter of that year it closed down. It was kind of a craphole to begin with, but once people stopped using the building, raccoons and teenagers took it over, sneaking in at night to do the things that raccoons and teenagers do, which is primarily making a big fucking mess.

Big fucking messes tend to be pretty flammable and so it was no surprise when some boys set the place on fire. Well, one boy set it on fire, if you were to believe the stories. No arrests were made, no parents found out, but the incoming freshman class entered Covington High convinced that on the last night of eighth grade,

Dylan Hovemeyer had accompanied Joe Dalton and Keith Lutz to the abandoned QuickChek with the intention of smashing shit. You know, as a celebration of their manhood. Only Dylan brought an unexpected guest to the party: a Molotov cocktail made from an Arizona Iced Tea bottle filled with lighter fluid and wicked with the T-shirt we got for graduating from the middle school that said GO GET 'EM, YOUNG SCHOLARS.

Apparently, Young Scholar Hovemeyer got 'em and got 'em good. That is, if 'em was a stack of old newspapers that he pelted with the burning Molotov cocktail before Joe and Keith had any idea what was what. The three bolted out of there with flames licking their haunches and promised never to speak of the incident, a truce that lasted a full fifteen hours.

In the end, everything worked out for the best. The building's owner probably got insurance money. The police never implicated the guys. And now there's a Chick-fil-A on the lot and everybody loves Chick-fil-A. Except for the fact that they're closed on Sundays. You can thank Jesus for that raw deal.

Story Number Three: Dylan is the father of three kids.

This was the least corroborated of the stories, but the other two stories certainly helped make it believable. Remember, by the time he was in high school, Dylan was known as a redneck pyromaniac with a dead father. In other words, he had nothing to lose, and so whenever something suspicious happened, he was a suspect.

A fire alarm pulled on the first day of finals? Gotta be that Dylan kid.

Laptops stolen from the computer lab? Paging Mr. Hovemeyer.

Spontaneously combusting students? You bet his name was whispered more than once.

But even before the spontaneous combustions, there was the curious case of Jane Rolling. Jane had always been a bit chubby. Not obese. Just consistently soft. Well, during junior year, she got softer and softer and softer still. Then one day, she stopped showing up to school.

"Triplets!" Tess told me a few weeks later.

"She was . . . with child? That whole time?" I said.

"With *children*. Yes. Three. All boys."

"That's boom-boom bonkers," I said, because junior year was the year I said nonsense like "boom-boom bonkers." Trying to land my own catchphrase, I will freely admit.

"What's even more *boom-boom bonkers*," Tess said in a mocking tone, "is the identity of the father."

I shrugged because there was better gossip than Jane Rolling's love life.

"How about Dylan?" Tess went on. "Manure-dad Dylan. Fire-starter Dylan."

"Damn," I said. "That's right. They dated. Used to cuddle on the front steps before first bell. It was . . . nausealicious." Yep, *nausealicious*. Another junior year gem.

"So there you have it," Tess said. "The delinquent has reproduced in triplicate."

"Guy's got powerful sperm."

"I thought you passed bio. It's more about Jane's eggs. Girl's got a chicken coop down there."

"Well, I don't envy either one of them," I said, which wasn't the whole truth. Having a trio of babies is not without its advantages. Once they learn to walk and talk, you can teach them song-and-dance routines and who doesn't love a little soft shoe and three-part harmony?

Jane didn't come back to school, of course, and Dylan became more of a lurking, mysterious presence than ever. I guess he talked to other kids. I guess he had friends. But to people like me and Tess, he was simply a bundle of rumors and suspicion, dressed up in jeans and ringer tees.

Literary Analysis: Dylan was sad. And dangerous. And fascinating.

back to the action

Monday was Halloween and school was back in session. The majority of kids and teachers skipped the getups entirely. I spotted a few "laser loafers" in the hall as a tribute to Brian, but that was the extent of the masquerading. Everyone was trying to pretend that things were back to normal, or at least the type of normal where you play football again.

All sports seasons had been put on pause after Brian, because obviously fit and limber kids need free time to grieve and freak out, the same as the rest of us sloths. Certain parents weren't thrilled about the hiatus, though, and they had a point. Our teams were usually state ranked, playoffs were around the corner, and there were college scholarships at stake. Not for Tess, necessarily, but it was still a vital part of her high school experience. While I didn't give a single shit about sports myself, I could at least appreciate that many of my peers depended on them for their health, sanity, and future.

The majority appreciated that too. After an open session of the PTA that Sunday, democracy declared *Play Ball!*, starting Friday with a football game against crosstown rivals, Bloomington. It was a rescheduled version of the previous week's homecoming game, there were apparently "playoff implications," and while there would be no dance and no parade with floats ferrying high school royalty, the stands would be full of current and former students and anyone who wanted to give a defiant finger to our predicament.

For most kids, football games weren't ever about the football. These sporting events were excuses to hang out in the bleachers and catch up with friends, or lounge behind the bleachers in the softball fields, where blankets could be spread out and kids could watch the stars in the sky instead of the ones on the field. These brutal battles were distractions from our cloak-and-dagger variety of partying, where booze mixed with Gatorade was smuggled past lazy-eyed security guards. These rousing contests were perfect for covert kissing in the shadows and heart-to-hearts scored to the sounds of cheering parents and girlfriends.

The homecoming game was going to be my first date with Dylan. It was his idea and the arrangements were made by text, since there wasn't much time in econ to discuss such things. As the week chugged along, the three stories and their subplots fizzled in my head and mixed with the dizzying memory of his hand on my hand. I know, I know. Getting all worked up by a little hand-holding? Total middle school. Elementary school, even. But when you think about it, hand-holding can be really sexy, especially when you're holding the hand of someone who may or may not be any number of things.

Was I leery of Dylan? Obviously. Was I excited about seeing him again? Uh . . . yeah. During lunch on Wednesday, Tess made me promise to be careful. "If he's half the things we think he is," she said, "I'm not sure you want to be alone with him."

"That's why the football game is perfect," I said. "Plenty of people around, but no one listening in on us."

"I wish I didn't have practice that night. I want to watch over you."

"That's sweet. But that's also creepy. I'll be fine. What are you worried about? That he'll fill me with quadruplets during halftime or that he'll douse me in gasoline to celebrate every touchdown?"

Tess took a potato chip from my bag and poked me playfully on the nose with it. "Do you really want to get close to someone who has three kids? Plus all the other stuff? Do you want to have a look inside all his baggage?"

I snatched the chip from Tess's hand, stuffed it in my mouth, and as I chewed, I said, "I've got plenty of baggage myself."

"A carry-on at best. This guy would have to pay hundreds of dollars to check his."

"Is Walsh doing a unit on metaphors in AP English or something? Because I don't think you get extra credit for using such pathetic ones, especially outside of class."

"I should poison your drink," Tess said with a fake sneer as she watched me take a slug from my strawberry smoothie.

"Should, but never would," I said as I wiped my mouth. "You know why?"

"Why?"

"Because you would be sad. You would feel . . . All. The. Feels."

Tess raised a finger. "How dare you? You know how I hate those words."

"You won't hate those words when they're on the cover of my novel, the blockbusting award-winner that I dedicate *To My Darling Tessy*."

"Royalties," she said as she patted me on the cheek. "Dedications are sweet, but cutting me in on the profits would be a whole lot better."

"Fine," I replied. "I'll be your sugar mama until the end of days. I'll keep your toes dipped in sand and your body draped in silk."

She put out a hand out and I shook it. The deal was officially sealed.

fun and games

Front row center.

Or so said the text from Dylan that arrived Friday afternoon. I got a ride to the game with the Dalton twins because Dylan hadn't offered one. I figured there wasn't enough room on his skateboard.

The Daltons shared a red RAV4 bought with money they made bussing tables at Covington Club, the restaurant at our local golf course. At least that's where they told their parents they got the cash. In reality, the majority of their income was the redirected allowances of kids who partook in illegal plants and pills. Kids like the late great Katelyn Ogden. Like me.

Joe Dalton was older than Jenna Dalton by a few minutes, but he was definitely the younger at heart. And mind. Since he was supposedly one of the guys with Dylan the night the QuickChek burned down, I could have asked him if the whole Molotov cocktail thing was true, but I wasn't sure I wanted the answer to spoil my evening. So instead I sat quietly in the back, while he drove and argued with Jenna about whether it would be better to retire to Florida or Buenos Aires.

Joe was advocating, poorly, in favor of Florida. "Bikinis, bottle service, and alligators, Jenna! Doesn't get any better!"

Jenna, on the other hand, was selling Buenos Aires like a real estate agent, highlighting "the mild climate, the European flavor, the dancing till dawn, and the steaks as big as laptops."

After a while, they seemed to forget I was there and were trading inside insults, which are like inside jokes but even worse because as Joe hollered, "You're such an Aunt Jessica!" and Jenna yelled, "Go puke on Donald Duck again," I had no idea who was winning. It was getting unbearably loud and so I started fantasizing about the two of them screaming themselves to death and leaving me all their drug money so I could hop on the back of Dylan's skateboard and the two of us could catch the next plane to Argentina where we'd forge a new life full of red. Red wine. Red meat. Red-hot love.

When we reached the lot for the football field, I slipped out with a "mucho appreciation, amigos," and hightailed it to the bleachers. The fight song was pumping and the seats were as full as I'd ever seen them, but sure enough, there was Dylan in the front row with a bag of popcorn next to him, saving me a seat.

"Here I am," I said, and sucked in a deep breath. I was not in shape. I had never been in shape.

He pulled the popcorn to his lap, revealing a buttery stretch of aluminum for me to sit on. "And there you go," he said, but he failed to wipe any of the sludge away. It didn't bother me, necessarily, though it did leave me with a decision. I didn't see any napkins, and I didn't want to be a pain in the ass from the get-go and ask him to fetch me some. I especially didn't want to call him out for being either clueless or inconsiderate. So I was left with a choice between having a buttery hand or a buttery butt.

Protip: Always avoid the buttery butt.

And that's what I did. I ran a hand across the seat a couple of times while Dylan was watching the referee flip a coin. As I sat, I flicked the butter down into the chasm beneath the bleachers. "What the, what the—?" muttered some poor dope who must've been beneath me, but that was all I heard because the crowd went absolutely apeshit when our team won the coin toss. *The coin toss.* It was going to be that kind of game.

"So," I said once the cheering petered out. "You prefer the bleachers to, I don't know, somewhere we don't have to actually watch the game?"

"I'm looking forward to the game," he said without even a hint of sarcasm.

"You are?"

"Sure. I've been a fan of the Quakers since I was a kid."

Yes, you heard that right. We are the tenacious, the proud, the fearsome . . . Quakers! It goes back over three hundred years to when this area consisted of a few scattered communities of Quakers who didn't make it as far as Pennsylvania. The lazy Quakers, if you will. We're a public school now, without any religious or philosophical affiliations, except for a mascot who basically looks like the guy from the oatmeal box, except with a Quakerly sneer in place of a Quakerly smile.

"So always a Quakers fan, huh?" I said, because I didn't know what else to say to something like that. And then it dawned on me. "But wait, didn't you move here during sixth grade?"

"I've always been here," he said. "Sixth grade was when I started taking classes. I was homeschooled until then."

"Oh. That's news to me."

"News to most people," he replied, and as he spoke, he kept his eyes on the Bloomington players preparing to kick off, sizing them up like my grandpa used to size up horses at the track. "My dad died of a stroke that year. Out in a field while laying down some fertilizer. He was a dairy farmer, but he also helped my mom teach me. Once he was gone, it was too much for Mom to do alone, so I was transferred to the *general population*."

He put his hands out and motioned to the crowd, which leapt from the bleachers as Jalen Howard caught the opening kick and returned it to the forty-yard line.

"That must have been tough," I hollered over the noise.

Dylan shrugged. "Another Hovemeyer for your dad's favorite graveyard."

It was a callback to the night at my house. And it was funny. Not because Dylan's dad was dead and buried, but because my dad is definitely the type of guy who would have a favorite graveyard. After all, he has a favorite public restroom (Covington Town Library, second floor), a favorite fire hydrant (the shiny blue one on Gleason Street), and a favorite park bench (the warped beauty in Sutter Park he calls Ol' Lucy).

So I laughed. And Dylan smiled.

"I never pegged you for a football fan," I said.

"Drama," he said. "There's always a different story. I like drama. I like stories."

Our quarterback, Clint Jessup, threw an errant pass that went into the bleachers and the crowd let out a collective sigh. "What's the story this time?" I asked.

"Depends on your religion."

"Meaning?"

He turned to me and his beaming face opened him up like a sunrise opens up a landscape. "This is a resurrection story. We're back."

the thing about comebacks

We *were* back. Our team had gone into the game as underdogs. Bloomington was a perennial powerhouse and we'd missed far too many practices to realistically compete. But compete we did. Leads were exchanged, and new numbers were constantly lighting up the scoreboard.

There was a certain amount of excitement and it was fascinating to see Dylan glued to every pass and tackle, but it confirmed to me that no matter how much drama there was, I still didn't care about sports.

What I did care about, however, was Harper Wie, Perry Love, and Steve Cox. They were players on our team. Benchwarmers, basically. Which was important. More than any touchdown, I wanted to see the three of them sit next to each other on the bench.

Why ever would you want to see something so mundane, you ask? Well, it goes back to junior year. In general, I don't have a problem with football players. At Covington High, they're mostly nice guys. They don't beat up people in the bathrooms. They don't cheat their way through classes (as far as I know). They don't record their dalliances with cheerleaders and post them on RaRa-Bang.com or whatever the amateur porn site *du jour* is called. Sure, they're not saints, but they're usually too busy being football players to be much of anything else. Harper Wie, Perry Love, and Steve Cox were the exception. Or at least they were for a brief moment, and sometimes all it takes is a brief moment.

It was a Friday last fall and they were wearing their jerseys, as is the custom on game days. They were sitting together in the cafeteria when I walked by them and I heard Perry say, "Oh, what a glorious fag he was, the faggiest fag in all the land, and his fagginess will be missed, the fag."

Or something to that effect, give or take a fag or two.

It made the two other guys burst out in laughter and made me immediately want to wring their necks. It wasn't really Perry's choice of words, which were more or less baby shit—gross, but juvenile and inconsequential. It was the target of his slurs. It had to be Mr. Prescott, our art teacher. He had passed away the week before and the school newspaper was planning to run an obituary. Perry was the editor and I had it on good authority (the authority being Tess, who worked on the paper too) that Mr. Prescott was gay. Not closeted, but not exactly advertising his lifestyle. The staff had been discussing whether to include this fact in his obituary. He was survived, they'd learned, by a partner named Bill. The two had been together for years, but they didn't bother to get married, even when they were legally allowed. Maybe they didn't care about marriage. I don't know.

Now, the death of Mr. Prescott was undoubtedly sad. But he was old. In his eighties, I think. Retirement was like marriage for him, I suppose. Never in the cards. Being an art teacher is a pretty mellow gig, after all. And it wasn't like he was my mentor or even my favorite teacher. But still, there's something about young men making fun of old men that really gets to me.

Go ahead and make fun of people your parents' age. Make fun of your peers. Make fun of babies, even. Old people, though? Completely off-limits. And recently dead old people? Please. Why would I even have to explain how fucked up that is? Which—flashing forward to my football date with Dylan—is why I wanted to see them lined up together on the bench. Harper Wie, Perry Love, and Steve Cox, in that exact order.

Still don't get it? Let me explain.

Football players have their last names sewn on the backs of their jerseys, and it may not be the world's perfect pun, but when you get Wie (pronounced We), Love, and Cox lined up and you snap a pic and post that shit on Instagram . . . well, it isn't exactly justice for them being a triumvirate of homophobic, ageist pubes, but there's a certain poetry to it. At least that's what I was telling myself.

So there we were, Dylan and I on a date—him watching football and me watching the bench. My phone was set to camera and resting on my thigh like I was a regular gunslinger. I couldn't settle for Wie Cox, which actually happened a couple of times. Because while that might have played well in Scotland, I needed the bingo, especially since Perry Love was the ringleader of the bunch.

During the moments my eyes weren't poised on the bench, they were resting on Dylan. For most of the game, he was calm, studying the action and—when there wasn't any action, which was most of the time—studying the coaches or the huddles. He seemed to be analytical about it all at first, subtly shaking or nodding his head as he dissected decisions. But as the game went on, and the crowd got more riled up, something changed in Dylan. He didn't become the frothing-at-the-mouth chest-painter I imagined most rabid sports fan to be. He became something much more charming.

He became a kid. Whenever our team made a big play, he'd lean forward in his seat, gripping the edge like gravity was going to give out at any moment. Whenever Bloomington snatched back the advantage, he'd clench his teeth and rap the seats with his knuckles and send little tremors through my thighs. And in the fourth quarter, whenever things got particularly tense, he'd reach over and grab my hand, and shake it gently.

There had been chatting during the game. I had asked questions about what was happening and he had explained (in what were supposedly layman's terms) about formations and strategies, though I don't remember even a word of it. What I do remember was his tone. It wasn't condescending. It wasn't "let me explain some man stuff to this precious little doll." Again, he was a kid. He was excited and proud. He might as well have been talking about his Legos.

So every time he grabbed my hand, I was holding a kid's hand and it was cute and innocent and it wasn't at all like holding Dylan's hand in my living room a few days before. The gentle shakes were the ones I recognized from my youngest cousins, the can-you-believe-that-we're-at-a-water-park-and-there-arewaterslides-and-oh-boy-I-could-pee-my-pants-right-this-minute! variety of shakes.

Kids grow up, though, and the kid version of Dylan went through puberty in the final seconds of the game. The scoreboard read Bloomington 38 and Covington 33. We had the ball at the fifty-yard line. Twenty seconds left on the clock. I'd seen enough movies to know that this was why people loved sports. Underdogs making good and last-second scores. Everyone on our team was wearing two black armbands, for chrissakes. Emotion to spare, my friends. *To spare.*

And Bloomington wasn't taking it easy on us out of sympathy. They were snarling, punching, and gouging. "It's a sign of respect," Dylan explained. "No true athlete wants to be a charity case. This is the way it should be."

The crowd was singing the alma mater, which pretty much never happens because it's a creepy bit of propaganda about "merging together as one, for the honor of mighty Covington." Still, in this context, it was appropriate. We had suffered together and together we were fighting through it, one throbbing mass of cheers and tears. We didn't need to win this game necessarily, but we needed people to remember this game. Even a girl who doesn't care about sports can be on board with that.

Our quarterback, Clint Jessup, was doing a hell of a job, but with twenty seconds left on the clock, he buckled over and started puking on the field. I'm not sure if there are rules about such things, but I think that even in football, puking puts you on the sidelines for a play or two. Because that's exactly where Clint headed. Helmet on the ground, head in his hands, he stumbled to the bench.

"They don't have any timeouts left, so they gotta go with Deely," Dylan said with a groan. "Deely has never even taken a varsity snap."

Deely was Malik Deely. From pre-calc. And support group. The one cool head in our woeful bunch. He was the team's backup quarterback, which, from what I could gather, meant he stood around holding a clipboard all game until the last twenty seconds when he was expected to come in and save the day because our number one guy was too vomity.

"Don't worry, Malik can handle pressure," I assured Dylan and Dylan gave me a you-better-be-right look, and it was that exact moment that he changed, that the hand-holding changed, that the charming became charged. He squeezed my fingers—a little too hard at first perhaps—but when he eased up, he soothed things by stroking them. He ran a fingertip over my palm, almost as though he were writing a message on it.

Maybe it was the crowd pulsing around us or the sweaty anxiety all over the field, but it was an unbearably sexy moment, at least for me. And when Malik Deely lined up behind his teammates and started barking out the play, I was basically at a point where I wanted to pull Dylan in and stuff my face in his neck and nuzzle, nuzzle, nuzzle. Weird, I know, and may not seem all that hot to you, but when you want something at a certain moment and you're not sure whether you can have it, but you know that it's within the realm of possibility if only you have the courage to go after it . . . well, I don't care who you are or what that thing you want is, the simple fact is this: It's fucking hot.

Problem this time was that I didn't go after it. It didn't seem right to distract Dylan. Because as Dylan ran that fingertip over my palm, and I thought about scorched convenience stores and dancing triplets and infinite nuzzling, Malik Deely took his first varsity snap.

I'm not exactly a sportscaster, so I'm not sure the best way to describe what happened next, but here goes.

Malik had the ball, raised up like he was ready to pass, and he moved left and right, looking downfield to see if there was anyone open. Two of the defenders from Bloomington pushed past the guys who were supposed to be blocking them and they closed in on Malik.

"Jarowski!" Dylan yelled, as did almost everyone else in the crowd, because the lumbering lunk named Jared Jarowski had broken free. But it was too late. The defenders were pouncing on Malik and Malik was bringing the ball to his chest and curling into a fetal position.

A collective gasp. And then . . . a collective cheer. Somehow, Malik slid out from under the two defenders without being tackled and there was an open patch of grass in front of him.

"Go! Go! Go!" Dylan hollered, tapping my hand with each *go!*

Malik went. He burst forth with the ball tucked under his arm. He reached the forty-yard line, then the thirty-five, then the thirty.

Defenders pursued. Malik spun out of danger and kept running. He stuck an arm out and knocked a guy over. He hurdled another guy. He was at the twenty-five, then the twenty.

I'll admit it. Football wasn't entirely boring. I could see the clock was in the single digits. I was as wrapped up in it as anyone else. A few of the guys on our team made some amazing blocks, throwing their bodies in front of Bloomington players who were nipping at Malik's heels.

"Please no flags, please no flags, please no flags," Dylan chanted as Malik hit the fifteen and then the ten.

It was almost too good to be true. A touchdown would win it for us. We didn't even need to make the extra point. Get the ball into the end zone, spike the thing, dance a dance, and call it a day. But when Malik reached the five-yard line, it happened.

He dropped the ball.

The crowd howled. The ball bounced once. Almost everyone within a five-yard radius dove for it. Malik didn't need to dive though, because on the ball's second bounce, he caught it. A shuffle, two leaps, a dive, and he was in.

Touchdown!

Nuts is not the word for what the crowd went. *Psychotic* is more like it. The stands shook as Quaker fans threw themselves on each other, over each other, and into the field. The band tried to break into the fight song, but the pandemonium sent their trumpets and tubas flying and the only sound they made was the clang of brass on bleachers.

I was hugging Dylan. I hardly realized it. Our hands were now clutching at each other's sides and we were hugging and hopping up and down and I was laughing myself to bits and it was magnificent in so many ways. The noise. The vibrations. The feeling of his chest pressing against mine.

Down on the field, teammates were surrounding Malik and

howling in his face like a bunch of Vikings, as players from Bloomington lay scattered on the grass, collapsed with exhaustion or doubled over and head-butting the ground in frustration.

In the stands at the opposite sideline, where the collection of Bloomington fans were either sulking or politely clapping in appreciation of our perseverance, I spotted two familiar faces. Special Agents Carla Rosetti and Demetri Meadows, dressed like they were on the job, stood side by side, intently watching something. But it wasn't Malik.

Rosetti raised her arm and pointed while Meadows raised his phone and tilted it sideways to take a picture of our team's bench. I figured our bench had cleared the second Malik had scored, but I was wrong. There were two players standing in front of it. Frozen.

The backs of their jerseys read WIE and COX. But there was a gap between them, an open space. Scanning the remaining players on the field, I realized I had missed my moment. So had Agent Meadows. Because a few seconds before, Perry Love had been standing in that open space.

WIE LOVE COX.

Terrible, terrible joke. I can't believe I thought it would be funny, or suitable revenge. But whatever it was, it would never happen again. Because Perry Love was now splattered all over their jerseys.

and wouldn't you know it?

Perry Love was gay.

Not the going-on-Grindr-and-meeting-some-businessman-for-a-midnight-tryst-in-the-dark-corner-of-a-Panera-parking-lot variety of gay. Not even the get-drunk-at-a-party-and-make-out-with-Kylton-Connors-on-a-pile-of-coats-because-Kylton-Connors-almost-looks-like-a-girl-and-Kylton-Connors-is-discreet variety of gay.

No, Perry Love was the variety of gay where his parents probably sat around every Christmas, scratching their chins and saying, "What should we get for our gay son, Perry, this year? He's not into those typical gay things like pocket squares and Pomeranians, but that boy of ours is as gay as they come. Let's at least get him a gift certificate to a coffee shop and maybe he can finally meet a nice fella and take him out for a chai. He deserves a nice fella . . . and a chai, don't you think?"

Perry Love was out, in other words. So out that you didn't even know he was out. Well, other people did, obviously. Just not me. The football team knew it and was cool with it. To be clear, there was never some big coming-out in the locker room, never an inspiring video online about how a young man's bravery is supported by progressive teammates who look beyond the petty prejudices, and simply see another comrade in the noble pursuit of concussions, no shared links saying: *Your Faith in Humanity Will Be Restored as Soon as You Find Out What Happened When This High School Football Player Told His Teammates That, Yeah, He Probably Has the Hots for at Least a Couple of Them.*

Perry was nothing more and nothing less than a mediocre and gay football player and he had been so since day one of high school. Apparently he came out in the summer after eighth grade to a handful of friends, Harper Wie included. Impeccable timing, it turns out. We were all redefining ourselves that summer, adding or stripping off layers before we plunged into high school. So when Perry slipped quietly into the deep end of gay teendom, it didn't make a splash. I suppose I was too busy gossiping about obvious transformations. Back then, I was discussing Greyson Hobbs's shrinking waistline and Diet Dr Pepper addiction, Poul Dawes's sudden skater-dude awakening, and Tammy Hartwell's shift from a bog of dour and frump to a volcano of smiles and cleavage.

Perry was never flamboyant, never had a boyfriend. He might never have even kissed a guy, but he was out and he was white and his last name was Love, which is a good American name and makes for especially sad headlines, such as, HOPES DASHED BY THE

DEATH OF LOVE. (Those words actually graced the home page of JerseyReport.com the morning after his demise.) And because of all these factors, discussions of the spontaneous combustions took a sudden turn. If there were no bombs and foreign-flavored folks to blame, then what the fuck were we dealing with here?

what we were dealing with

It's been covered ad nauseum, but I think it helps to go back to the moments after the latest spontaneous combustion. What had been a private phenomenon, experienced and recounted by a few unlucky kids, was now a public event, experienced and, more importantly, recorded by many.

When the flood of videos were uploaded to YouTube that night, there may have been an ethical dilemma among the bleary-eyed gatekeepers who have to sift through all the gore, porn, and adorable hedgehogs. Was this exploitative? Nothing but snuff? Or was it news, a necessary document to help us understand this fucked-up world, like images of burning buildings and rhinos with their horns cut off?

The official verdict was "News! Glorious and bloody news!" Yes, we are a world of Zapruders offering up death from a variety of angles and aspect ratios.

What's remarkable about the videos is the lack of awareness on display. It didn't go down at a string quartet, after all. Since the place was full-on pandemonium already, most didn't notice what happened, including many with their phones pointed at the field. Chances are, some of them even drove home minutes later, saw the stream of police cars headed the other way, and wondered, "What's all the hubbub?" as their images of Perry Love's exploding body finished uploading to the cloud.

I'll spare you the details of the scene because you can watch the videos and, frankly, it's hard to know whether my perspective is an honest one. Ecstatic flailing and terrified flailing are actually pretty similar, and depending how I've felt on particular days, I've pictured the atmosphere differently. I do remember Rosetti and Meadows fighting their way through the crowd and rushing the field with everyone else. I remember the hollering and the whooping. I remember Meadows diving on Steve Cox and I remember Harper Wie fainting. And, of course, I remember Dylan whispering in my ear.

"Did something happen?" he asked. *"Did everything happen?"*

My response was to grab his hand and lead him to the side of the bleachers. An older couple, who had chosen not to enter the fray, noticed us holding hands, and smiled the smile of approval as we slipped by.

Like that, we were a couple. So said the elders.

We slid off the bleachers and I pulled Dylan away from the field, in the opposite direction of the kids who had heard the booming announcement of "TOUCHDOWN!" and emerged from their cocoons of cuddling and parking-lot hot-boxing to become one with the tribe.

"We need to be there!" Dylan shouted. "We need to experience this!"

"We need to go!" I shouted back. "We need to get the fuck out!"

I sped up and our hands broke apart. I was in the wide open—past the reach of the lights, past the throb and the thump—sprinting, the chill of the autumn cutting through my shirt, my cardigan flapping and threatening to break free.

"Slow down!" Dylan shouted.

I did the opposite. I put my arms out and head down and I charged toward the patch of woods near East Campus. The leaves had all turned and even in the moonlight I could see the brilliant yellows, oranges, and reds. I ran my hands across the first few trees I passed, feeling the grizzled landscapes of bark, and I imagined this was a haunted forest, a forest that would eat you if it could, that would chew you with its mouth open and swallow half of you in a big gulp, but let your legs writhe in the foggy air.

When I reached a little hill where the trees weren't so thick, I stopped, turned, fell to my butt, fell to my back, looked up at the web of branches and the blanket of stars, and began to wiggle and laugh.

Dylan was soon above me, feet planted next to my hips, arms crossed, a witness to my weirdness. I laughed even harder.

"It happened again, didn't it?" he asked. "Who was it?"

"Does ... it ... matter?" I said between gasps.

"Of course," he said. "It matters to someone. To many people, probably. To me."

I thrust my arms into the air and he grabbed my hands and pulled me up and against his body. Leaning forward, my nose grazed his cheek, and I kissed him, a tiny peck on the neck. "I'm pretty sure it was Perry Love," I told him.

"Crap. I liked that kid."

I kissed Dylan again, and the little hairs on his neck tickled my lips. "I hardly knew him," I said, which was the nicest thing I could say at that point. When we lost Katelyn and Brian, it had torched my insides. With Perry, I felt . . . not nothing, exactly, but this particular horror was more communal. It seemed obvious. We were all going down together. Sure, that was worth crying about. But it was also worth laughing about.

"I didn't see it," he said. "I saw you looking toward the bench instead of the end zone and then I saw the blood and then . . . dammit, I wanted to be there for Perry."

I kissed him again and whispered, *"Be there? What do you mean?"*

"When you die, don't you want someone to see it? People say that everyone dies alone, but that's a bunch of bull."

"We do everything alone, essentially," I said as I kissed him again. I was going to keep kissing him. This wasn't going to be another Brian Chen incident. These lips would not be ignored.

He put his hands on my shoulders and nudged me off his neck. Looking me in the eyes, he said, "To have that moment etched in people's memories, in the very biology of their brains, that's not dying alone. That's a magical thing. And you've been there for three people's last moments."

"I'd hardly call it magic," I replied.

"Yet you're laughing. And you're here in these woods, with me, as alive as you've ever been."

He was right, obviously. I had an undeniable spark in my body. A feeling of lightness, of thereness. So when he leaned in and finally kissed me, it was one motherfucking blockbuster of a kiss.

Sirens in the distance answered one another's howls and the wind gusted as I pawed that boy's body. It wasn't all contoured and smooth. There were riffles and lumps. Not a perfect body, but I didn't want a perfect body. I wanted this body—whole, intact— there in the patch of woods not far from where three of my classmates had blown up.

it will come as no surprise

There was chatter about patterns. When one kid blows up, it's an anomaly. When two blow up, it's a disturbing coincidence. Three and you've got yourself an epidemic. So what happens when a kid blows up at a football game that's supposed to symbolize a town's return to normalcy?

Things get weird.

Football season was officially canceled. No surprise there. No real complaints, either. It was easy for terrified players to shoot down arguments from meatheaded fathers waxing nostalgic on how "kids were tougher back in the day."

"Tougher, eh? Did your teammates randomly splatter all over you *back in the day*? No? Well then, shut the fuck up, Dad."

School was closed indefinitely. We all learned this via the press conference held on Saturday morning. Press conferences were nothing new to us, but Sheriff Tibble didn't use the steps of the library to deliver his shrugs and empty promises this time. He moved the production to a vacant field past Brighton Orchards. It was the only way to accommodate the people who had arrived as soon as the death toll had reached *what-the-fuck?*-able numbers.

You'd think a town full of exploding teenagers would scare people away, but no, there was a mass migration here. Scientists came in search of samples—water, dirt, blood, anything they could stick under a microscope. It had been a calm year for hurricanes, tornados, and other natural disasters, so the storm chasers and aggressively charitable types came rolling through in RVs, hoping to get off on our tragedies. I don't think I need to mention that the religious fanatics swarmed the streets and public buildings like a proverbial plague of . . . religious fanatics. My favorite of their charming picket signs?

THE DEVIL INSIDE YOUR CHILDREN HAS FOUND HIS WAY OUT!

It was inevitable that their signs also zeroed in on the whole Perry "Gay" Love angle. Soon almost everyone would focus on that angle. It was the one obvious and tangible difference he had from the rest of the herd.

But what did that mean about Katelyn and Brian?

"I kissed Katelyn once," Jenna Dalton told me the Sunday after the game, when she picked me up at Covington Kitchen on the way to an emergency town hall.

"Not listening," said Joe, who was sitting shotgun and sticking his fingers in his ears. "Do not wanna know who my sister has or hasn't kissed. No thank you. No way."

"Like *really* kissed?" I asked.

Jenna shrugged. "Yeah, I mean we were on molly and it was dark but, you know, tongue and everything."

"But you're not gay," I said.

Jenna shrugged again. "I don't know what I am. I don't know what Katelyn was either. It was a good kiss. I can say that for sure."

Other girls had also kissed Katelyn and were now telling. The only thing it proved, of course, was that Katelyn was into a bit of experimentation, but when the stories hit the comment sections, suddenly she was gay too. And when photos surfaced of Brian Chen in fishnet stockings, it was *case closed* for an assortment of morons and homophobes.

The seeds were actually sown at that emergency town hall, when Tina Parcells, self-proclaimed "social media guru and internationally renowned mommy-blogger," grabbed the microphone and asked, "Has anyone tested their DNA?"

Our mayor, the perpetually harried Roger Giancola, answered from the podium. "I do not know all the science behind an autopsy, but you must remember that we don't exactly have a lot of . . . autopsy material."

There were groans from the crowd, and I looked around hoping none of the Ogdens, Chens, or Loves were present to hear their dearly departed referred to as "autopsy material." I didn't see any of them, but it didn't mean they weren't there. The town hall was held in the State Street Theater, just like Katelyn's memorial, but it was even more packed than that had been. Priority seating was given to town residents, and the rest was standing room only. When the place reached fire-code capacity, the crowd spilled out into the streets, where there were giant speakers, a projector, and movie screen rigged up to broadcast the proceedings. There were also live streams provided by major news outlets, which meant some kid in a yurt in Mongolia could fire up his laptop, snuggle under a yak blanket, and join us, so long as he had a decent Wi-Fi connection. It was like the World Cup. Only not boring.

"You only need a drop of blood to do DNA tests," Tina said. "It's as if you haven't watched a movie or TV show in your entire life."

Mayor Giancola's tone became decidedly perturbed. "I've watched plenty of movies. I'm quite the cinephile, as a matter of fact, but I don't see what DNA has to do with the crisis we're currently facing."

"You and the sheriff keep telling us that there's no evidence of explosives," Tina said. "So if it's not an external problem, then it's an internal one. I've been told Perry Love was a homosexual. And while I don't want to take anything away from the bravery required to live such a difficult lifestyle, I've been told that homosexuality is genetically determined. So maybe this whole thing is as well. Look at their DNA is all I'm saying."

That wasn't *all* she was saying. By introducing this line of reasoning, she was telling people to consider Perry's sexuality, and by considering Perry's sexuality, they also had to consider Katelyn's and Brian's. The rumors about Katelyn had already been spreading by the time the town hall started, and within a few hours after it, the fishnet picture of Brian was trending.

Never mind that the picture was taken by his mom one innocent Saturday morning last spring when Brian was thinking about auditioning for the community theater's production of *Hedwig*. Never mind that even if Katelyn was gay and even if Brian was gay—and part of me kinda hoped that he was after that bus kiss snub—there's nothing about being gay that makes a person more combustible. Most sane and reasonable people realize this.

Alas, the world is neither sane nor reasonable, especially when ad-click revenue comes into play. Only the most callous and cynical "journalists" were trotting out link-bait like A NEW GAY PLAGUE? But that didn't mean others weren't implying the same thing.

I tried to stay away from all that noise, but what was there left for a girl to do? There was no school on the horizon, and Tess could only afford so much gas, and Dylan . . .

again, sorry

I've been a cagey little weasel, haven't I? You're probably wondering what happened after that kiss in the woods, aren't you? Did Dylan throw me down on the moss and ravage me? Are our clothes still hanging from the trees? Does the moon blush, thinking of the raw carnality she witnessed?

Sorry to disappoint, but it was only kissing and petting, but kissing and petting aren't nothing. Especially when helicopters show up and start stabbing the woods around the school with spotlights. Kissing and petting feel downright illegal at that point. And trust me, it's always best to be fully clothed when you run out of the woods and find your peers huddled up and asking each other, "Again? Really? Again?"

Really. Again.

The police couldn't round up and interview everyone at the football game. They certainly couldn't rope off the scene. So when Joe Dalton spotted me, he rushed over and said, "We're hightailing it out of here before shit goes crazy. Jenna's pulling the car around to Rumson Road and we're heading to Laura's house to get blind. You in?"

"Who's gonna be there?" I asked, because guest lists are important when blindness comes into play.

"Me, Jenna, Laura, Holly, Greer, and Rasheed," Joe said.

A more-than-acceptable roster, so I turned to Dylan and asked, "Do we join them?"

It was like Joe didn't even notice Dylan until I addressed him, like Dylan was some mythical beast that only materialized when its name was spoken. "Oh, hey, man," Joe said. "Sure. You should come too."

Dylan pursed his lips for a few seconds, then replied, "Nah. Go on ahead. Get somewhere safe. I'm going to stick around here for a while."

I was in a bit of a pickle. I wanted to be with Dylan but I wanted to leave. The buzz of the night was wearing off and I was sinking back into the sludge of awareness.

Really? Again?

"Come on," I said. "Nothing good will come out of staying here."

"Have fun," Dylan said, and before I could object, he kissed me on the cheek and jogged away, in the direction of the flashing lights.

I could have chased after him, I guess, but I didn't want to. He had left at the exact right moment, leaving me in a state of anxious anticipation. At Laura's house, all I needed was some gin and SunnyD to pick the buzz back up, and while everyone was trying to piece together what happened on the field, I was musing about what might happen next with me and Dylan.

What happened next was a text, arriving at nine a.m., as I bur-
rowed under a blanket on the living room couch. It read:

Everything,

I wrote back immediately.

Me: Deep.

Him: I meant that last night I felt everything.

Me: Not every THING. Next time. Maybe.

Him: When's next time?

Me: Not today. Parents got me doing a double shift at
the hug factory.

Side note: My parents weren't big huggers but, after Katelyn,
they rolled up their sleeves and did their due diligence, smother-
ing their daughter whenever her face got all droopy. It worked at
first, but ever since Brian, it was the opposite of what I needed.
Still, Mom and Dad wanted me home that Sunday to be their little
stuffed animal. I think they'd come to depend on the hugging, in
fact. This was no longer about me.

Him: When then?

Me: Not tomorrow either. Working at Covington
Kitchen. Keeping busy helps.

Him: Should I stop in for an Oinker?

Me: Yaaassss! Wait. No. Not because I don't want to see you.

Him: Too much of a tease?

Me: Exactly. Monday?

Him: MONDAY!

As you already know, my deli gig was interrupted on Sunday by the emergency town hall. Cell reception was terrible at the theater, so even when I tried to connect with Dylan, I didn't get through, and I certainly couldn't spot him in that sea of anxiety. I'd love to break down all the bullshit that was shat out at that meeting, but I think covering Tina's DNA witch hunt is enough. Because it represents when the theories went off the rails.

That Sunday evening, my parents were still huggy, so I was constantly retreating to the bathroom for alone time and giving in to the stupid urge to pull out my phone and shake a virtual fist at all the trolls. TV was even worse. A tour of cable news resulted in teeth-grinding and blind-pulling because I was sure that some helmet-haired reporter was creeping through our shrubbery, about to thrust her head through our window and say, "So is it terrorists, homosexuality, or the overall crappiness of your hometown that's tearing your generation apart, young lady, and do you mind holding your answers and tears back until my cameraman gets the proper lighting in place?"

So I went dark for a few hours. I didn't text Tess or Dylan because if I couldn't see them in person and hold on to them, then it wasn't worth it. All I could do was get in bed and wait for sleep to grab me and whisk me along to a future closer to my date with Dylan.

a little further in the future

On Monday morning, less than three full days after Perry Love spontaneously combusted, Cranberry Bollinger's dad waltzed into his daughter's room to wake her up and found Cranberry sauce all over her Miyazaki posters.

Fuck. Sorry. Bad joke. Old habits die hard. But come on, the girl's name was Cranberry.

It was and has always been Cranberry, as far as I know. My earliest memory of her is the first day of fourth grade, when Ms. Caldwell took attendance and said, "Cranberry Bollinger. Is Cranberry Bollinger here?"

"*Here,*" came a soft voice from the back and we all turned around to see a purple-haired, dark-skinned girl wearing a black T-shirt with a ghostly face on it. I didn't know until years later that the ghost face represented a Guy Fawkes mask, the symbol of Anonymous, everybody's favorite zit-faced army of hackers.

Yes, Cranberry was a hacker, a gamer, a cosplayer. Even back in fourth grade. I would tell you more about her if I knew more about her, but I don't. She was always just Cranberry, the girl whose name launched a thousand corny puns.

"Don't get bogged down, Cranberry."

"Hey, Cranberry. You know what my favorite cocktail is? A Cape Codder. Because it's a mix of vodka and you."

"Yo, Ocean Spray!"

She seemed to take it in stride, usually rolling her eyes and saying, "Hilarrrrrious!" or "Only heard that one about a billion times."

Granted, most of it was harmless. Can't pack much punch into cracks about cranberries. It wasn't like she was named Cherry, Peach, or some other sexy fruit. Cranberries aren't sexy and neither was Cranberry. She was awkward. She was quiet. Outside of class, her headphones were always on and her head was always buried in a tablet. And yet... and yet...

She had a boyfriend. A *serious* boyfriend. Her consummate companion since ninth grade was Elliot Pressman, a fellow hacker, a fellow gamer, a fellow cosplayer. In other words, Cranberry was not gay. She was a lot of other things. She was black. She dyed her hair—pink being the latest and last incarnation. She was aggressively nerdy. But she was not gay.

Elliot Pressman could certainly attest to that fact.

When word got around that Cranberry was gone too, everyone turned to Elliot's Tumblr to offer condolences. What we found there was a tribute to a girlfriend. Tender and, well, I should let it speak for itself:

Cranberry, my love. While I was making love to you
last night with the moonlight streaming in through
the windows and caressing our naked torsos, and as
the sweat from our bodies pooled up on the floor, and
when our moans of pleasures shook the heavens, I
knew our love was eternal and . . .

Okay, that's about enough of that. It goes on and on and you get
the picture. Turns out Cranberry, bless her heart, was a wildcat in
the sack, a lover for the ages. At least by Elliot's estimation. Not
that he had many points of reference, but there are worse ways to
be remembered by your boyfriend. No wonder I was once jealous
of the girl.

That was a while ago, late spring of sophomore year. Tess and I
were in chemistry. I was doing my best maintaining-my-B by gazing
out the window at a gym class softball game. Cranberry and Elliot
were in the outfield, but they weren't exactly waiting for their call
up to the big leagues. They were lying next to each other in the grass,
holding their phones aloft. Their other hands were buried in their
softball gloves, but since Elliot was a lefty, and Cranberry a righty,
they could hold hands with the gloves. How very cute and hygienic.

Ms. Schultz, our boxy and Botoxed gym teacher, must've had a
romantic streak, or maybe she'd stopped giving a damn—rumor
had it, she was perpetually on the verge of retirement—because
she didn't budge or blow her whistle when the couple ignored the
pop fly that dropped a few feet from them. Greg Holder sprinted
in, scooped the ball up, and fired it toward second base, but not
before shouting something at the couple.

"Get a room"?

"Email me that selfie"?

"Long live your everlasting love"?

I don't know, because I couldn't hear. But I could certainly feel the pangs of my insignificance as I sat there in a class that promised the world could be broken down into formulas.

Okay, fine. Then what the hell was the formula for what these two lovebirds had?

When the bell rang and broke me out of a daze of self-pity, I turned to Tess and said, "I would kill to have a boyfriend like Elliot Pressman."

"Really?" Tess said as she packed up her notebooks. "But he's so . . . Elliot."

"Sometimes all you need is an Elliot. A guy who'll hold your hand with a softball glove while you update your status. A guy who won't expect you to do things like talk to him or bathe."

"So who'd you kill for your Elliot?"

"Cranberry, I guess."

"Oh no. Not Cranberry. Cranberry is innocent. Cranberry is harmless."

"For me to find happiness, Cranberry got to get got," I said, and I held my hand out like I had a gun and tilted it sideways for the gangsta effect.

Of course, our incredibly kind chem teacher, Mrs. Otieno, was standing behind me when I did it, and I turned around and witnessed this tolerant woman, hanging and shaking her head. Not in disgust, exactly. In exasperation.

I felt like a total shit.

I don't know if Cranberry's spontaneous combustion made a lot of people feel like total shits, but it certainly made them rethink things. Besides eradicating the gaysplosion theories, it shattered any ethnicity arguments. We had a black girl, a white guy, an Asian dude, and a . . .

What exactly are people from Turkey? Turkish, of course, but are they European or Asian? Are they Arab? It doesn't matter, right? Because it obviously didn't matter then, which I think frustrated a lot of people who were hoping for some excuse for their racism.

"Well, leave it to them [*insert your least favorite skin tone*] folks to start poppin' off like bottle rockets!"

The more valid proximity arguments were becoming problematic too. The first three explosions took place on school grounds and so many, including myself, suspected something was in the air at Covington High. Magnetic waves? A grand confluence of cellular data? The chemicals wafting from the cafeteria food?

Cranberry lived at least five miles from school, in a split-level near the highway, so it was clear that even if the problem originated in the high school, it wasn't contained to the high school. A virus seemed a likely culprit, but the powers-that-be weren't quite ready to go down that path. There was something else to focus on.

drugs

"Drugs?" Mom asked me Monday afternoon as I waited in the armchair by the window.

"What's that?" I replied. My eyes were fixed on the driveway. Dylan was supposed to arrive at any minute.

"Drugs?" Mom asked again.

"No thanks," I responded. "I did a bump of coke with breakfast."

"Ha-ha, hilarious," she said, and reached to put her hand on my shoulder, but pulled back when she remembered how I'd been avoiding hugs lately. "I mean with this Cranberry girl. I looked her up online and she, well, her hairstyle choices were interesting."

"So she's on drugs?"

"Hey, all I'm saying is that the druggies stood out when I was in high school. A girl with orange hair? Come on."

"Did you really call people druggies?"

"What do you call them?"

"Katelyn Ogden."

"Wait, so Katelyn did . . . ?"

"Not like meth or anything. But I understand that she dabbled."

Protip: When your parents ask you to confirm rumors that you know are factually true, it's best to start your confession with "I understand that . . ." Because, one, it's not a lie. You do understand. You understand the hell out of it. But, two, it distances you from the rumor. You're analytical about things, not emotional, which means you're not all wrapped up in the mess. You're an observer.

"Dabbled?" Mom asked. "Who else dabbles? Shit. Tess doesn't dabble, does she?"

"Tess neither dabbles, tinkers, nor flirts," I said. "Don't worry about darling Tessy. She is squeaky clean."

I wasn't thrilled about the momentum of this conversation because it was obviously barreling toward me, a serial dabbler. I had yet to tell my parents about my dabbling, though I suspect they had their suspicions. Luckily, the momentum was stopped in its tracks by an ice-cream truck that pulled into our driveway.

When Dylan had texted earlier that he was coming to pick me up, he hadn't specified the mode of transportation. I had wondered for a second if he expected me to also have a skateboard, but I quickly convinced myself that he wasn't that naive. I'd never seen him driving a car, which led to me picturing horse-drawn carriages, Segways, and even bicycles built for two. I definitely did not expect a rusty old ice-cream truck, though I suppose I should have.

I leapt from the couch and through the front door to intercept Dylan as he made his way up the walkway. "Nice ride," I said. "A bit cliché, don't you think?"

He didn't take the bait and turn around to look at the boxy white truck with the faded Popsicle and sugar cone decals on it. He simply shrugged and said, "Date a lot of ice-cream men?"

"Of course you don't show up in a Hyundai or something," I said. "You've gotta be the kid who rolls up in something quirky, endearing, and yet strangely manly."

"First time I've driven it actually. I usually take my mom's minivan or my brother's pickup, but they're both occupied."

"You've got a brother? I didn't know you had a brother."

"There's a lot you don't know about me."

Mom was in the doorway, watching our exchange, sizing up the chariot that was going to whisk me away. I wondered what she knew about Dylan. Surely the rumors hadn't reached the adult sphere. But you never know what she overhears at the deli.

"Nice to see you again, Dylan," she said. "I'm guessing that thing doesn't have airbags."

Dylan shook his head and said, "Seat belts though. And it reaches a maximum speed of forty-five miles per hour when it's going downhill, so there won't be any drag racing, I can assure you of that. Strictly an around-town vehicle."

"Like a trolley car," I added. "You're not afraid of trolley cars, are you, Mom?"

She shook her head. "I'm not sure what to be afraid of these days."

While I would have loved to shrug off her worries as typical parental jitters, how could I possibly do that? It was a tough time to be a kid, but, good God, I couldn't imagine what sort of panic had overtaken our parents' brains. The best I could do was redirect things with a joke. Only it wasn't really a joke. It was more of a test.

"Don't worry, Momma Bear," I said. "Dylan is only taking me to meet his three kids and then we're going to burn down a convenience store or two."

She rolled her eyes. A good sign. She detected hyperbole.

Dylan, on the other hand, rolled with the punches, which I wasn't sure how to interpret. "That wasn't the plan, actually," he said. "But I guess if we have time, we can fit those things in."

Grumbling audibly, Mom accepted this all as teenage snark. "Be safe," she said.

Be safe. In the history of moms, has there ever been a more useless declaration? My mom isn't stupid, of course. She knows saying "be safe" won't make me any safer. She knows that hugging me won't make me any safer either. Still, she rushed over and hugged me because even if I wasn't gaga for that stuff lately, and even if that stuff wouldn't prevent me from blowing up, she couldn't let me leave her sight without at least squeezing the ever-living fuck out of me.

what to do
on a second date

The ice-cream truck bumbled down quiet roads on the western edge of town, out where things get all "are you sure we're still in New Jersey?" I figured we were just driving around, going nowhere, because that's what was discussed over text.

Him: What ya wanna do?

Me: Doesn't matter. Getting out is enough.

As we rolled along, our conversation started with the ice-cream truck's origins. Turns out Dylan's father drove it on summer evenings in the nineties to keep the farm afloat, a fact I found both noble and depressing. So I changed the subject to Perry Love and Cranberry Bollinger. Neither of us had known them well, but Dylan had noticed the incongruity I mentioned before.

"Cranberry wasn't anywhere near the school," he said.

"Hallelujah, right?"

"I guess."

"Young Mr. Hovemeyer, were you hoping our halls would be all Jackson Pollocked up each and every week?" I asked as Dylan guided the ice-cream truck onto a dirt road.

"No, no, no," he said with a furrowed brow. "But it seems like it should be a communal experience. Something we should all be going through together."

"You're weird."

His response was a crooked smile and a "yeah, well . . ."

Without another word, he pulled the truck over and parked in brown grass next to a hulking blue silo with a dent in the top that made it look like it had been struck by a meteorite. He hopped out and circled around to the passenger side—to open my door and help me down, I guess, but I had beaten him to it. I was already waiting in the waist-high grass.

"We feeding some chickens?" I asked.

"You'll see," he said. Then he opened the back hatch of the truck and yanked out a green duffel bag, which he hefted over a shoulder. "Follow me."

The silo door wasn't much bigger than a dog door, but the duffel fit through, and Dylan did too, twisting his body and snaking his way inside. "Come on in," he said. "It's perfectly safe."

I stuck my head through the door and I couldn't see farther than the reach of the sunlight. A couple of feet at best. "It's dark as hell in there. There could be raccoons with switchblades. There could be Jehovah's Witnesses, waiting to pounce."

"Completely empty," he assured me. "Besides, I have a light."

He reached his hands toward the door and I figured what the hell. I'd never been in a silo before, and while that's not exactly bucket-list worthy, it's something to do when you're with a boy who intrigues you, scares you, and turns you on in equal measure.

By the time I'd slipped through, stood up, and dusted myself off, Dylan had moved toward the center of the silo. I couldn't see him, but I could hear his echoing footsteps and the hiss of the duffel's zipper. Any guess as to what was in that duffel bag?

Samurai swords?

The bones of an ex-girlfriend?

Pie? Lots and lots of delicious pie?

Wrong, wrong, and unfortunately wrong. You weren't paying attention, were you? Because Dylan had already told me what was in the duffel.

"Let there be light," he said.

White shapes erupted on the curved walls of the silo and the place transformed. From darkness, disco was born. Sitting on the floor was a spinning orb that shot out the light. If I had inspected it closer, I would have discovered that it wasn't some fancy club or theater equipment. It was a regular illuminated globe, a miniature plastic world poked full of holes and mounted on a battery-powered turntable. Honestly, I didn't care what it was, only what it was doing. It was showing me Dylan's smiling face and his reaching hand.

As I grabbed his hand, music kicked in, perfectly on cue.

I knew the song. It was a song Tess and I used to sing when we were riding our bikes down the shore and dreaming of our future. It was a song that everyone in New Jersey knows. I suspect the rest of the world knows it too, and they probably make fun of it. Out here in the northwestern corner of the Garden State, we don't ever pronounce it "Noo Joisey" and we certainly don't appreciate all the uninspired cracks about "The Dirty Jerz" and "The Armpit of America." And yet we will freely admit we have an irrational attachment to certain songs. This one was perhaps the most obvious example of that.

Yes, I hate to break it to you. It wasn't some obscure but transcendent indie track, or some dusted-off gem from the good old days that boys are supposed to play you to make you rethink the past while you fall in love with their musical archaeology. It was an enduring emblem of cheese. I'm embarrassed to even say the title, because it's one of those eighties' anthems where even the drummer sings on the chorus. But dammit if it didn't slay me right then and there in that silo, ricocheting off the walls with all the light.

"When my dad died," Dylan said as he pulled me toward him, "I used to come in here and put on this music and I would dance by myself."

He was dancing with me now, slowly turning me against the spin of the lights. "That's the saddest fucking thing I've heard in my entire life," I said.

He shook his head. "I liked it. It helped."

"This is your silo?"

"No. Bank owns it, I think. Used to be owned by a family called the Rogalskis. But their farm went bankrupt and they took off. Not sure where to."

"Do you still . . . farm?" I asked, which suddenly seemed like a weird thing to be asking a boy I was dancing with.

"Dad had life insurance," he said. "We're doing okay without milking any cows these days."

As the chorus erupted, he dipped me slightly. He wasn't the best dancer, but his moves were certainly practiced.

"You've done this before, haven't you?" I asked.

"Like I said, I used to dance in here all the time."

"I mean with another girl."

"Oh," he said as he dipped me again, this time a bit lower. "Yes. I have. Does that matter?"

It didn't. His hands on my hips and my hands on his back, the pulse of the music, the ridiculous riot of light—that's what mattered. But still I pressed things further, because that's who I am and what I do.

"Did you lay that girl down and make sweet, sweet love to her?" I asked, channeling the same muse that inspired Elliot Pressman's ode to Cranberry. "Did your bodies entwine right here in grain dust and mouse turds?"

"Not in the silo. We did things in the field behind it."

Crazy, right? No bullshit, no "oh baby, there's you and there's only ever been you"? Maybe it should have bothered me, but it didn't. He was fully clothed and yet he was naked.

"Why are you telling me this?"

"Because you asked."

Is that all it took? Okay then. "Did you really burn down the QuickChek?" I asked.

He laughed. "Short answer: no."

"Long answer?"

"Hell no. Keith Lutz is a pyro and brought me along when he and Joe Dalton wanted to burn some stuff. Always good to have a scapegoat on hand. A farm boy with a *shitty* father is a perfect one."

"Is the other rumor a lie as well?"

"What's the other rumor?"

"You know. The doozy. About you having three kids and all that."

"I don't know."

"You don't know the rumor?"

"I don't know about having three kids. There were never any blood tests that I'm aware of."

"Wait a second," I said, and though I was tempted to stop dancing, I didn't stop dancing because I was enjoying the dancing. "Did you take Jane Rolling here?"

"She was my girlfriend. We did things together. That's what you do. You've had boyfriends, haven't you?"

I have. Never for much longer than a month or two, but at the time I would have called them my boyfriends. Carson Sears. Patrick McCoy. L. T. LaRouche. (That's right. I dated a guy named L. T. LaRouche. Do with that information what you will.)

But me having a boyfriend was besides the point. There was a more pressing matter. "Dylan Hovemeyer," I said. "Are you using the same moves on me that you used on some girl you knocked up?"

"We also went to the movies," he said. "We went to dinner. Are those things off-limits too? I wanted to have a nice afternoon with you. Isn't this nice?"

The chorus kicked in again. He couldn't possibly have planned the timing, but goddamn, goddamn. Those lights did their thing, the music boomed, and it *was* nice. There was no denying it. As there was no denying this:

"You're a father," I said. "A dad. I'm dancing in a silo with a dad."

"I'm only a kid trying to figure things out. Hoping that you don't blow to smithereens."

For that whole time in the silo, I had forgotten all about the spontaneous combustions. I guess that says something. I had spent so much energy in the previous weeks trying to push those images and ideas out of my mind ... when all I needed was a power ballad and a homemade disco ball.

I was a little mad, a little confused, a little stunned by how things had gotten here, but mostly I was sharing the same thought. I was hoping to God he wouldn't blow to smithereens, right there in my arms.

And he didn't.

you're probably wondering

Did we do the deed? If by "do the deed," you mean did we make out furiously until we were cut off by Dylan's phone ringing—if by "do the deed," you mean did he then give his phone a glance and say, "I gotta take this"—then yes, the deed was most thoroughly done.

There wasn't much to the phone call. A few "uh-huhs" and "I understands" and then it was back to the ice-cream truck for us.

"Do you mind if I ask who that was?" I said, as I slid into my cracked vinyl seat.

"I don't," he replied, and he backed the truck onto the dirt road and jammed it into gear. "It was a woman named Carla Rosetti. I've got to go and meet with her right now."

"You mean Special Agent Carla Rosetti? Of the FBI?" If he couldn't hear the excitement in my voice, then he could certainly feel it in the vibrations I was sending through the thin frame of the truck by stomping after every word.

"The same," he said, and he reached to turn on the radio, to fill the truck with music so we didn't have to talk, I guess. But there was no radio. So he rapped his knuckles on the dash, then gave the wheel a firm squeeze.

"She's, like, my hero," I told him.

"Well, your hero wants to talk to me about Cranberry Bollinger."

"Madness! What do you have to do with Cranberry?"

"Nothing, but I ran into Carla on Friday night. After you left with the Dalton twins. She wants to clear a few things up."

"Wait, wait, wait. You refer to Special Agent Carla Rosetti as Carla? Like you two are best buds or something?"

"Not best buds. But we go back."

"You *go back*? With Special Agent Carla Rosetti? You didn't skip the light fandango in a silo with her, did you?"

God, what a moment that would have been. I could picture Rosetti folding her coat and placing it gently on the floor, and then grabbing Dylan and waltzing perfect circles around the silo. She would lead of course; and she wouldn't even take off her holster because she's always on the job.

"No fandangoing," Dylan assured me. "But she did arrest my brother, Warren."

"Hold up. How did I not know this?"

"Probably because you don't know everything," he said. He was teasing, of course, but I was beginning to wonder when I'd gotten so far out of the loop. If I didn't know the sexual preferences and arrest records of my peers, then what sort of nonsense was I filling my brain with?

"I probably just forgot," I said. "So remind me. What did Warren do?"

"Nothing. They say he posted threats on Facebook. The arrest didn't happen around here though. He was at prep school in Connecticut. After Dad died, Warren wanted to escape for a bit. Mom had the money to fund his escape."

"What were the threats?"

"To"—Dylan provided the requisite air quotes—"*burn all you fuckers to the ground.*"

Holy shit, right? Where was that radio now?

"*All* us fuckers?" I asked carefully. "Or particular fuckers?"

"That wasn't specified," he said with a sigh. "But when you attend a fancy boarding school in Connecticut and you're the one kid there who doesn't come from hedge-fund money, then the world notices. And the world calls in the FBI. That's how Carla entered our lives."

Crossing my wrists, I put my hands out like I was ready to be cuffed and asked, "Did she, like, stun gun him and toss him in the shackles?"

"Wasn't like that. There were lawyers. Deals. He got community service and a one-way ticket home. He was sixteen at the time, so he dropped out."

"So where's Warren now?"

"Living in a little cottage on the south side of our farm. Working at the Fast Lube."

"Damn. Has Special Agent Carla Rosetti spoken to him?"

"You bet."

"So why does she want to speak to you?"

"Because she thinks I'm the one who made that original Facebook post."

"And why would she think that?"

"Because I did."

the benefits of cyberstalking

I'd already done my Googling. I knew more than a bit about Special Agent Carla Rosetti. A few highlights, collected from various websites and newspaper archives.

• At the age of eight, a pigtailed Carla Rosetti placed third in a pumpkin-growing contest in Blacksburg, Virginia. 246 pounds. A massive, massive gourd, my friends.

• Thirteen-year-old Carla Rosetti was a member of her high school's Model UN team. She represented Bhutan. Presumably, she rocked that shit, and for at least an afternoon, Bhutan was the greatest country in the world.

- In an 87–34 drubbing of Christianburg High, Ms. Rosetti, then a senior, but only fifteen years old (!), scored a game-high 27 points. In your face, Christianburg!

- At the University of Maryland, criminal-justice major Carla Rosetti was quoted by *The Diamondback* as saying the refurbished student center was "pretty boss" and that it seems like a "chill place to hang with friends." Thanks for the heads-up, Car-Car. If I'm ever down that way, I'll check it out. Definitely sounds boss. Totally chill.

- After nabbing the infamous "Pawtucket Pyro," FBI newbie Carla Rosetti received a commendation from the governor of Rhode Island. It may be the smallest in the Union, but they sleep better in the Ocean State thanks to our favorite up-and-coming field agent.

- Carla Rosetti rocks a purple taffeta bridesmaid dress. Congrats on the nuptials Jamir and Heidi. What a beautiful farm that was! What a beautiful wedding! And that picture of you two hugging the llama? Priceless.

- Carla Rosetti has killed a man.

Okay, this one needs a bit more background. The guy's name was Gordon Laramie and he was one of those mouth breathers with an Armageddon hard-on. A few years ago, he was hiding out in the remote woods of northern New Hampshire, stockpiling Chunky Soup in an underground bunker he'd built out of shipping containers. He'd laced the perimeter with land mines acquired from some shady French Canadians. When a couple of hikers lost their way one foggy autumn morning, they stumbled upon Mr. Laramie's hideout and over one of the aforementioned land mines.

A land mine is a lot lazier than a spontaneous combustion. By that I mean it doesn't always finish the job. In this case, it blew the right leg off one hiker and the left leg off the other. Luckily, they were both paramedics and had the Rolls-Royce of first aid kits on hand. They managed to shoot themselves full of morphine and apply tourniquets to each other's stumps. Then they strapped their bodies together with belts and duct tape and used their two good legs to walk a mile to a logging road, where they flagged down a guy on a quadrunner who strapped them to the back, alongside the nine-point buck he'd just bagged. He rushed them to a ranger station, where they called in a medevac helicopter and the FBI.

Because of her experience with arsonists and explosion enthusiasts, Carla Rosetti arrived that evening with a bomb squad and SWAT team in tow. She commanded the team from a distance—stationed in an ATV decked out with video surveillance—and they stormed the underground bunker aided by assorted gizmos.

Of course, Gordon Laramie proved to be wilier than assorted gizmos. Expecting their arrival, he had devised a ruse. Earlier that day, he had kidnapped Ruben Howe, owner and proprietor of the Grahamville General Store, and locked him in the bunker. The SWAT team was rocking infrared goggles, so when they detected movement underground, they assumed they had their man.

Their man, however, was creeping through the woods, donning the skin and antlers of a recently killed moose as a disguise. As the SWAT team was descending into the bunker, Laramie was creeping up on Rosetti and her small team of unarmed technicians, his makeshift crown of antlers rattling against the low-hanging branches.

Now, I'm not sure how many people have had a good old-fashioned shootout with a man wearing a moose skin and antlers, but I'm guessing it's only one.

You know who.

The details of the shootout are sketchy at best. In interviews she did for an extended piece about the case in *Salon,* Rosetti described the situation as the "fog of war," and repeatedly talked about "simply doing her job."

Well, she simply did her job pretty damn well, because that evening they carried Gordon Laramie out in a body bag and a hyperventilating, but safe, Ruben Howe out in a stretcher. Apparently they found a manifesto of some sort, but Rosetti never shared that with the press. After all, you don't want anyone else influenced by the rantings of a madman.

Reading the *Salon* piece, I imagined the moose-frocked Laramie running at Rosetti with a shotgun blasting, her diving behind a tree, and chunks of bark exploding in the frosty air. I imagined Rosetti pulling a pistol from her boot, rolling over and unloading—*pop-pop-pop*—as the fog settled in. I imagined the fog clearing, and Rosetti standing over Laramie's dying body and pulling out an e-cigarette, taking a drag and it lighting up all blue at the tip as she said, "Moose season is officially . . . over."

another part of the story

Ten minutes after Dylan dropped me off at my house, Tess was
picking me up and I was giving her a rundown of the date.

"So many red flags," she said as she drove us in the direction of
the police station. "So, so many."

"I know, I know."

"Let's forget all the Jane Rolling stuff and focus on the whole
'burn all you fuckers to the ground' Facebook post, why don't we?"

I smiled sheepishly, and said, "He was a child. Twelve."

"Psychopaths have childhoods too. Full of fire and dissected
roadkill. And he let his brother take the blame for him? What's
that all about?"

"His brother wanted to take the blame. Warren wanted out of
Connecticut and this gave him an out. Dylan was helping him. Or
at least he thought he was."

"Keep telling yourself that."

I would. I would keep telling myself that, because that's what

Dylan told me before he dropped me off. It won't surprise you to hear that I'm a skeptical person. I don't even believe half the garbage that tumbles from my own mouth. So putting my faith in Dylan was a big deal.

"Dylan hasn't lied to me," I said. "Not yet."

"How do you know?"

"Because this is precisely the stuff he should be lying about."

"So he's a fountain of honesty. And yet here you are, secretly stalking him."

We were now parked alongside the road, between two news vans, a half block from the police station. Dylan's ice-cream truck was in the station's parking lot. We hadn't arrived in time to see him go inside, but where else could he be?

"If Dylan asks me, 'Did you follow me to my rendezvous with Special Agent Carla Rosetti of the FBI?' then I will say, 'I understand that Tess might have driven me near the vicinity of the police station while you were inside with aforementioned government employee.'"

"Oh, honey," Tess said. "You're in deep, aren't you?"

"Hit the deck," I shouted, and I grabbed Tess by the shirt and pulled her below the horizon of the dash.

"Whoa," she howled. "A simple 'slide down, please' would have worked fine. I'm guessing you spotted them?"

Head poking up and on a swivel, I checked the windows. "They're getting in her car. She drives a Tesla."

"She's so rad," Tess said. "I bet she plays poker. Hangs out at high roller tables wearing aviators and chewing a toothpick. I bet they call her Lady Nightshade."

"No doubt," I said, and I sat up. "They're pulling away. We're gonna have to tail 'em."

Tess checked her mirrors, pushed the bangs out of her eyes, checked her mirrors again, slipped the car in reverse.

"Come on, come on," I said. "Haven't you ever tailed anyone before? Step on it!"

Ever since forever, Tess could scold me with nothing more than a sigh. She sighed long and deep and said, "We will follow them. But we will be safe. A car chase is not how I plan to go out."

"Fine," I replied with a groan. "You know that I love you, right? Bunches and bunches."

"You better," she said as she pulled into traffic. "Bunches and bunches and bunches and bunches."

We were four cars behind Carla and Dylan. If a couple of stoplights didn't go our way, we'd lose them. Which wouldn't be the end of the world, considering that Dylan said he'd fill me in on everything, but that was the equivalent of reading a recap of a TV show instead of watching it. When it's information versus experience, you always choose experience.

As we tailed them around the corner, past the Wawa and the Little League field, a text from Dylan lit up my phone.

Why are you following us?

"Dammit! They made us," I said.

"That's Lady Nightshade for you," Tess replied. "Can't get anything past her."

I started to type a response:

We're out for a drive. You just happened . . .

Then I thought better of it. Deleted and retyped.

Me: Busted! Sorry. Curiosity.

Dylan: It's cool. Carla wants you to join us. She'll drive slow.

Tess must have seen my eyes go googly. "What's up?" she asked. "Double date."

a meeting of minds

The parking lot next to the long-abandoned factory off Wood-erson Road was thick with weeds. And the weeds themselves were thick. Like, celery thick. The sound of them smacking the undercarriage of Tess's Honda was a jungle sound. Why the hell were we out here?

Because Special Agent Carla Rosetti was calling the shots, that's why. As we pulled in, she was already parked, out of her car, and putting up a hand like a traffic cop. Something that looked like a DustBuster dangled from her other hand.

"Reach for the sky," she hollered as we exited the vehicle.

We did our best, tippy-toeing and stretching out as Rosetti waved the device over Tess's body. The thing was connected by a cable to her phone, where an app flashed and blipped.

"Metal detector?" Tess asked. "Because I have a tin of Altoids in my pocket."

"Won't matter," Rosetti said. "This detects radiation. Explosives. The nasty stuff. It's what the Secret Service uses. Top of the line."

Rosetti moved on to me, leaning in as she swept my body for . . . who knows what? Spontaneous combustion juice? As she bent over and her hair brushed my face, I gave her a good sniff.

A little weird, I admit. But also informative.

Rosetti wore perfume. Nice perfume. Not that I expected her to smell like coffee and gunpowder, but it was surprising how subtle and soft her scent was. Undergarments were now something to wonder about. What manner of lace was rubbing up against her holsters?

"Both clean," she said as she moved the device past my ankles and stood up. Man, did I want her to spin the thing in her hand and blow on it like the smoking barrel of a pistol, but all she did was slap it to her hip and carry it back to the Tesla.

Dylan had joined us at this point, hands in pockets, looking adorable and a tad nervous.

"Nice to see you again, Dylan," Tess said.

"And you," Dylan said, and he did a little bow. Which ignited the polite young lady in Tess and she responded with a little curtsy. I joined in by dancing little pirouettes, because . . . well, because I'm odd.

"Enjoying ourselves?" Rosetti asked when she returned from her car.

Pirouettes are usually best not left unfinished, but Rosetti deserved my respect, so I stopped one halfway through, planted my feet, threw my arms to the side, and said, "Sorry. I get carried away."

Rosetti waved a dismissive hand and said, "You're a child."

So harsh, but at that moment, unfortunately true. I didn't say another word.

"And who are you?" she then asked Tess. "Friend?"

"Um . . . I'm Tess McNulty and I like to think of myself as more than—"

"What's your deal, Tess McNulty?" Rosetti asked. "Give it to me quick."

The poise that had guided Tess through so many math olympiad victories and slam-dunk babysitting interviews leaked from her body like the whites from a cracked egg. "Well," she said. "I'm, well, I told you my name and I guess I'd say . . . well, I'm hoping to go to RIT in the fall. Oh, and I was on the field hockey team but, you know, the season was canceled and . . . I like music and movies and . . . stuff?"

Rosetti did her shittiest to feign interest, stare-squinting, and clearly waiting for Tess to shut up. When she was finally given an opening, she said, "Tell me this, Miss McNulty. Do you blow people up?"

"No, ma'am."

"Good to know. Moving on."

"Why are we here?" I asked. It was the middle of the day, sunny and perfectly pleasant, but the place was giving me the creeps. It wasn't the weeds or the cracked bricks of the building, or even the overall hauntedness of the place. It was the odor: metallic and animal at the same time, a rusty rot.

"Glad you asked," Rosetti said, and she pointed at the building. "Do you know what this used to be?"

"My dad always told me they made fertilizer," Dylan said.

Rosetti smiled and said, "Dad was a good liar. Or maybe he never knew the truth. Truth is, this place was into far dirtier things than that. And when you're located on a river and you do dirty things, well, I don't know all the details, but let's just say there was a time in the fifties when kids downstream were born with their organs on the outside."

I couldn't see it, but I could hear the rush of the Patchcong River through the trees. We were at the bottom of the gorge on the edge of town, not far from the reservoir where all the county's water originated.

"Shit," I said. "So you think we're all drinking tainted water and that's why—"

"No," Rosetti said. "They dealt with all that years ago. Cleaned up and covered up. But this place *is* a symbol. Something is tainted in your town. But it's something new. Even nastier than what came before."

It made me think of that novel I had been working on. You know, *All the Feels*? It was set in the town of Cloverton, New Jersey, where seedy secrets are the stock in trade, and the seediest secret is the one kept by the protagonist—the intrepid and smoking-hot Xavier Rothman. I decided that if I was going to write more of it, then I should add a character with Rosettiesque qualities. A scenery-chomping detective with supersleuth abilities.

"Okay, so then why are *we* here?" Dylan asked.

"Because I wanted a moment in private, away from the media,

the police, my partner. I wanted to talk to my favorite pyromaniac, his always-in-the-wrong-place-at-the-right-time girlfriend, and our resident . . . field hockey star."

Tess looked away and whispered, "*I wasn't technically a star.*"

"So what do you think is tainting us?" I asked.

"Don't know yet," Rosetti asked. "But I have my suspicions. We can rule out chemtrails and other broad factors. But something has gotten into your bodies."

A pickup truck rumbled past, and a guy stuck his head out the passenger-side window and yelled something. Vulgar by inflection, though I couldn't make out the words.

"Ignore them," Rosetti said. "Ignore all of them. This town is full of people who think they know why this is happening. But all we really know is that this is happening to *you*. All four incidents have involved students in your senior class. The odds that this is random aren't even odds at all."

"So you're saying we're fucked?" I asked.

"I'm asking for your help. I want you to come to me with all the rumors, all the gossip, all the things you know and hear about your peers. I want to feel like I'm undercover among your classmates, something I am obviously not equipped to do."

Rosetti pulled at her suit jacket to straighten it. She was thirty-six years old—or at least that's what my research had told me—and she had been something of a prodigy, having graduated at sixteen. Which meant she hadn't been a high school student in twenty years.

"So we're tattletales?" I asked.

"Volunteers," she said.

"So we're not suspects?" Dylan asked.

"Everyone is a suspect," Rosetti said. "However, I don't think the three of you have been plotting together to take down the senior class if that's what you mean."

"Give us some credit," Tess said. "We can plot. We're clever."

"Not that clever," Rosetti responded. "What you are is scared. And scared people all want the same thing."

"Which is?" I asked.

"To survive," she said. "So bring me something. Whatever it is that's finding its way into your bodies. And we'll get rid of that fear."

My mom's voice whined its way into my head and I blurted out, "Drugs. Maybe it's drugs."

"Okay then," Rosetti said. "Bring me drugs."

hate to break it to you

Buying drugs is the easiest thing in the world. At least for me. Parents of the world don't want to hear this, but it's true. All I had to do was send a text to one of the Dalton twins. Nothing more than a single letter usually did the trick. *P* for pot. *M* for mushrooms. *E* for ecstasy. *O* for oxy. *S* for surprise me.

They would then text back a time and place. *4 Chipotle* for instance. I'd show up, they'd hand me something inconspicuous, like a bag with a burrito and the stuff tucked beneath the foil. Then we'd chat a bit and go our separate ways. They always operated on credit and I evened up with them in the cafeteria, slipping them cash long after the transactions took place.

It served them well. No parents, teachers, or, most importantly, cops ever caught wind. Regulars knew the drill and newbies were vetted and referred by those regulars. People got their jollies and the Daltons got richer. Free enterprise won the day, like every other day in history.

Two days after Cranberry died and I was deputized (my word, not hers) by Special Agent Carla Rosetti, it was poised to be another winner for free enterprise. I texted Jenna Dalton.

Me: *A.*

Her: A? What's A?

Me: All of it.

Her: All of it? Like everything?

Me: Yep. Make me a sampler. Like a gift basket.

Her: Tough week, right?

Me: Perry. Then Cranberry. FUCK!

Her: Fuckin fuck. At least there's no school. Can you do noon? Dunkin.

Me: I'm so there.

I would go alone. Both Tess and Dylan were with me during the texts, but it made no sense for them to come to the handoff, because I always met the Daltons alone. Not that the Daltons would be all "I smell a rat" or "pat her down for a wire" or anything, but they might notice something was off. They might not give me what I needed.

I needed all of it. Rosetti assured us that she wasn't going to arrest anyone. She didn't even care who was supplying the drugs. Not yet, at least. For now, she only wanted samples of the drugs most likely to be consumed by our peers.

It's no exaggeration to say that the Daltons were the primary drug source for our school. As I've already pointed out, Katelyn was a loyal customer. I couldn't tell you about Brian, Perry, or Cranberry, but if they had taken a hit off a joint in the last two years or popped a pill so they could stay up all night to dance or study—or dance while studying, for that matter—then chances are the original source was the Daltons.

The plan was that I would procure every drug they had and, if one of those substances proved to be volatile, then Rosetti would go after their supplier. "I don't care about a couple of schoolyard hustlers," she had told us. "I'm after big fish. Because the big fish is often bigger than you might ever suspect."

As much as I wanted to think of the Daltons as big fish, I had to admit that big fish don't do deals in doughnut shops with girls who show up on pink bikes. That's right, I rolled up to the big drug deal on the beach cruiser my grandparents bought me for our annual trips down the shore. Because, again, that's what I always did. I didn't want to arouse suspicions.

Joe was waiting in the parking lot when I arrived, fastening a bike rack to the back of their RAV4. "Slap that bad boy on here," he said. "We've got your stuff, but we're getting the fuck outta Dodge. Cool?"

"The coolest," I said.

at the edge of dodge

If the Daltons were big fish, this probably would have been the moment for them to drive me to an alley behind a strip club and pistol-whip me as the rap blared and a sneering, arms-folded bouncer named Sergei stood guard. But no, they definitely weren't big fish. Jenna played a comedy podcast (that none of us laughed at) as she drove us down a private road past the Covington Club until we were hidden behind a patch of shrubs alongside the twelfth green of the golf course.

"No one should bother us here," she said when she cut the engine. "Security guard doesn't come until at least eight, if he comes at all."

"We're so glad you texted, Mara, because we need this as bad as you do," Joe said as he sparked up a fully packed bowl.

"Man, do we need this," Jenna added.

"Have at it, sis," Joe said without exhaling, and he passed the bowl to Jenna.

Spark, spark. Suck, suck. Cough, cough. Then, having had at it, Jenna thrust it in my face. "Hit that shit."

In any other situation, I would have been all "well, if you *insist*." This, however, was a situation where the burning weed was perhaps a burning fuse. Call me silly, but I had begun to put stock in the Say No to Drugs theory. It made more sense than anything else at that point.

"Rain check," I told Jenna.

"More for me then," Joe said, snatching it back for another hit.

"We got shrooms," Jenna said. "Acid. Some meth."

"What?" I said. "No. Hell no. When did you start selling meth?"

Jenna passed me a Dunkin' Donuts bag. The top half consisted of Munchkins disguising what was beneath—a plethora of prescription bottles and plastic Baggies. "You said you wanted everything," Jenna said.

"I did," I said. "I do. I just didn't know you guys were selling hard shit."

"Ever since kids started blowing up, hard shit sells," Joe said, launching a billowing sail of smoke my way.

I held my breath as it caressed my face, seemingly crooning, *Suck me in, sweetie, and I promise I won't turn you inside out.* I waited a full ten seconds after it passed and then drew in a small breath and whispered, "I think I better take the stuff and head home."

"Ah, kid," Jenna said. "I know you're sad, but we can't let you get high alone. And if you haven't done some of this stuff, you're gonna need a spirit guide. Especially with the acid."

"Don't worry," I said. "Dylan will be with me. We're gonna . . . we'll be together."

"Dylan?" Jenna asked as she took another hit. "As in Hovemeyer?"

Joe snagged the bowl back and went in for round number three. He closed his eyes and held the smoke tightly in the fists of his lungs. "You didn't know," he grunted. "Dylan and Mara are like—"

God bless headrests.

The splatter hit the windshield. It painted Joe's window velvet red. It drenched one half of his twin, the right half, plastering Jenna's long brown hair to her face. It streamed back, splashing on the seat next to me like a spilled cherry soda. But yeah, God bless those headrests, Joe's in particular, because it shielded me from what was left of him.

The car shook for a second, as if hit by a gust of wind. Then Jenna began to moan. "Ohhhhhhhhh."

"Oh my God," I said. "Jenna? Are you okay? Tell me you're okay."

"That wasn't . . . that wasn't . . . that wasn't . . ."

The explosion was loud, but not so loud that my ears were ringing. I still had my wits about me. I'd been down this road before. "Jenna, honey," I said. "This is not good. But we've got to get out of here. I know someone who can help."

"That wasn't . . . he wasn't . . . oh God, oh God, oh God."

I reached forward and put a hand on her shoulder. "Jenna," I said. "We've got to go. We've got to get to my friend. She'll take care of us. We'll be okay."

Not that I really believed the words, but I had to say something.

Jenna looked into the passenger seat, winced, and then collapsed on the steering wheel. "He didn't do anything wrong," she cried. "He was a good boy. He was the best boy."

"Can you drive?" I asked. "Because I'm going to make a call and I'll lead us somewhere safe."

Rather than wait for a response, I reached forward and turned the key. The engine rumbled, which made the car vibrate and the blood shake and shimmer in the autumn sun. I suppose I could have gotten behind the wheel myself, but that would have required me unbuckling Jenna, pushing her over, and actually having the will and desire to drive a car.

Jenna's body suddenly went rigid and she gasped. Of the girls I knew, she was by far the toughest. She could deal with anything and anyone. Parents. Cops. You'd think she was twice her age because of how goddamn smooth she usually was. At that particular moment, it seemed like she was fighting to channel her calm and cool, but she was also trembling. And when she flipped on the windshield wipers, they didn't help push away the gore. So she cried, "It's staining the glass. It won't ever wash off!"

"Deep breaths," I said. "It's on the inside. The wipers won't work. Use your sleeve. Clean a patch so you can see out."

She filled her lungs again and became a good little soldier, doing as asked, sopping her twin brother up in her cable-knit sweater and creating a gauzy but mildly transparent ruby circle.

"Okay, now press your foot on the brake," I told her. "Because I'm gonna put the car in drive. All you have to do is, you know, steer and accelerate." I reached forward and eased the gearshift down to the D.

Another deep breath and she said, "I can do this."

"Yes, you can. Yes, you can."

The car lurched forward and off we went. Phone in my lap, I searched my contacts under the *C* and *R* for Carla Rosetti, but didn't find her there.

"Where do I go? Where? Where?" Jenna pleaded.

"Head toward Wooderson Road," I said, because that old factory was chosen to be the rendezvous spot with Rosetti. "Go fast, but be safe."

Be safe. It was that mom nonsense again, but it was all I could think to say to a girl who had just watched her twin explode. I know it wasn't like they were identical or anything. They didn't share matching DNA. But they did share a womb, and it must have felt like part of her body had torn apart right then and there. A part she loved and hated in equal measure. What could I possibly say to that?

Be safe, and that's it. I let the dull roar of the car do the rest of the talking. The golf course coursed by the window. Then, in a tone-deaf but entirely endearing voice, Jenna began to sing.

"When the red red robin comes bob-bob-bobbin' along . . . along!"

"What are you doing?" I asked.

"Driving," she said.

True enough. Though only barely. She was keeping the car on the road, but not in the correct lane. Luckily, we had this stretch of the pavement to ourselves until we reached the Old Post Road. Then we'd be in the thick of antique shops and farm stands.

Jenna fell back into the tune, but louder this time, singing,

"There'll be no more sobbin' when he starts throbbin' his old, sweet song."

"What I meant was, why are you singing?" I asked.

"It's my calming song. It's my happy place."

"Does it help you drive?"

"It does."

"Okay then. Carry on."

In retrospect . . . a lot of things. I'm not going to play the in-retrospect game here or anywhere else. Because it doesn't change a thing. What I am going to do, however, is celebrate good choices. Jenna's song was a good choice. Sure, it was dopey and weird. Sure, she was a crappy singer, but it calmed her down and it calmed me down too. It helped me focus.

As Jenna sang, "Wake up, wake up, you sleepyhead," I remembered something.

"*S*!" I hollered. "She's under *S* for Special Agent Carla Rosetti of the FBI!"

As Jenna sang, "Get up, get up, get outta bed," I placed my call.

We passed the Covington Club, its stately whiteness all horror show through our smudged windows. The phone rang, and as Jenna sang, "Cheer up, cheer up, the sun is red," Rosetti answered.

"Agent Rosetti," she said, because chicks like her don't ever say hello.

"Thank God," I said. "We're heading to the rendezvous spot early. There's been another."

As Jenna sang, "Live, love, laugh, and be happy," she turned the car onto the Old Post Road, put her foot on the gas, swerved to avoid an oncoming UPS truck, and promptly blew up.

Bam. Red. Wet. Fuck.

Not again.

Without a driver, the car would go no faster, but it would continue under its own momentum. The phone slipped out of my bloody hand and I lunged forward to try to grab the wheel, but I was still strapped in, so the belt yanked me back against my seat. As I reached down to unbuckle, the car hopped a curb and even though the windows were now completely red and opaque and I couldn't see a thing, I knew impact was imminent. I braced myself.

That's when the blood-soaked RAV4—occupied by me and a shit-ton of narcotics—crashed through the front window of the Covington Quilt Museum.

what you have to understand

I had broken a promise. Back when I was starting freshman year, Dad had said, "Can you do something for me?"

"Probably," I had replied.

"Make sure I don't ever receive a phone call from either the police or the hospital. That's all I ask from you."

"Consider it done."

As I climbed my way to consciousness amid the huffing and beeping machines of a hospital room, I saw the old man slumped in a chair in the corner. To defuse things, I made a joke. "So which one called you first?"

His phone and the TV remote were resting on his chest, and when he sat up, they fell to the floor, which changed the channel on the TV from a football game to a newscast with a scroll across the bottom that my blurry eyes couldn't read but my blurry brain guessed was about the death toll in Covington, and how it was now up to six. Jack the Ripper killed only five people, in case you were wondering. (Though I don't know why you'd be wondering about Jack the Ripper. Weirdo.)

"Baby," Dad said as he leapt to his feet. "Sweetie. Cutie."

His foot must've been asleep because he hobbled over and put his hands on my face and held my cheeks, really held them, like he was trying to hold me together, which maybe he was.

"Where's Mom?" I asked.

"In the café talking to your friend," he said as he pulled his hands away and gazed in my eyes.

"Dylan?" I asked. "Tess?"

Dad shook his head. "The FBI agent."

Notice how he didn't introduce Rosetti as "that hard-ass fed who's super pissed at you for messing up her perfectly good drug sting." He said "friend." As in friendly. Which wasn't a side of the special agent I knew, but one I wanted to know. What with her being my hero and all.

"Am I . . . is everything . . . ?"

I sat up, which was actually easier than I expected. I ached. I was dizzy, but dizzy was hardly a new sensation for me.

"You have a mild concussion," he said. "Some bruises and sprains but, thankfully, you're still you. You're still you."

But who was I at this point? The girl who'd been splattered by four spontaneous combustions? The girl who'd been pulled from a mangled car? The girl who survived? Which is a horrible thing to be sometimes.

"Was it only the twins?" I asked. "The car didn't hit anyone, did it?"

"Quilts," Dad said. "Expensive ones, I guess, but quilts are nothing but quilts."

I'm sure the proprietors of the Covington Quilt Museum would protest such a notion, but I suspect the proprietors of the Covington Quilt Museum doth protest too much. They were undoubtedly part of the next wave of fist-shakers who quickly jumped on the bandwagon that I had helped launch. Because as the blur slipped from my eyes, I could finally read the breaking news.

PRESIDENT CALLS SITUATION "A NATIONAL TRAGEDY"
AS SEVENTH VICTIM OF THE COVINGTON CURSE CONFIRMED.

And there was a picture of Kamal Patel in all his stonerific, assholish glory.

sorry, not sorry

Kamal Patel blew up halfway through a gravity bong hit, his body liquefying and cascading down into the orange Home Depot bucket of bong water that Laura Riggs was holding steady with her bare feet. It was a special bong hit, a bong hit of purpose, though Kamal hardly required his bong hits to be purposeful. And it's no coincidence that this hit took place hours after the deaths of the Dalton twins, because it was meant to eulogize them.

Upon learning of Joe's and Jenna's spontaneous combustions, Kamal, Laura, and Greer Holloway gathered in the rickety remains of a tree house perched in a willow on the edge of Laura's backyard. This is where, in seventh grade, they first got high together. Those three and the Dalton twins all huddled around a balloon full of nitrous, giggling their way into a new hobby.

It was a defining moment for them, and I remember hearing whispers in middle school about the "crack tree house" and all the debauchery that took place up there, including make-out games and partial nudity to go along with, well, not crack, but a mix of mild sedatives and hallucinogens.

Back then, the stories terrified me. By sophomore year, when they finally tickled my curiosity, the crack tree house had been replaced by Laura's basement, which had the added comforts of indoor plumbing, Wi-Fi, and parents who did not give the first shit about teenage hooligans hanging out downstairs amid clouds of carcinogens. They had one of those we'd-rather-it-happen-in-our-basement-than-out-on-the-streets attitudes, which is great in theory, but in reality the streets can be fucking cold at night and the streets don't have fold-out couches. So, as far as environments conducive to shenanigans go, basements are always preferable to streets.

Actually, I hate to refer to what went on down there as shenanigans. It was at first, I guess, and it was most of the other times too, but a few undeniably dark things happened in Laura's basement as well.

They *all* involved Kamal Patel. Now, I can't tell you too much about Kamal without getting all stabby. I'm not ashamed to admit that I hated the bastard. The fact that girls like Laura and Greer still hung out with him made me question my feelings about them too. He was that toxic a person. I only hoped they didn't know the stories.

The stories were multiple and despicable. For the sake of protecting those who should be protected, I'll simply say that more than one girl passed out in Laura's basement over the years, and more than one girl woke up alone in the dark with Kamal Patel on top of them, his stank breath creeping down their neck and his knuckly hands creeping everywhere else.

Christ. The tears shed because of that slime, the shame tucked away and only shared with those who promised not to say a thing. Including me. And yes, I'm saying a few things now, but I'm only naming one name. Kamal Patel.

To many, Kamal was a lovable stoner. To me and a few others, he was a predator, and whenever I was invited to Laura's house, I always had to ask "Who's gonna be there?" If his name was on the guest list, then I made my excuses and had my fun elsewhere. Not because I was afraid of him, but because I was disgusted by him.

So when I saw his picture on the TV screen in my hospital room and learned that he was lucky number seven in our ever-growing list of spontaneous combustions, I certainly didn't shed a tear. If anything, I felt relief. Not that he deserved death, but he certainly deserved it more than the others. Still, what Kamal deserved had little to do with what this meant. A bloody car full of drugs plus a bloody tree house full of drugs equals a community about to rip itself apart.

because of that

The exodus gained steam. On the drive home from the hospital the next afternoon, I lost count of the U-Hauls. Neighbors were packing up the valuables and heading to Grandma's house or the beach house or anywhere far from here where they could afford to stay until the madness blew over. Sure, there'd been some refugees in the days leading up to this, but running away was now a full-blown fad.

Like always, my parents weren't about to follow any fads. With all the reporters and camera crews still in town, Covington Kitchen was busier than ever. The legend of the Oinker was spreading and seeing Oinker Oil on the shelf of every grocery store in the country suddenly seemed like a possibility. Besides, the evidence seemed incontrovertible: Stay away from the drugs and everything will be a-okay.

"We don't care if you tried it once or twice," Mom said to me on the drive. "Just promise to never, ever do that shit again?"

I've made a lot of promises I never planned to keep, but this one was legit. "I swear. I'm not about to fill my bloodstream with that TNT. No thank you, ma'am. As for what happened—"

"I know, I know" she said with a hand up. "You were only trying to help. Agent Rosetti explained everything to me."

My parents aren't litigious folks, but a government employee sending their daughter into a drug-mobile with a couple of teenage time bombs should have been enough for them to at least consider a lawsuit. So I had to ask, "What exactly is *everything*? My memory is . . . fuzzy."

"Well, we certainly don't need you to relive the moment again, but she said that you were incredibly brave and intuitive and you had only the best intentions. She also said that next time you should contact her first before you go trying to collect evidence. I'm still shocked that the Daltons went down such a dark path. But these are desperate times."

"The desperatest," I said.

By bending the truth, Rosetti was covering both of our asses, so I couldn't exactly be pissed. I only hoped that she had recovered at least some evidence from the car, something that would help put this madness to an end. My hopes were fulfilled almost as soon as I arrived home.

Now, as we all know, a group of dolphins is called a pod, a group of crows is called a murder, and so on. Henceforth, I'd like all groups of people who call themselves reporters but are actually only bloggers writing listicles to be known as a *scumbag*. Because that's what was waiting in front of our house, an absolute scumbag of . . . listiclists. And they brought with them tidings of the investigation.

They were sitting in folding chairs along the edge of our yard, their phones and faces moving from their laps to the car as we pulled into the driveway. They didn't besiege me. That might've been acceptable, or at least instinctual, like hyenas going in for the kill. Instead, they strolled over saying things like, "What's poppin', Mara?" and "Have a sec for a powwow, girl?"

Dressed in their ridiculous floppy caps and fingerless gloves, they were all acting like they were my friends, and yet I knew absolutely nothing about them other than that they were probably in their thirties and still lived with roommates in some neighborhood in the city that they would refer to as "authentic." I could only imagine what they'd dredged up about me and how they were going to use that information against me.

"She needs some rest, for fuck's sake," Mom said and, working up some mom sorcery, put her hand out and kept them at bay as I slipped through the front door.

Though not before I heard a nasally voice cry out, "Tell us, Mara, have you ever had sexual relations with Dr. Wonderman in exchange for drugs?"

The answer to that question was an unequivocal "are you trying to make me vomit? Because I'm already nauseous from the concussion and questions like that tend to push a girl over the edge."

Oh, Dr. Wonderman. Make no mistake about it, the man is vile. Everyone who knows him will tell you this, and almost everyone in Covington knows him, because almost everyone in Covington has straight teeth, thanks to our dethroned king of orthodontia.

Dr. Wonderman works wonders! read the billboards, and they weren't false advertising. The guy did a bang-up job when it came to braces, retainers, and other dental torture devices. I'm a satisfied customer myself, having spent all of sixth grade with a set of ceramics putting my bicuspids through boot camp.

The irony is that the man himself had a horrid set of chompers. I guess it speaks to that old riddle: If there are two barbers in town, which one do you ask to cut your hair? The one who has a terrible haircut and filthy barbershop or the one rocking a tight do and a spick-and-span establishment?

You take the slob, in case you haven't figured it out. Also, you move out of town, because I don't care where you live, you need more than two dudes who know how to cut hair. How about a Supercuts, at the very least?

Which is all to say that Dr. Wonderman had an orthodontic monopoly in Covington. There wasn't even competition around to straighten his own teeth. And it turns out this wasn't the only monopoly he had. For as I was contemplating the sickening notion of Dr. Wonderman in nothing but striped socks and tighty-whities, I was greeted by Harold Frolic's wagging finger. The family lawyer was now part of the family, it seemed, and he had been waiting in our living room for my arrival. He strode toward me saying, "Don't speak to any of them. Don't speak to anyone about Dr. Wonderman."

Dad was there too, pacing back and forth across the room and adding, "Mr. Frolic came over as soon as the news broke."

"Another one?" I asked.

Frolic shook his head and replied, "They arrested Dr. Wonderman in his driveway a few hours ago. He was packing up his Corvette and heading out of town. They confiscated his phone and an obscene amount of illegal substances. Please tell us your phone number is not on his contact list?"

"Do you mean to imply that I chat with my disgusting, fifty-year-old, married orthodontist on the regular?" I asked.

If Frolic was amused by my witticisms, he didn't show it. "Thanks to assurances from Agent Rosetti, the police aren't investigating you in conjunction with what they found in the Daltons' car," he said. "But should they find out you've been in contact with Dr. Wonderman, then—"

"Harold," Dad piped in, as he stepped between me and Frolic. "If my daughter said she's not associated with the man, then she's not associated with the man. End of story."

Frolic put up his hands in surrender and replied, "Only doing my job here. Because things are about to get messy."

"*About* to get messy?" I said. I swear I could still taste the iron from the Daltons' blood on my teeth and this prick was pretending like there was still some tipping point to reach.

Mom cupped my ears with her hands and kissed my forehead. "Rest," she said. "Let us figure out what strategy we have to take."

The fact that our family even required a *strategy* was insane to me, and I made my frustration known with a hearty huff and dramatic turn for the door. But, honestly, I was more than happy to take the cue to leave. Because as soon as I was in my room, I was on my laptop trying to get a hold of Dylan. My parents had declared my hospital room off-limits and the police had confiscated my phone, so I hadn't been in contact with him for two days. Mom had informed Tess that I was okay, so I suspected the news had reached Dylan, but I still needed him, like I needed sunlight, like I needed laughter, like I needed . . .

Actually, needing someone isn't like needing anything else, because nothing else makes you feel the way you do when it's been too long since you've heard a certain voice and then you hear that voice and that voice fills in all the cracks of your splintered little soul.

"She lives," Dylan said with a smirk as he peered across the cosmos and through my laptop screen at me.

"It's gotten . . . how has it gotten like this?" I asked.

"I'm glad it was you who was with the Daltons. To have your face as the last image they saw, that's a blessing."

"Tell that to their parents. God, I'm so confused and so scared right now. Have you heard about Dr. Wonderman?"

"The man is trending. Someone tweeted a picture of him and Carla."

It took me about five seconds to find it, and as iconic photos go, this is one of a handful that everyone associates with Covington. It's that shot of a bedraggled Dr. Wonderman hunched over in cuffs and surrounded by a SWAT team dressed in hazmat gear, except for Special Agent Carla Rosetti, who's leading the perp walk and throwing caution to the wind, dressed in black and rocking the pumps. In the background, a bomb squad surrounds Baggies of drugs laid out on a driveway.

"Just so you know, I'm not touching that stuff anymore," I said.

"I know."

"And if they're claiming Wonderman is the source, then I never had a clue."

"I know."

"So do you think it all ends now? Or do you think there's something lingering inside of people . . . like me."

"I don't know."

"Do you ever partake?"

"Never have."

"Thank God. You do realize you have to get over here right this minute. Or the minute after my parents go to bed, which is like ten thirty."

"Ten thirty-one then."

at 10:31

Dylan tapped on my window and then climbed through like boyfriends have been doing since windows were invented. I'd been napping on and off throughout the evening, trying to chase away the headaches and the veiny pink webs from my eyes. Tess and I had chatted for a bit in the afternoon, though she kept dodging the obvious: if I had to pee in a cup right that very minute, then my blood would come back chock-full of illicit substances, which seemed to indicate my status as a ticking time bomb.

The closest she came was saying, "You survived, Mara. No matter what you do, you survive. And you will survive. Everyone knows this."

I know it can be empowering to some, but I hate that word in all its forms. *Survive. Survival. Survivor.* Blah! So temporary and meaningless. "Congratulations! You didn't die! At least not yet! But you will! Oh, trust us, you most certainly will!"

I didn't want to be considered a survivor because who wants to even think about surviving? That's what starving animals think about and I assure you there's no glory in being some skinny-ass raccoon. Fighting against death may be noble, but it's no way to live. What I realized when I hugged Dylan in my bedroom is that I wanted to die oblivious to death. I wanted to be so distracted by life that I hardly knew what death was. Quite the herculean task given the situation, I know. Still, it's my best explanation for why I did what I did. Which is put my hands down the side of Dylan's pants and get a firm grip of his butt cheek.

My forearm could feel the muscles in his stomach clench up, a comforting result. A hand down his pants wasn't an everyday occurrence for him, and it certainly wasn't something he felt entitled to. "Hey there," he said, in the same wide-eyed, wondrous way that someone greets a furry little forest animal.

"I know this isn't even close to your first time," I said. "But if you're really good at it, then take it down a notch. I'm strictly junior varsity over here."

He giggled, a breathy spasm that made his chin dip and his eyes squint closed. "I don't know who you've been talking to, but I'm pretty sure I didn't make the varsity cut."

"But you already have . . ."

The triplets. I didn't say it because I didn't have to. This was a boy who knew actions had consequences. Or potential ones. "Why the hell hasn't he just gotten the damn blood tests?" I suddenly thought, and with his cheek in my hand, I felt angry at him for the first time. And I felt angry at myself. How'd I let things get to this point?

"Ow, ow, ow," he said, turning his hips, and I realized that I was squeezing him a bit too hard.

"Sorry," I said, and pulled my hand out. I flopped onto my bed.

"Is everything okay?" he asked as he contemplated his cock-eyed jeans.

"Of course not."

"We don't have to do anything you don't want to," he said, which is the right thing to say, even if it's not incredibly sexy.

"You're a dad," I said, and I grabbed a pillow and hugged it. "With three kids. And you make bomb threats. And you actually think there's value in seeing people explode. None of that is right. None of that fits. None of that is what I need right now."

He nodded. "So what do you need?"

"I don't know," I said as I rolled over and faced the wall. I felt like I was carsick for a moment, then a headache rushed in. "I need you to tell me that I'm not making another mistake in my long and storied history of mistakes. I need you to tell me that I shouldn't be putting my hands down Clint Jessup's pants instead of yours."

"Do you want to have your hands down Clint Jessup's pants?"

"No. I mean, probably not. I guess there are worse fates. Even Tess has the hots for that dude and she usually goes for the cerebral types. It's just . . . I could explode at any moment and is this what I should be doing? Getting all wrapped up in you?"

"You should be doing what makes you happy. That's what I'm doing."

I pushed the pillow down toward the bottom of the bed and scooted closer to the wall. "Lie down next to me," I told him.

He did, with his face pressed into my shoulder.

"This is the part where you put your arms around me," I said.

He did, and grasped one of my hands. His hand was still cold from being outside. My hand was shaking a bit.

"How many?" I asked. "Girls, I mean. Besides me."

He stroked my fingers. "Well, I guess you could count Jane."

I tried not to wince but I'm sure I winced. "Yes. Jane certainly counts."

He kept stroking my fingers and didn't say anything else.

"And?" I asked.

"And that's it. Jane."

Now it was me who was silent. At least for a few seconds, which is about as much silence as I can stand.

"Don't you want to know my number?" I asked.

"Yes. And no."

I lifted his hand and rolled over so I could look him in the eye. "Three. Do you want to know their names?"

He bit his top lip, then said, "Probably not. Do any of them have neck tattoos? Any of them immortal beasts of indeterminate age?"

"Not that I'm aware of."

"Then I'd rather not know."

I sat up, pulled my phone out from under my pillow, and set an alarm for five thirty a.m. "You can sleep here tonight, right? Slip out early before my parents get up? Is your mom expecting you back?"

"There aren't exactly curfews at my place."

"Maybe that's it," I said with a forced chuckle. "Kids who break their curfews go boom."

"Makes as much sense as the drug thing."

"What do you mean?" I said as I settled back in for the cuddle. "It's pretty obvious that's the link. Someone posted pictures of Wonderman's house in Florida. Did you know he has a mansion down there?"

"So? So do a lot of people."

"A lot of shady smuggler types. Who knows where this stuff originates? Who knows what was put in it? Who knows anything?"

"If you're going with scientific explanations, then you have to look hard at the science. And I don't think the science can possibly hold up."

"If you're not looking at the science, then what do you look at?"

"Spiritual answers," he said, kissing me on the head. "Karma."

"What goes around comes around, huh?" I asked. "Well, I'm not exactly a saint."

"It's okay if you get high and all that," he told me. "I don't love that you do, but it's okay."

"Really?"

"Really. You know what I worry about more? Jennifer Lawrence."

"Don't we all? Never hear about that poor gal, anymore, do we?" I deadpanned, assuming, like anyone would, that he was joking. Even though I didn't get the joke.

"Fact is, a lot of us have it coming," he said with a sigh. "I don't know if we can be forgiven."

Then I kissed his neck again, as if the kissing would fill his veins with forgiveness. And immortality. Turn him into an enduring man-beast of indeterminate age. "Promise me that it won't ruin you and your whole life if it happens to me first."

"It won't," he said. "Not because I don't care about you, but because I'm lucky to know you at all."

"It would ruin my life if it happened to you."

"It wouldn't. You're tougher than that."

"You don't have any idea about how weak I am."

"Because you're scared? That's not weakness."

"No. Because I'm weak. And impulsive. And foolish."

"Says who?"

"Says me."

"Well, you're not the best judge of yourself."

My head was spinning again, so I put it on his chest and said, "As much as I want this to happen tonight, it can't. It's a lame excuse, but I'm using it. I have a migraine coming on. Maybe the worst one ever."

He twirled my hair in his fingers and said, "Don't worry. We have all the time in the world."

Really? Because it sure as hell seemed like our world was already on borrowed time.

where our world was headed

'm usually a deep sleeper, but that night we slept the broken slumber of two people who aren't used to sharing a bed, and Dylan was out the window before my parents got up. A quick peek at the news got me up to date.

Dr. Wonderman had been denied bail. The DA claimed he had foreign bank accounts and every reason to flee what could end up being seven individual murder charges. A lab was still analyzing the drug samples found at Wonderman's home, in the Daltons' car, and what was now known as "the tree house of horror" (née "the crack tree house"). The war on drugs had hit our shores and was raging. All over town, police were kicking down doors. Well, knocking very forcefully on doors, at least.

Meanwhile, the FBI was gently ringing my doorbell. Special Agents Carla Rosetti and Demetri Meadows arrived at our house around eight a.m., accepted Dad's offer of a "cuppa mud" (really, Dad, that's what you went with, "cuppa mud?") and we all sat on kitchen stools as Rosetti supplied more updates.

"I had a look at your lab work this morning, Mara," she told me. "And the doctors assured me there was nothing abnormal."

Dad was a bit too angry to notice the happy surprise that slapped my face. "Wait, wait, wait," he barked. "We're thrilled to hear the news, but medical records are confidential between a doctor and a patient."

"So you're saying Mara's healthy?" Mom asked and put a hand on Dad's shoulder.

Rosetti gave her a curt nod and turned to Dad. "Mr. Carlyle, I do respect that confidentiality, but I'd be disingenuous if I pretended we didn't have full access to medical records as part of our investigation. Besides, I figured Mara would want to hear the news from a friend."

Now *she* was using the word *friend*. Voicing it out loud. In public! It felt like I was being asked to the prom. I almost fainted. Still, I managed to squeak out a thank-you.

"It makes me as happy as it makes you," Rosetti said. "But let's move on to the task at hand. You were close to the Dalton twins?"

"I was friendly with them," I said.

"Shouldn't we have Frolic here?" Dad asked, which seemed more a rhetorical question than anything. No doubt he was sick of the guy too.

Meadows finally piped in. "Mara is not under investigation for anything," he said as he swigged his cuppa mud. "In fact, she might be the best thing that's happened to this investigation."

I turned to Rosetti for confirmation and she nodded confidently. "Okay, then what can I do?" I asked.

"We've got a list of Wonderman's contacts," Meadows said. "Now we need to know who the Daltons were selling to. We don't have time to sift through all their social media chums."

"You're asking me to be a narc?" I said.

"We're asking you to save some lives," Rosetti said. "No one will be arrested. Everybody will be thanking you when this is through."

Mom reached across the counter and grabbed a pen and a torn envelope to write on.

"No need," Meadows said, holding up an iPad displaying the yearbook pictures of all my classmates. "She can tap faces."

I tapped thirty faces, give or take, which made them disappear from the screen. Talk about ominous. For each face I tapped, my parents either nodded knowingly or they sucked in little wincing breaths. At this point, I don't remember all the faces that I tapped, but I can confidently say I never tapped Billy Harmon's face.

Because why would I tap Billy Harmon's face? How could I tap Billy Harmon's face? If Kamal Patel was a plague on our school, then Billy was the antidote. May all gods of all religions bless Billy Harmon. Which is all a roudabout way of revealing that when Rosetti and Meadows took off to go rescue the owners of those thirty tapped faces from their tainted pills and poison pot, I got to enjoy a few days of concussion headaches, long naps, and genuine hope, before the unthinkable happened.

Tess sent me the world's most devastating text on the morning of November 15, a previously inconsequential day on the calendar that I guarantee will be remembered for decades to come. The news that kicked things off was so bad that all I could do was throw my phone across the room (at the couch, mind you—it was still another year until I qualified for an upgrade). And things were only going to get worse.

"What's the matter?" Mom asked.

"Billy Harmon," I said with a shaking head. "Billy Harmon."

The incredulity must have echoed for hours through our increasingly empty town.

the calm

Tripping over half-full cardboard boxes, I made my way through Tess's house later that afternoon. Mom had driven me and had stuck around to talk to Paula, who was in the kitchen emptying the fridge of everything but the condiments.

"Mara can come with us if she likes," I heard Paula say as I looked for Tess in her room. All I found were packed bags and a wall covered with maps and drawings of flowers, animal anatomy, and chemical compounds. The names of the deceased, along with numbers and symbols, were scrawled on multicolored sticky notes in Tess's looping, elegant handwriting. The notes were on nearly every surface. Now, I was no dummy (I was in pre-calc, after all), but I wasn't even going to try to figure out what this mess was all about.

Side note: If it's the left side of the brain that determines someone's abilities with numbers and logic, then it was a wonder Tess could hold her head up straight. Stuff like computer code and sudoku came naturally to the girl. Pre-calc? Pshaw! She'd placed out junior year and was already taking college courses. It was one of the few aspects of Tess's life that she didn't share with me, which was okay by both of us. Once her mind got spinning, she needed someone who could keep up, and she was always better off picking one of her online friends or the kids she knew from the Rubik's Cube cotillions and whatnot.

The window by Tess's bed faced the backyard and that's where I eventually spotted her, swinging in a sap-stained hammock strung up between two pine trees. We'd spent many an autumn day in that hammock, watching videos or reading books side by side, howling at the moon when it rose in the evening sky. So when I went outside that afternoon, I didn't even have to invite myself up. I climbed in beside her and snuggled.

"*I loved that little guy,*" Tess whispered.

"We all did," I said, and I kissed her on the forehead.

"He wasn't a saint, you know?"

"He was the closest thing we had."

"He swore. He made dirty jokes. There were people he didn't particularly like."

"Like who?"

"Doesn't matter. Point is, he was human. Still, it makes no sense that this would happen to him."

"Did anyone see it?"

"His dad and Tyler sorta saw, but they were spared the goriest parts, thank God. They were wheeling him over to the porch to have breakfast and he was hiding under an orange quilt, joking around, pretending to be a pumpkin. The quilt puffed, and fell,

and that was that. I guess they knew his days were numbered anyway, but they couldn't possibly have expected this. Connie called
me before she even called the police. Said she considered me family. She was so friggin' calm. Like she always is. I don't know if it's
even sunk in yet."

"What sort of pills was he on?" I asked.

"I thought you knew. The Harmons are Christian Scientists.
They don't vaccinate or take medicine of any sort. Billy was as
clean as they come. The whole family believes in the healing
power of God."

"If God blew up Billy Harmon, then God is the goddamn devil."

With a sigh, Tess held her phone out so we could both see it. A
video of Billy Harmon was cued up, one of his daily vlog posts. He
didn't have tens of thousands of followers, but he had enough that
there were already a few comments asking about the delayed up-
load of the latest installment.

"This was his last post," Tess said. "From yesterday."

In the video, Billy was smiling as wide as he could, which wasn't
very wide considering that he barely had control of his face.
At the age of six, he'd been diagnosed with a rare degenerative
nerve disorder that made his muscles clench in different configurations throughout the day, which meant it looked like he was
constantly in pain. And he was in pain, but it was pain he could
bear, apparently. Unfortunately, the condition also meant that he
could do very little for himself, was confined to a wheelchair, and
had a life expectancy that didn't reach much past his teens. There
were something like twenty other people in the world with this
condition, which had a tongue-tying scientific name, but ended up

being known as Billy Harmon's Disease because he was the only sufferer with a YouTube channel.

"Good morning, friends," Billy said in his slow, devastatingly tender voice. "A lot of people have been asking about what it's like to live in Covington during these dark times and they ask how I can keep smiling. All I can say is look out the window. Is it sunny where you are? Rainy? Snowy? Does the weather make you angry? Does it make you sad?

"The weather gives me joy, to be honest. Rain feeds plants. Snow blankets the world in beauty. Hurricanes, tornadoes? Sure they destroy, but they're moods of the earth, aren't they? The earth is moody like any of you. And I love the earth like I love all of you. Even if you're moody. *Especially* because you're moody.

"I don't know what's causing my friends and classmates to explode. And while I mourn their loss, I also accept that this is part of the weather now. I hope that doesn't sound callow. I've wept as all of you have wept. But I've also laughed because I have memories of these wonderful people that no one can ever take from me. And I look out of my window and I smile. Because after the hurricanes and tornadoes, the sun always comes up, the plants always grow, the world spins on.

"And as long as the world spins on, we can still dance. No matter who we are, we can always dance."

A jaunty jam kicked in, animated confetti fell over the screen—along with a flashing *Dance Party!* insert—and Billy Harmon danced.

Dancing for Billy Harmon consisted of twisting his lips and struggling to move them back and forth. It was sincere, schmaltzy,

and sad. In other words, quintessential Billy Harmon. We loved
the kid in the same way we love inspirational quotes photo-
shopped onto pictures of sunsets over the beach. Not because
they're profound. But because they assure us, temporarily at least,
that life is simple, that an aw-shucks attitude paired with a splash
of color can defeat the sting of tragedy, no matter how tragic that
tragedy is.

Which is bullshit, right?

Still, consider the messenger. Fate basically said, "Let's totally
fuck with this guy!" and the guy shook fate's hand and bought it
lunch. Along with his YouTube channel, Billy had self-published
an e-book called *Harmonese*, featuring fifty life-affirming haikus. I
never had the stomach to read the thing, but no matter what Billy
said or did, you had to respect him and you had to love him. And no
one loved him more than Tess did.

Billy's jam was still jamming, but Tess had had enough. She
tossed her phone to her feet, hugged me, and said, "We're going
to Uncle Andy's tomorrow. Mom's working remotely. Now that
Billy's gone, she's afraid that it'll happen to me."

"You can't leave me here alone."

"Mom said you can join us."

"And leave my parents?" I said as I chewed on my thumbnail. "I
don't think I could do that. But aren't we supposed to be together
forever, you and I? Isn't that written in the stars?"

"I won't ever question the stars," Tess said as she kissed me on
the forehead. "But for now we've gotta do what's right for our families. And it won't be that bad for you. At least you've got Dylan."

"I hardly know Dylan. I've known you my entire life. You can't go anywhere. You're Tess McNulty. You're Covington's finest citizen. You're invincible."

"I seriously doubt that. There are some quant guys I've been trading data with online and—"

"You talk so sexy sometimes."

She pinched me to scold me and said, "I'm serious. There are some compelling patterns in the numbers. Birthdays. Moon cycles. I may be as susceptible as anyone."

"Moon cycles and birthdays? So it's like a period?"

"Have you ever thought that maybe you shouldn't joke about stuff so much?"

I considered invoking Billy, saying, "Didn't we watch the same video? Billy wants me to joke, right? Kids blowing up is like the weather. We should joke about the weather, shouldn't we?"

Instead, I muttered a baby-voiced "sorry." Because while I might have known what Billy said, I had no idea what he really wanted. That was Tess's department.

Since sixth grade, when she first volunteered to help around the Harmon home, she'd been Billy's confidant. They'd had tons of private conversations to which I'd never been privy. And yes, that made me jealous sometimes, but I also knew it was something Tess needed—a friend who expected nothing but her presence. Sometimes people teased her and asked her if she and Billy were dating, but that didn't offend Tess. Not one bit.

"If he survives until his twenty-first birthday, I'll marry him," Tess told me once. "Gladly. I'd be lucky to call a guy like that my husband."

Their relationship never got physical, as far as I know. I don't know if it could even get physical, considering his condition. But it was intellectual, emotional, and everything in between. If there was one silver lining to the whole ordeal, it's that his condition never reached the point we feared it might. It was entirely possible that Billy's disease could have gotten so bad that it left him in the sort of pain that made life unbearable.

Tess didn't reveal many of their secrets, but she did tell me once that if Billy ever decided to go to Oregon where assisted suicide is legal, she had promised to drive him. No questions asked. I promised to go with her, because I was her friend and the kid deserved a dignified death. Whether I would have actually gone is another question. It was the right thing to do in theory, and maybe that's what was so hard about this. We could be happy that Billy didn't suffer, but it sucked that he didn't go out on his own terms.

"One in sixty-five thousand," Tess said with a sigh as the hammock rocked back and forth.

"Excuse me?" I replied.

"Eight seniors have blown up. Like Rosetti noticed, only seniors. If we're talking about only Covington High students, the probability that this would happen to only seniors is about one in sixty-five thousand. In other words, one in four to the eighth power. Take that probability out into the general population of Covington and it's like one in seventy-five to the eighth power. Which isn't even a number you can fathom. Take it out into—"

"You're saying it's not random," I said. "I think we all realize that."

"I'm saying it is focused to the point that it seems to have a purpose. And I don't think it's going to stop anytime soon."

the storm

That evening someone threw a Molotov cocktail through the front window of the police station. I know what you're thinking, but stop. Dylan had an alibi. A solid one. Me, if you must know. We were chatting on our laptops when it happened and he lived at least a mile from the police station. Unless he's got a supersonic bionic arm, I doubt he could throw that far.

The more likely culprit was Keith Lutz. Why? Because minutes after someone threw a Molotov cocktail through the front window of the police station, he tweeted:

> I THREW A MOLOTOV COCKTAIL THROUGH THE
> FRONT WINDOW OF THE POLICE
> STATION! #ForBilly

Oh, that hashtag. Boy did it get out of hand quickly.

#ForBilly started as a tribute to a fallen hero, a quick way to find a collection of selfies of kids blowing kisses skyward. In less than twelve hours it mutated, became a flag to wave while screaming, "Watch me tear this town apart!" (A sentiment I can safely assume Billy never would have supported.)

Still, how could you blame anyone? We felt powerless. We felt expendable. The people who were supposed to guarantee our safety—the parents, the teachers, the politicians, the cops— they weren't doing a thing. If they couldn't keep a guy like Billy together, then there wasn't much hope for us, was there?

So after Keith firebombed the police station, Shaw Feeney put a brick on the gas pedal of her brother's snowplow and sent it down Main Street. #ForBilly. It took out the tables in front of Covington Kitchen, along with two streetlights and seven cars, before it flew off the Centennial Bridge and into Patchcong River.

Meanwhile, a gang of kids armed themselves with baseball bats and donned a variety of disguises—a grim reaper, a sumo wrestler, and a Disney princess to name a few. Then they broke into the school and smashed the night away. #ForBilly. Nothing was spared: trophy cases, the PA system, even the statue of our beloved mascot, the Snarlin' Quaker. They clogged pipes. Broken sinks spurted like cut veins. They set fires and sprinklers spit to life. By midnight, the place was flooded.

The Molotov cocktail didn't do much damage and there weren't any injuries as a result of it or the rogue snowplow. So when word got out about the school, the police sat on their hands.

"As long as they're not hurting anyone, let them do what they want," Sheriff Tibble apparently said. "This is beyond us now."

As chaos goes, it was meticulously documented. Live-streams of the destruction were carried by all major news outlets. Google maps gussied up with icons showing movements of rioters were shared like war plans spread across a general's desk. Dylan and I watched it unfold online from the comfort of our respective homes. I suspect most of the country did. And the #ForBilly hashtag evolved again, into a catchall for civil disobedience around the world.

- Kids in Indonesia stole the cars of government officials and went joyriding. #ForBilly.

- South African students chained themselves to gates in front of the homes of Johannesburg's elite. #ForBilly.

- A German punk band named Scheiße Schneesturm (or Shit Blizzard) broke into a museum and shot up priceless paintings with paintballs. #ForBilly.

When the morning of November 16 came, everyone expected the same thing. The president would declare martial law, and the National Guard would roll into Covington to keep everyone in line. That wasn't an entirely inaccurate prediction, but all the closeted sadists hoping for an escalation of atrocities were sorely disappointed.

Because what we got was a fleet of shiny buses, two dozen doctors dressed in Ebola suits, and a team of Navy SEALs—also in Ebola suits, but packing considerable heat—knocking on doors.

Deploying actual troops was unprecedented, and likely illegal, but there was no noticeable uproar or insurrection. Tess and Rosetti may have been among the few who crunched the actual numbers, but plenty of others had noticed that this was happening only to seniors from Covington High. And that's who the SEALs and doctors were visiting. Meanwhile, a collection of carnies and road-ies were raising giant quarantine tents out at Brighton Orchards.

A doctor named Pei rang my doorbell at dawn. She was a kind-eyed soul, someone whose voice sounded trustworthy even when filtered through a medical mask.

"We are setting up a state-of-the-art facility where we can keep your daughter and her classmates safe and we can finally put an end to this awful ordeal," she told my parents as she handed them release waivers. A bus idled in the road.

Now, let's be honest. A few weeks before and this shit wouldn't have flown. But given the state of our town and the fact that the death of Billy had made even the most innocent among us seem vulnerable, my parents saw no choice but to sign the waivers and send me off for some prodding. Almost all the parents did. They trusted the doctors more than they trusted themselves at that point. Most of Covington's anti-vaxxers and die-hard conspiracy theorists had hit the road long before this, way back in the wake of Brian's death. All that was left now were the optimists, pragma-tists, and capitalists like my parents.

Tess texted me when a bus blocked her driveway and a doctor told her she couldn't leave.

Tess: Guess I'm not going to Uncle Andy's.

Me (as my bus pulled up to the tents): See you at the circus!

There was already a perimeter, an electric fence circling the nylon village at a hundred yards. The ubiquitous reporters and bloggers were waiting on the outside, along with the parents who followed the buses. Everyone was leaning in, trying to get a glimpse behind the tent flaps.

Inside the tents, it wasn't a circus at all. It was orderly. Names and handprints were taken. Fingers were pricked and blood was dripped into boxes on thick, gridded paper. And we were all given these surprisingly comfy robes, told to change into them, and go relax in the tent labeled COMMONS, where we were to await further instructions.

There were sofas and armchairs spread throughout the commons. There was also coffee, bagels, juice—continental breakfast, basically—and every thirty minutes a fresh crop of kids arrived. Tess showed up. Then Dylan, thank God. Even Keith Lutz and Shaw Feeney were among the blurry-eyed masses. I was glad that Greg Holder asked them, "Shouldn't you guys be in the slammer?" so that I didn't have to.

They both responded with shrugs and Shaw said, "Gave us each a get-out-of-jail-free card. Mainly because they don't want to expose us to anyone else."

By noon, the total number of rounded-up seniors was 89. The official class enrollment was 239—not counting the 8 we'd already lost. You didn't need a genius like Tess to do the arithmetic: 150 of our classmates had fled Covington. We were the pathetic stragglers.

making an impression

It's a shame that my parents weren't catering because the soggy Wawa sandwiches they gave us for lunch were decidedly subpar and certainly didn't serve as an appropriate appetizer for what came next. Two SEALs led our not-so-merry band of pathetic stragglers into a small tent labeled COMMUNICATIONS and we sat on metal folding chairs. One SEAL plugged a laptop into a projector as the other positioned a small white screen and a tripod-mounted camera in front of us.

When the projector spat out its light, we were greeted by the smiling face of our president against a backdrop of—what else—an American flag.

"Good afternoon, you brave, brave souls," the president said in that regal yet motherly voice of hers. "God bless you, each one of you. I cannot imagine the pain you have endured."

There were gasps and whispers, following by clapping and a few people standing up. I think Skye Sanchez—the most promising political prospect in our class—might have even put her hand on her heart.

"The president can see us?" Harper Wie asked.

The burlier of the two SEALs motioned with his rhinoceros chin at the camera, which was quite clearly poised on us.

The president chuckled and pointed at Harper the way she points at people during her State of the Union addresses. "I can see you, pal," she said. "Looking good. All of you. And I can assure you that I have your back. The nation has your back. We are all rooting for you. Have been since day one. We will make sure you are cured of this terrible virus."

This wasn't the first time we'd heard the word *virus* used, but hearing the president say it was something else entirely. We traded worried glances and the SEALs tightened the masks over their mouths.

Practiced concern fell over the president's face and she put out her hands in a gesture of acceptance. Granted, she was a couple hundred miles away, but she sounded genuine when she said, "If I could be there right now to hug each and every last one of you, I would. I know this is difficult and I can't promise there aren't still difficult times ahead. But the doctors I have dispatched are the greatest in the nation, and we will spare no expense until you are—*oh, for fuck's sake!*"

The nylon walls of the tents rippled from the blast and the burly, rhino-chinned SEAL plowed into the bloody screen like he was taking a bullet for our virtual commander in chief. Meanwhile, the other SEAL—I'll call him the hot one, because he was, even all covered up like that—unholstered a pistol and pointed it at Harper Wie's bloody, but empty, seat.

"Oh, for fuck's sake! Oh, for fuck's sake!" the president cried as she pushed her wheely chair back from her Oval Office desk and threw up her hands. Her terrified face was now three times as large and projected on the dripping walls of the tent. "Turn it off. Good God! Off, off, off!"

People do what the president says, so the image of her face was immediately replaced on the tent wall by a screensaver of an eagle, only the eagle looked as bloody as the rest of us.

Yes, Harper Wie was officially victim number nine of the Covington Curse.

what they did to us

This is what happens when the president sees in real time what it looks like when a young man spontaneously combusts. You stay put. You don't leave those tents under any circumstances. You do as you're told because you're the problem, and the doctors and the men with guns are your only salvation.

That night we slept in cots in a tent marked DORMITORY. Clear orders stated that there was to be no "romantic canoodling," but we were allowed to bunk down in coed configurations. So Tess was on one side of me and Dylan was on the other, and I held a hand each.

"How many times have they tested your blood?" Tess asked.

"At least four now," I said. "Along with a CAT scan, an MRI, some X-rays. Then whatever the hell that thing was that they used on us today after . . . Harper."

"What else can they find?" Tess asked. "What else can they do?"

"I didn't get a close look at the waivers our parents signed," I said. "Did it grant the doctors full and unfettered use of medieval torture devices on us?"

"The three of us are seventeen, right?" Tess said. "But there are eighteen-year-olds here. Their parents didn't have the authority to sign them away like that."

Dylan had been relatively quiet up to this point. "I suspect the waivers were bogus," he finally said. "To make the parents feel like they have even a little bit of control over this situation. Which they don't. The president is involved. That's all we need to know."

That's when I lost it, giggling and making my cot rumble. "Did you see her face? Oh my God, that was priceless."

"*Shut up*," Tess whispered.

"What? Why? It was funny. The president said 'oh, for fuck's sake.' Granted, it was quite a thing to witness, but—"

"Don't you realize that Harper was my first?" Tess said.

"You slept with Harper Wie?" I asked.

"No, you idiot," she said. "This was the first time I actually saw it happen."

"I didn't even see it because he was sitting behind me," Dylan said. "Technically, I didn't see Perry either. Just the commotion and the videos later."

I didn't really count Perry myself, but that still made this my fifth time. I'd seen more of these than anyone. I'd forgotten that. As much as this was a shared experience, I was the reigning champ of spontaneous-combustion-witnessing.

"Am I a horrible person?" I asked, because it was and still is a perfectly valid question.

"No," Dylan said immediately.

It took Tess a bit longer to respond, but she finally said, "No."

Which was quickly countered by a shouted "Yes! You are all horrible. And horribly loud. We are trying to sleep here!"

I knew that voice. It was Claire Hanlon, still the most annoying of my pre-calc compatriots. A fight with her could last all night and she did have a point. It had been an exhausting and emotional day.

After losing Harper, we'd all been whisked off to the HYGIENE tent, where we showered and put on clean robes—like a hotel, they seemed to have an endless supply. Then SEALs led us to the EXAMINATION tent, where five separate doctors asked us to list our sexual partners, to detail our daily diets and the consistency of our stool over the last few days, and then to go ahead and declare if we'd been bitten by any skunks, bats, or monkeys lately. Then the doctors told us to strip down—in privacy, thankfully—and step into a glass chamber that looked like the ones on game shows that blow tornadoes of cash around giggling contestants, only this one assaulted our body with strobe lights and a fine pink powder before smacking us with a blast of air that smelled vaguely of maple syrup. Next they covered us with electrodes, plopped us down on treadmills, and told us to walk for three hours, or fifteen kilometers, or until we collapsed. Whatever came first.

When the day was through, did the doctors tell us what they were looking for? Come on, don't be so naive. They simply served us dinner, which consisted of pizza and a blue sludgy drink that was called a smoothie but tasted more medicinal than fruity. Then, in a fresh new communications tent, they showed us streaming video of our parents relaying their love and words of encouragement at a candlelight vigil that was being held along the electric fence.

Before lights out, the head doctor, a lanky woman known to us only as Doc Ramirez, assured the group. "We're making progress. You'll be home before you know it."

So, yeah. Exhausting and emotional and Claire was right to be mad. We shut up and tried to sleep.

before we knew it

Our numbers doubled. Over the next week, 89 became 113, which ballooned to 158 and then topped out at 210. The government was searching beyond the borders of Covington for fugitive members of the senior class and they were having plenty of luck. Nobody wanted to be harboring combustible—and possibly contagious—students. If local private detectives and police forces didn't find someone, then bail bondsmen and good old-fashioned vigilantes stepped in and did the job.

Since we were cut off from the world—no internet, no phones, only paper and Sharpies to write letters to our parents—we didn't know exactly what was happening out there. The new arrivals filled us in as best they could.

"Rest of the world is completely freaking," Bree Malone told us one morning in the commons. "I'm lucky I surrendered. Turns out Carlos Bazalar was hiding out at his grandparents' hacienda in Peru or wherever, and these two kids with machine guns drove in on dirt bikes and *pop-pop-pop-pop*. Mowed. Him. Down. No joke. And Gayle Heatherton? That bitch was spotted watching some high school talent show in Ohio. Entire auditorium cleared out in three minutes flat and a kid got trampled and broke both legs. A gym teacher tied Gayle to her seat with jump ropes thinking it would keep her there. Nothing left but red sludge when the police arrived though. Yessir. The Covington Curse does not respect state borders."

"Damn," I said. "Really? Carlos never hurt anybody. And Gayle? All the way in Ohio? She was the best person to argue with. That girl had opinions."

"She was a firecracker, all right," Bree said. "Shit. Sorry. No pun intended."

"So the rest of the world is convinced it's a virus?" Tess asked.

"I saw a poll on Fox and ninety-five percent of the country thinks we should be kept in quarantine," Bree said.

"Viruses don't tend to zero in on single classes of high school students in random towns in New Jersey," Tess said, a valid argument that many of us had already raised.

"You think that matters?" Bree asked. "People don't use logic when they're scared. And they're friggin' terrified of us. And not just us. Anyone who used to be in our class."

"Really? Former classmates?" Dylan asked.

"Yep," Bree said. "Rounding them up too."

Indeed. The ones who moved (even as far back as elementary school), the expelled ones, the ones who dropped out—they were on their way to join us as well. Including Jane Rolling.

the showdown

When Jane Rolling arrived on the eighth day of our quarantine, her face was red with fury. At least that's how Tess described it. She noticed Jane before I did and approached me in the commons to whisper, "*You've got competition.*"

"What hole did they dig her out of?" I asked. "I mean, where is she living these days?"

"Ask your boyfriend. I saw him hugging her before she went off to be deloused."

It'd be a lie to say I wasn't jealous, but I also knew that Dylan was entitled to hug whomever he damn pleased. And rather than be a passive-aggressive sneak, trying to squeeze information out of second- or third-hand parties, I decided to go directly to the source.

It did take me a few hours to build up the nerve. Hours spent pacing and peering around shoulders to see if I'd spot Jane. That was the thing about our quarantine. By day six, they had stopped running tests on everyone except the new arrivals, so the rest of us were basically hanging around. Which was kind of fun for the first day or so. Shooting the shit, catching up with people I hadn't seen in weeks.

Boredom set in pretty quickly, though. Yes, I had Dylan, but our physical contact was limited to hand-holding and quick kisses stolen in moments when the SEALs weren't watching. I thought constantly about that night in my room, wishing I'd endured the headaches and dizziness from the concussion and taken the chance on lust while I had it. I was feeling much better now, with only the occasional dizzy spell, which meant I was also feeling a hell of a lot more horny.

God, I hate that word. *Horny*. It's so lecherous and pre-teeny. And yet it's the best way to describe what I was feeling. Hot and bothered? Ugh. No. In heat? Gross. What am I, a farm animal? No, I was horny. Like we all are at some point.

That's what I tried to bottle up—my horndog jealousy of a girl who'd journeyed to parts of Dylan I had yet to explore—when I finally approached Jane in the canteen tent. She was eating soup and I sat down next to her with my chair flipped around and my arms draped over the back. I figured this made me look relaxed, but in control.

"*Hola*," I said, because suddenly I spoke Spanish or something.

"Hi," Jane chirped, her voice so much smaller and sweeter than I expected.

"Do you know who I am?" I asked and realized immediately that it might have sounded like I was threatening her, so I added, "I mean, do you know my name?"

She shrugged.

"Well, I guess I can make something up then," I said with a forced chuckle.

She sipped her soup.

"It's Mara, actually," I said. "You're Jane Rolling, right?"

"I am," she answered, which of course I already knew. Her round face and cropped black hair were unmistakable. I had been picturing them on the shoulders of rodents and pit bulls and pretty much any fugly beast I could imagine.

"Do you at least remember me from Covington High?" I asked.

"I recognize your face," she said. "And now I know your name is Mara Actually."

Her delivery was completely deadpan, and I both loved and hated her for that. If anyone was in control but playing it cool, it was her, and I don't think she even realized it.

"I'm just gonna get it out," I said. "I'm with Dylan now. We are like . . . a thing."

Another sip of soup—goddamn her—and then she finally looked me in the eye. "Okay," she said.

"Okay," I replied, and I made sure she heard me exhale. "Now that it's out in the open, I'm guessing I don't have to worry about you shanking me in the shower or anything like that?"

"Our *thing* ended over a year ago," she said. "I moved on. Bigger stuff to worry about."

"Right, right, right," I said, a right for each of her triplets. "Speaking of which, since we're both being all honest with each other, I have to ask you something."

"I doubt I could stop you if I tried," she said, which almost sounded like a compliment. Almost.

I fake-chuckled again. "You're right about that. So here goes. Why no blood test for Dylan? I mean, if it was ever a question of paternity, that is."

If I hadn't hit a sore spot, I had certainly hit *something*. Jane pushed the soup away and scooted closer to me. "*If you're worried about your boyfriend being a daddy, worry no more,*" she whispered. "*There is no doubt about it. They aren't his.*"

It felt like I was the one finding out I wasn't the father. I ran the back of my hand across my brow and flicked it theatrically. "Wooo. That's . . . that's fantastic. Thank you for that."

Jane shrugged.

The relief wasn't complete, obviously. "So why doesn't Dylan know?" I asked.

"Would it surprise you if I said he was a strange boy?"

"It would not."

"Well then, there you are."

"Okay. But it doesn't . . . I'm still confused."

"He doesn't want to know even the most obvious things," Jane told me. "Not really. Dylan believes in ideas more than facts. Want to break the boy's heart? Give him something real."

"I'm real," I said, patting my body to make sure. "I haven't broken him yet. So he should be able to handle the truth about the triplets."

Jane sighed a sigh that could feed a village and said, "Talk to him about it if you need the whole story. I've already told you more than I should have."

"Can I just ask you one last eensy-teensy itty-bitty widdle thing?" I said, and I put my hands together and tilted my head like I was a cherub.

And goddamnit if a tear didn't slip out of the girl's eye and hang there on her cheek, as if to chastise me for being so damn pushy. "You can ask me only one question," she said as she put a finger up. "You can ask me if I miss my kids more than life itself and if I give a damn about you and Dylan, and what you know, and why you know it, and if your love is eternal or whatever it is you want me to make you feel better about. You can ask me that and only that. So is that your question?"

I started to reach forward to wipe away her tear and then follow up with a hug, but I realized at the last moment it was absolutely the worst thing I could do. "No," I said as I pulled back and stood up. "I already know the answer to that one."

I let her be.

the revelation

We were allowed to write letters to our parents, but to keep the quarantine effective, those letters had to be typed and emailed by the SEALs. No physical things were allowed out and very few physical things, outside of captured refugees, were allowed in. The doctors wanted to keep exposure to the exterior world at a minimum, so that nothing could throw a monkey wrench into their "research." It certainly seemed suspect, but Doc Ramirez assured us they were close to reaching a conclusion and all of us lab rats made a pact to cooperate. Gayle's fate had proven that running away wasn't going to save us and Carlos's fate had showed that no one else in the world wanted us around anyway. This remained the best chance we had at survival.

We were still allowed to see our loved ones via video. Every evening at eight p.m. we shuffled over to the communications tent and watched the candlelight vigil. Our parents were often there, lined up along the fence, waving or singing or putting up their thumbs in support. Some held signs that wouldn't have been out of place at a marathon.

WE BELIEVE IN YOU, BREE

SO PROUD OF YOU, PIETRO

BE SURE TO HYDRATE, HELEN

Or whatever. My parents didn't make any signs, but at least one of them attended each evening. As for the rest of the crowd, it was a rotating cast of familiar and unfamiliar faces. With each successive day, the crowd got smaller, but getting a glimpse of them was still our favorite part of our routine. The camera panned back and forth, and different kids would cheer when they saw a loved one.

On the day Jane arrived, the camera panned over three tiny boys dressed identically in powder-blue suits. Friggin' adorable. They were standing at the fence, but they were only barely standing. Two older folks who must have been Jane's parents were holding their hands. The crowd let out the obligatory *awww*s when they saw these cuties. I didn't bother to look in Jane's direction. I didn't want my cold heart to shatter in two, after all.

But as the camera moved on, I couldn't help but turn to Dylan. A few spots down from the triplets stood a young man. I couldn't ever remember meeting the guy, but he had a face I recognized. Dylan's face. Same bone structure; same deep, dark eyes. Only this face was a few years older and its eyes never strayed from the triplets.

"Is that your brother?" I asked him. "Warren, right? He hasn't visited until tonight, has he?"

Dylan nodded, but he didn't look at Warren. He looked at Jane instead.

I put a hand to my mouth and resisted the urge to howl. What a supersleuth I was, because suddenly I understood. Jane and the Hovemeyer boys had gotten themselves into one hell of a love triangle.

just so you know

Dylan had snuck off to bed without even a good-night so I didn't have the chance to confront him with my discovery, and once morning arrived, we barely had a moment to rub our eyes before some SEALs shepherded us from our cots to the communications tent. There was no screen set up, no camera or computer anywhere. Only Doc Ramirez. Since she wasn't wearing a mask, we knew right away that something had changed.

"First off, I want to thank you all for your cooperation," she said. "We couldn't have asked for a better bunch of young men and women to work with."

Work with? That got more than a few laughs.

Ramirez put up a hand to quiet the crowd, and smiled as she said, "I know. I know. This hasn't been easy, but the good news is that you are all virus free and you'll be going home today."

Pure elation. Putting her hand up again did nothing to quell the happy noises. Ramirez had to wait this one out.

"We will be releasing a statement to the press later today," she said when the room finally settled down. "But I do have to warn you all of something. No matter what we say, the public will still be afraid of you. Simply because you are virus free, it doesn't mean we can guarantee that this, whatever it is, won't happen again. So we not only advise that you remain within the borders of Covington, we require it."

"We?" Skye Sanchez asked. "Who's we?"

"The US government and its armed forces under the authority of our commander in chief."

"You can't do that," Claire Hanlon said. "You shouldn't even have been able to detain all of us. I came voluntarily, of course, but don't doubt for one minute that my lawyer won't sue each and every one of you if you force me to do something against my will."

Though they hardly moved any other muscles, the SEALs inched their fingers closer to their triggers. Ramirez's smile fell away.

"Your lawyer can certainly try," she said. "But know that we are doing this with the full support of our president and congress. If anyone attempts to leave town, authorities will know and you will be detained."

"That's not legal and that's not possible," Claire said.

"It is and it is," Ramirez said. "Thank you again and good luck to you all."

With her head down, Doc Ramirez exited one side of the tent and a SEAL peeled back a flap on the other side. Sunlight poured in. Buses were lined up and ready to take us home.

thankful

Remember earlier how hugs were the last thing I needed? Now they were the first thing. As soon as I saw my parents, I ran to them and grabbed two armfuls. And we sobbed. And we said breathy *I love yous*. We did all the things a family does when it's been apart for what seems like years, but was really only a little more than a week.

"Graduation," Dad said. "Together, we make it to that point, and we're in the clear. Graduation."

"Where'd you get that?" I asked.

"There was a lot of talk along that fence," he replied. "This started when senior year started, so it makes sense that it will end when you graduate."

"Well, if you haven't noticed, school's out," I said. "Permanently, it seems. No cap and gown in my future."

"I wouldn't be so sure," he said. "There are murmurs about restarting classes for at least some kids. Gears are moving."

"The school is wrecked," I said. "The—"

Mom put a hand on my shoulder, kissed my cheek, and said, "Let's not worry about murmurs. For now, how about we close Covington Kitchen? Hang out. The three of us. Spend all our time together."

As appealing as it sounded at first, it was a plan destined to fail. A keen sense of your mortality can make you crave a lot of things, but those things rarely include endless evenings on the couch with the family. I loved my parents, so very much, but I loved them because they weren't always there.

"The Kitchen has to stay open," I assured her. "You'd be antsy and broke without it. I'd be bored and annoyed. Whoever is left in town would be pissed. And for what? So we could sit around watching Netflix?"

They nodded.

"You've always been so honest with us," Dad said.

"Well," I said. "I might as well keep the honesty train rolling then."

"Meaning?" Mom asked.

"Dylan is coming over tonight. By that, I mean he's spending the night in my room. Because I don't see the point in having him sneak in and, honestly, I don't know how much time we have left."

Dad stared at me for a moment. "It's Thanksgiving. You do realize that right?"

"It'll be after dinner," I said. "You'll be conked out anyway. From the trypto-whatever in the turkey."

"Is this something his mother is aware of?" Mom asked.

I shrugged. "If they have the awesome kind of relationship that we do, then I'd guess she is."

"I see," Mom said.

Dad stood up, kissed me on the forehead, and left the room.

"I'll take that as his approval," I said.

Mom hugged me hard and whispered, "We're so sorry."

"For what?"

"For you having to live this way, in this world. I know we're supposed to tell you it was harder when we were younger. But that'd be bullshit."

even more honesty for you

Rather than climbing through the window, Dylan rang the bell. Dad stayed in the family room watching a football game, either as a silent protest or a grudging acceptance that I was a grown human being who likes things that grown human beings like.

Mom hovered by the kitchen door as I pecked Dylan on the cheek and invited him in. "I'm so glad you're safe and healthy, Dylan," she said. "Happy Thanksgiving."

"I'm thankful to be here, ma'am," he replied.

"You didn't drive, did you?" she asked. "Because that would be dangerous."

"No, ma'am," he said. "My board is on the porch."

"It's a long way to skate," Mom said.

"A few miles," Dylan said. "But I've got strong legs."

That's when I realized that I'd never been to Dylan's house. I knew where it was, but I'd never actually been there or met any of his family. Suspecting what I did of his brother, I wasn't entirely sure I wanted to. Now that's a Thanksgiving dinner where every "pass the gravy" has subtext.

"Well, if you need a ride back," Mom said, "let us know. We'll get you home whenever you want. Even if you want to go early. You can take some leftover turkey with you."

"That'd be awesome," Dylan replied.

Mom watched us for a few more moments, then cleared her throat, but instead of saying anything else, she slipped into the kitchen. I sympathized with all the emotions she must have been feeling, but I was feeling plenty myself. As soon as she was gone, I did more than peck Dylan. I kissed him on the lips, deep and long, then grabbed his hand and pulled him toward my room as I said, "Come on. I wanna show you something."

In my room, with the door closed, I showed him something. I lifted my top. I wasn't wearing a bra, which gave him a full view of my soft and supple, gravity-defying, perfectly natural 36 Double-Ds.

Ha! Hilarious.

If you believe that's what they look like, then go ahead, you poor dear. All I will tell you is that in reality, they are far less spectacular. Though Dylan's reaction didn't indicate that. He stopped breathing for a second and reached forward slowly like he was about to touch a Deathly Hallow. I pulled my shirt down at the last moment, hopped on the bed, and patted the open patch of mattress next to me.

"A preview of what's to come," I said. "I know I'm being a horrible tease, but let's wait until my parents go to bed. It'd be weird to imagine them going about their evening while we . . . go about ours."

"Got it," he said. And then he sat on his hands to show he was willing, if not entirely able, to wait.

"I've been on an honesty kick," I told him.

"A good thing."

"Maybe. Maybe not. But if we're taking things another step, if we're taking things all the way to the end, then there can't be any walking on eggshells anymore. I'm getting stuff out there. And I want you to do the same."

He pulled out a hand and placed it on my knee. "Of course."

"Right now," I said, placing a hand on his hand. "I showed you my chest. Now I want you to get something off yours."

He looked me in the eyes, then laughed awkwardly and replied, "Wait. This was your idea. I'm not sure I know what you're getting at but—"

"The triplets," I said, and the words spilled out of me. "They're not yours. I don't know if it's blood tests, but there's proof that you aren't the father."

"I . . . wait . . . how?"

I kissed him on the forehead, softly. Then the bridge of his nose. Then the cheek. Finally the lips. A whisper of a kiss.

"And that makes me so relieved," I told him. "Because it means I have you all to myself. That's a selfish thing to say, I know. And I realize you might not have wanted to know the truth. You might have wanted to live in some sort of paternal limbo or something. But *I* know the truth and I couldn't keep it to myself. It's better this way. Trust me."

"Who told you?" he asked, not smiling, not crying, not doing much more than staring straight ahead.

"Jane," I said, as I leaned in and wrapped my arms around him, placing my chin on his shoulder and closing my eyes. "And hey, if your brother is the father, and if he and Jane had some fling behind your back, well then fuck him and fuck her. If he did it as revenge for something you posted on his Facebook way back when you were a little kid, then fuck him even more. And fuck her even more. Fuck everyone. Because again, what it ultimately means is that you can be with me. Truly. Completely. Without strings. That is a great thing."

All I could hear were Dylan's quivering breaths. And then, "So we're being honest?"

"We are now. And forever."

"She was Warren's girlfriend."

"What?"

"She was with Warren first. Well, the whole time, actually. They had to date in secret, because he was twenty and she was sixteen. But if she was gonna be at our house all the time, then she needed a cover for her parents. I became her cover. I think I was a beard. Only I was a beard for a girl who was dating my brother."

"Wait. You were never together?"

"We were and we weren't. We started pretending we were together and then after a while, we sorta were."

"And you slept with her? In the fields behind the silo?"

"We did . . . things."

"Things?" I asked, making my fingers into male and female bits and pantomiming some hanky-panky.

He shook his head.

"You are aware of how babies are made, aren't you?"

He nodded and said, "I didn't lie to you. I mean it got to a point that could be considered *something*. And anything is possible, right? I mean, I never . . . what I'm trying to say is that Jane was always Warren's girlfriend, even though certain things happened. Things I set into motion. It was supposed to be pretend, but I made it more than that. Because that's what I selfishly wanted. So I'm the villain in all this. Have been since day one."

Villain. I looked him square in the eyes, trying to see what he saw in himself, and I said, "Fuck 'em, anyway. So you're a villain? There are worse things to be."

"Like what?"

"Boring."

The corner of his lip inched up, a wee bit. "True . . . ," he said.

And I replied, "Lemme show you something else."

all the feels

Lying on the bed, my head on Dylan's chest, one of his arms wrapped around me, I said, "I'm going to embarrass myself now."

"No. You could never do that."

"Oh boy," I replied, as I lifted my phone. "Just you wait. I'm going to read you something. All I want you to do is close your eyes and focus on the words."

I couldn't see if he followed my instructions because I was looking toward the foot of the bed. But I trusted him. Completely. Which was a good thing in theory, but revealing a secret side of myself—my *artiste* side, if you will—was now far too easy. Believe it or not, a girl can often benefit from being a little uncomfortable.

I opened a file on my phone. I hadn't looked at it in months, but I'd read it so much in the past that I basically had it memorized. It was the beginnings of what, once upon a time, I thought would be my masterpiece.

"'Xavier Rothman had more feelings than he knew what to do with,'" I said in my reading voice, which was a notch deeper than my speaking voice.

"Who's Xavier Rothman?" Dylan asked.

"Shh!" I said. "It's . . . this is something I wrote. Listen."

"Sorry. Go on."

> "'Xavier Rothman had more feelings than he knew what to do with. He had his own feelings. Which were plenty. He was seventeen, after all. But he had other people's feelings too. He had his grandmother's feelings, God rest her soul. He had the feelings of Karen Vilner, God rest her soul too. He had the feelings of David Abrams, God rest his soul as well.'"

"That's a lot of souls God is resting," Dylan said.

"Shh!"

"Sorry."

> "'Ever since his seventeenth birthday, Xavier had a power. Whenever he touched someone, he took all their feelings. He absorbed them, sopped them up like he was a paper towel and their feelings were a spilled beverage. Then the people died. Because you can't live without any feelings. Xavier discovered his power before he did too much damage. It was a good thing he wasn't exactly a huggy person. It was a bad thing that he was in love. With Veronique. And he could never touch the only person he wanted to touch in the first place.'"

I set the phone on Dylan's stomach and took a deep breath. It was the only time that I'd shared that with anyone. I had a lingering suspicion that it was a steaming pile of terrible, but I was using it to prove a point.

"Is there more?" Dylan asked.

"Not much," I said with a sigh. "And that's all you need to hear."

"It's a short story?"

"A novel. The beginning of one. It's called *All the Feels*. I never finished it."

"Catchy title," Dylan said, though I could tell he didn't believe that.

"I read it to you because you said you're a villain. Xavier thinks he's a villain too. You know, on account of the whole touching-people-and-killing-them thing?"

"Yeah, that'd make a guy feel a tad guilty."

"It's a metaphor," I said. "In case that wasn't obvious. Or maybe it's an allegory? Point is, Xavier is wrong. No one should feel guilty about having feelings. Especially the intense feelings inspired by other people. So you had feelings for Jane. You couldn't help it, right?"

"Right."

"And now you have feelings for me," I stated. "Even stronger feelings. Feelings you will never, ever be able to help."

Dylan paused, then said the words slowly, clearly. "I love you."

Even though trusting him wasn't an issue at this point, I felt the need to tell him to "say that again."

"I love you," he repeated. "I love you, Mara Carlyle. I love what you say. I love what you think. I love that you have opinions. I love that life happens when you're around. I love you. I love you. I love you."

I leaned in and kissed him gently on the lips. Of all our kisses, this one was the best. It made my body tingle and his tremble, and for a moment, I was sure that this would be the end. Because sometimes life is that cruel and that poetic and that stunning.

But it wasn't the end. It was something closer to a beginning. For exactly like Xavier stole people's feelings, Dylan stole mine, drew them out of me like venom from a wound. For the first time ever, I said the words to someone other than my parents or Tess.

"I love you too."

Then I fell back on the bed and opened my eyes.

what we did

We didn't talk about what was going to happen next. We lay there for a few minutes, staring at the ceiling, listening, searching for an opening. When the sink upstairs had stopped running, and the house had fallen silent except for the gurgling of our tummies, I made another move, grabbing his hand and putting it under my shirt. The tips of my nerves were buzzing, sparking, firing. I flinched and I shivered.

Good God, did I want him.

"I'm on the pill," I told him. "But there are condoms under the book on the nightstand and I still think we should use them."

"You're okay?" he asked, and he kissed me right between the eyes. "Now's okay?"

"Is it okay for you?" I asked, which was a better question than "Are you ready to become a man tonight, young virgin?"

He was a virgin. That fact was just dawning on me. He said he'd only been with Jane, and if we were going to be technical about it, he hadn't really *been* with her. Which isn't a shocking thing on its own. Most kids I knew were virgins. It's simply that I had assumed the contrary for so long that it was hard to picture him any other way.

Until, that is, his hand was on my stomach, and he was nodding his approval, looking so goddamn nervous. I kissed his neck below the patchy stubble. Three times. To calm him. To assure him. Then I guided his hand down to my waistband and tucked his fingers under the elastic. He reached the other hand over and fumbled with the lamp, almost knocking it to the floor before finding the switch and flicking it off. There would be no helicopters to interrupt us now, no phone calls from FBI agents, no soul-crushing headaches.

Only the lips, pecking, kissing, falling together. Only the pawing over the lumpy and the smooth. Only his stubble scraping at my cheek and my hair falling across his neck and face, tickling his nose and making him squirm. Only my tongue on his lobe, then in his ear, making him squirm even more. Only his hands—slightly cold, but nicely cold—peeling off my top and his fingers running over my breasts and down to the slightly smaller folds of flesh below my ribs. Only my nipples in his mouth and his nipples in my fingertips. Only the rolling away, the spines arching, and then easing back straight. Only the kicking down of covers. Only the struggling with his belt and laughing and me asking if it "required a key." Only the tugging at the pants, the synchronized wiggle to free ourselves. Only his mouth, exploring my thighs, and that stubble again, now pressing against my hips. Only the draft across my hair as my panties shuffled into the tangle of sheets. Only his lips, exploring, and my fingers on his scalp, and me saying, "Just a little bit, not too much." Only him taking a breath and asking, "How do you like it?" Only me thinking, "Who the hell knows, I don't do this all that much myself," and only me responding, "However feels natural." Only the stopping, only him motioning with his chin toward the dresser, only me nodding. Only the crinkling of the condom wrapper and the smell of the condom, sharp and not unpleasant, but not anything like the smell of a person. Only me bending forward and kissing his stomach and him holding the condom up to the moonlight streaming through the window to determine the direction of the roll. Only cupping him and helping him slip it on. Only his hands on the pillow, only his arms straight, only the pause as he lingers above. Only my fingers repositioning him and me telling him, "Slow at first." Only the tension. Only the easing in. Only a little, and then a little more. Only the opening up. Only the flood. Only the quickening. Only the teeth and the nails. Only the creak of the bedframe that wasn't loud, necessarily, but still, was it too loud? Only me checking the door to make sure it was locked. Only me suddenly not caring about what's loud and what's locked. Only him saying, "Is that too much? Am I—?" Only me interrupting and assuring, "Keep going." Only the slipping out. Only the rush to get back in. Only the slipping out again. Only the rush to get back in. Again! Only the clutching. Only the clenching. Only the held breath. Only the waves and the throbs and the squints and the puffs and the gasps and the gulps and the falling apart. Only the kisses on the neck. Only the knowing, the fearing, the *loving* that it could have all ended right then and there in gloriously messy fashion, but it didn't, even if it nearly felt like it did. Only the giggling and the relief.

phew

Dylan left the next morning through the front door, picking up his skateboard on the way out and saying, "Thank you for letting me feel, you know, all the . . . you know."

Oh, I knew, but no thanks were necessary. I was the one who should have been thanking him, for introducing a colorful diversion from our predicament, a predicament that became darker as soon as I sat down to breakfast.

My parents didn't say a word about Dylan. Instead they informed me that authorities had captured my classmates Yuki Dolan and Cameron Quell as they were trying to leave town. Yuki was curled up in the trunk of her cousin's Miata and Cameron was on foot, jogging through the woods with a backpack full of supplies. No dogs or helicopters were needed to track them down. Officers had simply predicted their movements and were waiting for them. It was eerie and telling, and made me want to hide in the house.

It was an instinct confirmed by Rosetti. Later that morning, she sent me a text:

Stay put. I'm coming over to talk.

Me: To me?

Rosetti: You can invite what's-her-name too. I'm sure you tell her everything anyway.

She wasn't wrong there. Between the two texts, I had already shot off a message to Tess:

Lady Nightshade Alert!

Because Paula had confiscated her keys for fear she'd blow up while driving, Tess arrived by bike half an hour later. Mom greeted her at the door with a hug. "You can't believe how happy I am to see you, Tessy."

"I've lucked out so far, haven't I?" Tess said as she kissed Mom on the cheek.

When Rosetti rolled in a few minutes later, there was only a handshake and a quick explanation that she needed to "borrow the girls for a second or two" and then she'd be on her way. Mom saw no harm in that. Borrow away, as long as we were within yelling distance. So Tess and I wrapped ourselves in blankets, and we decamped to the back deck, where we watched the wind blow dead leaves into little tornadoes as Rosetti got, as she put it, "down to brass tacks."

I had no idea where that term came from, but I imagined a corkboard full of photos of the victims and strings leading from each of the photos back to a series of brass tacks that were skewering an envelope emblazoned with a big black question mark. While we'd been in the tents, Rosetti had obviously been out there doing some serious detectiving, and now was the time for the big reveal, for her to take down that envelope, tear it open, and knock our socks right the fuck off.

"So what is it?" I asked. "GMOs? Aliens? Lay it out there."

"It's what I've feared since the beginning," Rosetti responded. "And you deserve to know. You are victims of the most heinous violation of human rights I have ever seen perpetrated on this soil."

"We're what now?" I asked.

"You're being monitored and tracked," she explained. "Nanotechnology, injected and now embedded in your arteries. Most likely near your heart."

"You're kidding?" Tess said, placing a hand on her chest.

"You've been tagged like a wild animal and there is nothing you can do about it," Rosetti explained. "That's why the next thing I'm going to ask you is important. Since I've ruled out illicit substances as the delivery device, can either of you think of an instance when your entire class might have been subjected to invasive practices at the hands of government officials?"

"You mean besides what we just went through?" Tess asked. "You mean was there another time when we were sequestered for days in tents and given a full battery of batshittery?"

Rosetti smirked and said, "It would have been more subtle than that. A field trip to an army base, a—"

I shot a triumphant finger to the sky. "Washington, DC. Eighth grade. We all went to DC together."

"Every eighth grader in the Northeast does that trip," Tess said.

True but, nevertheless, the info raised Rosetti's eyebrows. "I suspect you were all in the same buses and hotels?"

"Probably . . . definitely," I said as realizations bloomed. Now *this* made sense. This wasn't some blowhard jumping to conclusions. This was about collecting evidence and presenting a logical case that would stick. Brass tacks, my friends.

"Go on," Rosetti said. "Give me details."

"Oh, oh, oh," I yelped. "We toured the Pentagon. We were all in this auditorium together and we listened to some military guy talk about national defense. I remember that."

"Interesting," Rosetti said. "Worrisome, but interesting."

Maybe it seemed obvious to you from the beginning.

Well, duh, Mara, why'd you swim through that sea of red herrings when we all knew from the beginning that there are drones and war-machine shit out there that can vaporize a person from two continents away? Obviously.

A very good point, and one I would have completely brushed off unless it came from the mouth of Special Agent Carla Rosetti of the FBI. Her stellar record of sleuthing and bad-guy-catching was the single thing I needed to pull the veil from my eyes. Tess was tougher to convince.

"So you're blaming the government?" Tess said. "Aren't *you* the government?"

"Have you ever had a job?" Rosetti asked her.

"I used to work at Boston Market," Tess said.

"And what'd you do at Boston Market?"

"I picked chicken carcasses. So they could use them in sandwiches. Carvers they called them, though there was very little carving."

This seemed to please Rosetti, and she leaned toward Tess and spoke to her in a tone of respect she had not previously bestowed upon my pal. "Hard, thankless work. And during your chicken pickin' stint, did you trust your employers? In other words, do you think the various levels of management at Boston Market always had your best interests in mind?"

"No, ma'am, I did not."

"Okay then. Crazy as it seems, I'm no different from you. Only it's the government I do my chicken pickin' for. What do you two know about false flags?"

Tess stared at her, studied her, as if searching for a lie.

While I said, "I don't know the first thing about false anythings, but I do know what you're saying makes a lot more sense than some magical explanation. And really, isn't that what everyone else is selling?"

"Exactly," Rosetti replied. "People see what they want to see, even when the evidence points in the opposite direction. My partner, for instance. I'm not about to share this information with Meadows because he loves this government more than he loves this country. The government has an agenda. Unfortunately, they're using kids like you to further that agenda. So you're the only ones I can trust. Together, we might be able to expose it."

"Seriously?" Tess said. "The last time you asked for our help, Mara ended up in the hospital."

"And for that I am supremely sorry," Rosetti said, nodding at me. "I will not ask you to take any more risks. I only ask that you stay in touch. Consider this more like a friendship. Sharing gossip. Girl talk."

Then she reached into her handbag, pulled out two flip phones, and handed us each one.

"Ooo," I said, holding my phone up to the light like it was a diamond. "Is this a burner?"

"It's clean, untraceable, and has my number programmed into it," Rosetti told us. "Call or text me whenever, about whatever."

"Can Tess and I program each other's numbers in it?" I asked. "So we can group-text the latest and greatest?"

"Fine, sure," Rosetti said. "But only the three of us. Dylan will not be involved with this venture."

"You want me to keep a secret from my boyfriend?" I asked, which seemed like an impossibility now that we'd shared everything we possibly could.

"Every girl should have at least a few secrets from her boyfriend," Rosetti said. "You're foolish if you don't. I picked you because you've proven to be smart and trustworthy. Don't let me down by proving otherwise."

Tess held the phone in her lap. She opened it and shut it, making it snap like alligator jaws. She did it a few times as her lips moved, the same way they do when she's doing an equation in her head. Then she looked up, and said, "I have my own theories, you know?"

Rosetti smiled. "I bet you do."

"Legit theories," Tess assured her. "Stuff I've spent a lot of time figuring out."

"And that's what it's for," Rosetti said, pointing at the phone.

Tess held the phone in her fist for a moment, then pocketed it, and said, "You might as well know, sometimes we call you Lady Nightshade."

passing time

Snatch. *Grab. Gotcha. Not-so-fast. Um-where-do-you-think-you're-going-kid?*

That was basically how the end of November went.

Every senior who tried to skip town was apprehended. Peacefully, thankfully, but a few situations were tense, with guns drawn and threats made that were more than idle. Disguises, Vespas, fake IDs—our fellow classmates tried everything, and they all failed. Which was still a better fate than spontaneous combustion, of course.

Thankfully, those had petered out. Harper Wie and Gayle Heatherton had been the last two. Coincidence? I doubted it. Something more than examinations seemed to have gone down in those tents. Rosetti was right: The implantation of tracking devices was glaringly obvious. But maybe Doc Ramirez and her team had taken additional measures to . . . defuse us.

Not that we could actually prove this. We were safe, but we were trapped. With no schoolwork to distract us, *downsized* from crappy part-time jobs, pariahs in a community of pariahs, we seniors were forced to avoid places in town where we were deemed a risk to the public, which was almost everywhere. The burners Rosetti gave me and Tess were essentially useless, because what were we going to text her?

> Sitting on my back deck, staring blankly into the yard.
> Once again, no CIA hiding in the leaf piles. Will report
> back at the top of the hour.

In short: It sucked. The silver lining: sex.

Time on our hands meant Dylan and I were now having our fair share. Imagine a relationship montage from a movie, but instead of a couple enjoying picnics, walks on the beach and what not, it's just a whole lot of gettin' it on. That was basically December.

Was the gettin'-it-on *good* gettin'-it-on? It was certainly diverse. Positionally, that is. Forward, backward, sideways, wrapped up around each other in the shadows behind an inflatable Santa in Claire Hanlon's front yard. Gymnastically epic stuff.

The only issue was, it never reached the dizzying heights of that first time. A little odd, because technically that first time wasn't very good. It was fumbly and messy. There's no question that we got better at the mechanics the more we learned about each other's bodies. Nevertheless, diminishing returns. Not that I worried too much about it. I often found *firsts* to be the best, and Dylan and I had plenty of other *firsts* to look forward to in our relationship. And let's not forget that I had a major conspiracy to feed my anxiety fix.

I wanted to show Dylan the burner, to explain my arrangement with Rosetti, and yet not much was happening on that front. I also didn't want thoughts of the special agent to dredge up memories about his family's past troubles. So during every carnal episode, I stifled the urge to shout out, "It's a government plot! We're guinea pigs! We must fight back. To war! To war! To war!" And after every carnal episode, I shifted our focus to other, less acrobatic endeavors. Socialization, for instance.

Our time in the tents had brought me closer to the other seniors than I had first realized, and I was starting to miss them. Also, I wanted to promenade Dylan and my true love in front of our peers, to have them whistle and pat our backs and say things like, "I always thought you two were perfect for each other."

But when New Year's Eve came and went with nary a social engagement other than another roll behind the inflatable Santa, I realized that it would take more than texting my old chums with pleas of :

> let's hang

—which were always answered with variations on:

> thanks but no thanks.

Everyone had resigned themselves to being homebodies and that was understandable. At first. But as the days bled into each other and I didn't hear a word about theories, let alone parties—I mean, come on, every night was essentially a Friday night—I began to think differently about my former classmates.

They were, to put it bluntly, a bunch of cowards.

well, not all of them

Tess was still Tess, of course. Remarkable, reliable, brave. On a sharp and sunny afternoon during the first week of January, I invited her for a bike ride, and she happily accepted. I hadn't been seeing her much lately either, but that's because she'd been too busy scouring Reddit for "promising leads." She'd invited me to join her, but I'd declined on account of it sounding about as appealing as taking a skinny dip in a septic tank.

We decided to ride our bikes as far from my house as possible, while staying within town limits, which we calculated would bring us to the Shop City Mall. The Shop City Mall had been closed for over a decade. Stores sat empty the entire time, waiting for a rebirth that was often promised, but never came. My parents had always blamed its demise on Amazon and Target, but I blamed the fact that Cinnabon is fucking gross and not a single living person has ever bought anything from a Brookstone.

We weren't in a rush, so we took the long cut through the center of town, expecting maybe to see some of our classmates out and about. But Main Street was a broken expanse of empty. They hadn't even fixed the guardrail on the Centennial Bridge or pulled the snowplow out of the Patchcong River after the #ForBilly riots. The stone steps of the State Street Theater were covered in a layer of dead leaves and I doubted that anyone had been inside since the emergency town hall, two days after we lost Perry Love.

We continued along the Old Post Road, through the tunnel of bare trees, and past the Covington Quilt Museum and its still-gaping, RAV4-shaped wound. Empty out there as well.

We didn't talk at first, because we never talked all that much when we rode together. It was rarely ever about that. And yet, as we got closer to the mall, I felt a need to confess. "I feel a bit weird keeping this from Dylan," I shouted through the wind at her.

"Keeping what?" she shouted back. Like me, she'd owned her bike for years and there were streamers on the handgrips that, though faded, still flared when she rode.

"The Rosetti thing," I replied. "The conspiracy investigation. I want to tell him about it. I want to tell everyone about it and live our lives. Have fun. Be social. Get on with our futures."

"About that," Tess said as she skidded to a stop. "If it makes you feel any better, I don't think it matters."

"What?" I asked, kicking up my own batch of dust. "Our lives? Our futures?"

"Rosetti's theory. Another in a long line of flawed ideas. You don't share every flawed idea you hear with Dylan, do you? So why is this one different?"

"Because it's not flawed. She knew Doc Ramirez put tracking devices in us from the get-go."

"Hardly the get-go. If you've done even a little digging, you'd know that the public has been asking for us to be tracked for months. It's been a standard part of stump speeches: *Contain the Curse!* It's all about giving the constituents what they want."

"So what? Doesn't mean Rosetti is wrong about anything. The government wants to exploit us because they know more than they're letting on."

"The government wants to contain us. Because they know less. Be wary of the government, but put your focus on the science. Something our friend Lady Nightshade is forgetting."

"So remind her. Have you been using the burner? At least sharing *the science* with her? I'm sure she'd like to hear about it."

Tess shook her head. "I'm not ready to share with anyone yet, because I'm not sure what I've found. You'll be the first to know, though. So hold on to that burner. If it's really untraceable, then it might come in handy. We might need a way to talk to each other if things get worse."

"Worse?" I said, almost choking on the word. "Well, thanks for the reminder that my life can still get shittier. In the meantime, what theory am I supposed to share with Dylan?"

"None of them," she replied as she adjusted her banana seat, which had gone a little crooked. "What I'm trying to say is don't worry so much about what you tell him. It'll only add stress to his life and then it will eventually turn out to be as meaningless as all this other nonsense. I mean, everyone has a theory. Even he has one, right?"

I shrugged. "A while back Dylan did say he thought it was all due to karma. But then he made some nonsensical joke about Jennifer Lawrence, so I figured he was kidding."

Tess snorted out a little laugh, and started pedaling. "Actually that's one of the more novel ones I've heard. I mean, that poor girl never did catch a break, did she? And Gayle Heatherton was the last victim. Makes you think, doesn't it?"

Déjà vu. I mean, what the fuck did Jennifer Lawrence have to do with anything? I wanted to ask, but by the time I caught up to Tess, we were climbing a hill and my lungs were fighting too hard against the crisp air.

When we reached the crest, the Shop City Mall was spread out below us in all its derelict glory. Tess kept going, so I followed, coasting down the road and howling into the wind, which is the only way to properly bike downhill.

As we blazed into the parking lot, we zipped our lips and jammed our brakes. Because, uh-oh, we were not alone. A man carrying a yellow hard hat hurried toward us, waving it as he ran. "Whoa, whoa whoa," he said. "What're you doing here. Gonna have to move along."

"Ummm, why?" Tess replied as she surveyed the empty lot. "This place has been closed forever. I doubt we'll be bothering anyone who's looking to shop at the Talbots."

The man used the hard hat to point to an entrance of the mall where at least a dozen other construction workers had gathered.

"Not shopping," he said. "Schooling. Didn't you hear? Board is re-opening the elementary and middle schools, but since the high school is a mess, everyone except those seniors will be taking classes here."

"Kids are taking classes in, like, the RadioShack?" I asked.

The man put his hat back on. "Whatever works. Got a food court for science labs . . . and food. Clear out the JCPenney and you have yourselves a gym. Plenty of room for whatever you want in there. The rest of you kids have been given a clean bill of health, so you deserve to go back to class. We should have it ready in a week or two and then you can get on with things. My daughter will be there. She's a junior now, so you probably know her. Lucia Watson? I'm surprised you haven't—"

Then the man shut his trap, took a step back. His eyes widened as it finally dawned on him who he was talking to.

Tess put her hands up in surrender and said, "Don't worry. It's not—"

"No!" the man shouted and he wagged a finger. "Get the hell out! You're not wanted. Not here, not anywhere."

"We're not dangerous to anyone but ourselves," I said. "I think that's been proven."

But the man wasn't having it. He ran back toward the other workers, gesticulating as he went. Tess and I mounted our pink steeds and scrambled to line up our feet with the pedals. By the time we were moving, the mob was upon us, shouting and shaking their fists like a good mob should. We made it out of the parking lot, barely, and chugged up the hill without looking back.

Now, I've never considered myself particularly cool, but I've been fortunate enough to have escaped any serious bullying in my life. I've been harassed, sure. What girl hasn't? Teased, without a doubt. But bullying—and I mean the constant and unrelenting variety—is something I don't have much experience with.

As my lungs and heart dug their claws into my ribs, I imagined this is how it felt to be bullied, to constantly fear that someone is behind you, chasing you up an endless hill, and if you stop moving, you'll fall back into their clutches. So you can imagine my relief when I reached the crest, and it was now the high school I spotted in the distance, speckled by a fresh flurry of snow.

Tess and I raced down the other side and away from the men and we howled even louder than before and it was in the midst of that howl and those snowflakes that I finally put two and two together.

"Well, aren't I officially the world's biggest idiot?" I said with a gasp when we were finally far away enough to feel safe. "Dylan meant our old classmate Jennifer Lawrence, didn't he?"

let's stop right now

I need to state the obvious: We did not go to school with the movie star Jennifer Lawrence. Let's continue stating the obvious: The movie star Jennifer Lawrence has ruined the lives of hundreds of women named Jennifer Lawrence. Well, maybe not ruined, but she's certainly made it so that whenever one of these Jennifer Lawrences introduces herself, some douchebag will inevitably say, "Or do you prefer Katniss?"

Hardy-har-har-har. I'm rolling my eyes right now in solidarity with the myriad and sundry Jennifer Lawrences out there. At the same time, I'm pumping a fist in support of all their admirers. Think about it. You're some regular guy who's curious about the little girl down the lane named Jennifer Lawrence, so you fire up the Google to check if there are any mug shots out there of her, or if she has a Tumblr dedicated to holocaust denial or something, and *bam!* the first ten billion results are pics and clips of some delightfully foul-mouthed, blond-locked ingenue who's captured the world's heart once again by, I don't know, tumbling down a flight of stairs and into the lap of a red-faced Dalai Lama at the Nickelodeon Kids' Choice Awards.

Or, to be more realistic, you could be a lovely and charming young woman named Mara who lives in New Jersey and whose boyfriend and best friend reminded her that they once went to school with a girl named Jennifer Lawrence who was bullied so much in seventh grade that she fled her hometown and now that lovely and charming young woman named Mara wants to know what the hell happened to that particular and exceedingly regular Jennifer Lawrence.

That's right. Our Jennifer Lawrence grew up right here in Covington, but she flew under the radar for a while. She had a handful of friends, as far as I could tell. Was nice enough, though not distractingly so. Did fine in school, I'm told. Wasn't gorgeous, wasn't hideous. There was nothing extreme about her whatsoever.

Then one day a website called JenniferLawrenceFarts.com went live. I don't know when I first heard about it—sometime during the fall of seventh grade I suspect—but I do remember laughing when I pulled up the home page and was treated to a series of photos of Covington's Jennifer Lawrence making the sort of funny faces that go hand and hand with flatulence. To drive the point home, there were speech bubbles inserted at butt height that said things like "Poot," "Pfft," and "Kaplowy-boom-boom-fizzzzzz!"

It was amusing enough, and I will say in all honesty that I figured she was in on the joke. A bit of self-deprecation can go a long way, after all. So the next day, when I saw her in the lunch line piling her tray with beans and rice I gave her a gentle hip check and with a wink, I said, "Fueling up the engine?"

"Excuse me," Jennifer replied.

I pointed at her butt, and said, "The engine. The old brownie baker."

The look on her face cannot be adequately described. Waves of shock crashed onto a beach of disgust and left a coastline of shame. In other words, she was devastated.

"Go suck a dong, Marigold," Jennifer Lawrence snarled.

I looked over my shoulder and asked, "Who's Marigold?"

Now add some confusion to the mix and her face nearly disintegrated. Tears streaming, she asked, "Isn't your name Marigold?"

I shook my head. She wept some more and stumbled away into the cafeteria. I haven't spoken to her since.

In the months that followed, other websites went live. JenniferLawrenceEatsHerOwnBoogers.com and JenniferLawrencePicks AWedgie.com, to name a couple. The pictures that appeared on them weren't nearly as salacious or as incriminating as advertised. Most of them were fuzzy, taken from a distance with crappy phones. But it didn't really matter. It became a contest in seventh grade to see who could capture the most unflattering pictures of Jennifer and post them online. I will readily admit that I got caught up in it and snapped a few shots. I never posted any of them, but I know it didn't help matters each time Jennifer spotted the girl she thought was named Marigold holding a phone up at the far end of the hall.

By spring, she was gone. Perhaps it was a coincidence. Perhaps one of her parents got transferred to a new job somewhere. But somehow I doubt that.

So yes, I was complicit in that patch of awfulness. Many of us were, maybe even Billy Harmon. Tess did say he enjoyed a good dirty joke, after all. But guess who was the ringleader, the web master? Gayle Heatherton, that's who. Our hapless talent-show-loving fugitive, my favorite debater, the most recent notch on the bedpost of the Covington Curse. She never publicly admitted it, but the domain names were all registered to an address that turned out to be her uncle's lake house. In Ohio, the same state she would later flee to and die in. And when that other Jennifer Lawrence became a big star, I heard Gayle made a few bucks by selling the domain names, which now host Tumblrs dedicated to pictures of the movie star's flatulent faces, nose-picking, and underwear-repositioning. I feel for you, Jenni-fer Lawrences of the world. I'm sorry that even your greatest embarrassments have been usurped.

So that's what Dylan and Tess were going on about. As for our Jennifer Lawrence, I figured the reason she wasn't rounded up with the rest of the former classmates is because the government was no better at Googling than anyone else, and she was still out there somewhere having a good laugh at our misfortune.

Or she was dead, blown to pieces like the others, and her obit-uary was buried so deep in the search results that it'd be almost impossible to find it. Which would be the ultimate slap in the face for the poor girl.

marigold and memoreasi

At Katelyn Ogden's memorial service we watched a slideshow created by her friend Skye Sanchez. *Created* is actually a strong word, because an app called MemorEasi had done most of the heavy lifting. It worked like this:

Enter someone's name into MemorEasi and the app would perform an image search. You could filter the results using hometowns, schools, etc., and once an image of the specific person you were looking for popped on the screen, all you had to do was tap and then the app would take the reins, using facial recognition software and sifting through social media accounts and databases to create a minute-long slideshow that featured pictures of that person and was scored to something corny and Josh Grobanish. All in about ten seconds flat.

After exhausting every other search engine to locate our old punching bag Jennifer Lawrence (okay, I only tried Google), I downloaded MemorEasi to my phone. I didn't have any information to filter the results other than the fact that she used to live in Covington. So I was graced with endless images of the movie star, the movie star, and, you guessed it, the movie star. But right when I was about to give up, one of these things was not like the others. A grainy photo of an entirely different person filled the screen.

I hadn't seen her in almost six years, but I was sure this was the same girl we had tortured, the same one who had thought my name was Marigold. She was smiling back at me. Older. Happier, I hoped, though there was no text to confirm that or tell me where she was or if she'd lived quite as long as I had. Only the photo. So I tapped it and MemorEasi did its thing.

Voilà, instant in memoriam.

The app found at least ten more photos, and a minute later, after Jennifer Lawrence's adolescence and its various haircuts had flashed before my eyes, I was crying. I'm not kidding. I was an absolute mess, mourning someone who probably wasn't dead, shedding more tears than I'd shed for all the victims of the Covington Curse combined. Ask me to explain it and all I can say is technology may be heartless, but that doesn't mean well-designed technology can't knock the wind out of you.

Of course, this is not to declare I was on board with Dylan's karma theory. (Because, come on, cosmic punishments for fart jokes? Ain't exactly sound reasoning.) I was still solidly Team Rosetti. But after hearing Tess's doubts, I needed a little reassurance. And after remembering what we did to Jennifer Lawrence, I needed someone to tell me things could still work out for us cowards and assholes.

Wiping the tears from my face, I pulled out the burner and called the special agent. "Do something," I told her.

"What?"

"Stop them. Catch them. Fix this."

"Mara," Rosetti responded calmly. "It's not as simple as that. It will take some time. It will—"

"Bullshit! Did you hear about what's happening at the Shop City Mall? Everyone except us gets to move on. No one cares about us anymore. We won't be able to live our lives, get a yearbook, go to prom, and do all the shit that we were supposed to do. It's like we're already dead. Roll the slideshow."

There was silence on the other end of the line for a moment and then Rosetti said, "I never got a yearbook. I never went to prom."

"Fine. So those things aren't big deals, but to me—"

"They *are* big deals," Rosetti snapped. "If only I still had the chance to experience them. But I was too wrapped up in growing up when I was your age. You still have a chance. Stop whining and take control of your life. That's what's happening at the mall. Initiative."

"But—"

"The people who did this to you expect you to wait around for the next thing to happen, for the next stage in their operation. Fight back by doing the opposite."

Once again, the woman surprised me. There was emotion in her voice, not all that different from the emotion that colored Dad's voice when he had told me that I needed to get to graduation, that I would be safe as long as I walked across a stage and picked up a diploma.

"So what do you expect me to do?" I said. "Make a few calls and open school next week? Easy peasy."

"That's the problem," she answered. "There are more than two hundred of you. Have you even tried?"

"No."

"Make an effort."

Her point was valid, and yet making efforts was not exactly my forte. I always had great ideas, of course. I would have been perfect for a think tank. Think tanks are a thing, right? Organizations where people sit around and come up with solutions to the world's problems? I would have been a shoo-in for one of those. However, if do-tanks are also a thing—as in, organizations that actually *do* shit—then you would have had to count me out. On account of, well, laziness.

I said an embarrassed "you're right" and "thank you for your advice" to Rosetti and I hung up. Then I tapped the fluffy pink icon for the MemorEasi app and watched the Jennifer Lawrence slideshow again. Ten times, with Rosetti's voice echoing through my head, in rhythm with the sappy background tunes.

"If only. If only. If only."

On the eleventh viewing, an idea struck me: Together we had the power to chase someone from our school, so maybe together we could have the power to bring people back.

I popped off a text to Laura Riggs—you know, the proprietor of the crack tree house and the basement of dark deeds?

> Me: How long would it take to put together a soiree at your place? Invites, booze, all that.

> Her (instantaneously): 4 hours.

Me: How bout a funeral?

Her (almost instantaneously): 5? Which am I hosting?

Me: Both I guess. Do you have room for a cauldron?

Her: Don't know what that means but probably.

What that meant was a big cast-iron pot that was collecting dust in the Covington Kitchen storage room. My parents used to mix their Oinker Oil in it when they were making small, artisanal batches of the stuff. Now I needed to mix up something else.

Reincarnation.

if only

Invitations were sent via Snapchat. The self-destructing image was of Laura Riggs's house—the front yard riddled with tombstone doodles—and the caption read *Your . . . Time . . . Has . . . Come . . . 8PM.*

Fear is a powerful motivator and I knew if anything was going to get the other seniors off their asses, it was an ominous reminder of their existential dilemma.

There was no way we'd be smuggling the cauldron out of Covington Kitchen without my parents noticing, so I had to ask Dad for a ride to Laura's. He dropped me, Dylan, and the cauldron off at seven, but not before saying, "Mom wants me to tell you to—"

"Be safe," I replied. "I know, I know."

"Have fun," he corrected me. "You guys deserve a night to let your hair down."

"We do indeed," I said. "But that's not what this is about. We'll call you in a few hours when we need a lift home. Or sooner if it backfires."

Dylan and Laura were the only ones who knew my plans, and while they were both willing to help because they didn't have anything better to do, I doubt they believed I'd actually accomplish my goals. Laura, dressed entirely in black, met us at the car and helped us wheel the cauldron on a dolly through her garage and down a makeshift ramp into her basement.

"Your parents don't care about stains and all that?" I asked her.

"OxiClean does wonders," Laura said. "Besides, my folks are down the shore for at least three days. A lot can be fixed in three days."

The cauldron was the size of a large beach ball and we filled it to the top with cheap vodka, peach schnapps, pineapple juice, and seltzer. We hung a tray with dry ice inside the rim to give it a smoky effect and tossed an aquarium pump in the liquid to whip up some bubbles.

"Hey, if anyone's down with Wicca and all that shit, it's me," Laura said. "But I don't know why we can't do a bunch of Jell-O shots and let the night lead wherever it leads."

"A bit of theater goes a long way," I said. "Remember Katelyn's memorial service? The pictures? The music? The spectacle?"

"Not to mention the crying," Laura said. "I hope that's not the scene you're going for."

"The reason the memorial was so effective wasn't because people loved Katelyn," I explained. "It's because they loved themselves, and the drama of the event made them confront all their lost potential. You know what I mean? 'If only I was a better person. If only I was a healthier person.' That sorta thing."

"*If only I had been there when it happened,*" Dylan added.

"Bingo," I replied.

"Fine, fine, whatever," Laura said. "Tell me exactly what you want me to do again?"

"Light some candles and fetch me your father's robe."

party hardy

Was it a wild party, the wildest in the annals of teendom? Were kids jumping from the roof into the pool? Were there flames, nudity, pissing on antique furniture?

Not even close. When the guests arrived, Laura greeted them at the door and told them, "Only one person goes in at a time." Then she texted Dylan the name of whoever was about to enter. Meanwhile, Dylan was down in the basement with his phone queued to MemorEasi.

Now, not all of our classmates were overexposed, but there were at least a few shots of everyone out in the ether. And MemorEasi was equally effective using only a handful of images. It panned and zoomed over faces in slo-mo. It applied smoky filters for an old-timey vibe. When combined with the tickling of ivories, the results were sufficiently tear-jerking.

So that's what our classmates confronted when they entered Laura's house: themselves.

Dylan would check the text from Laura, enter a name into MemorEasi, filter, tap the image, and then, as saccharine sounds wafted from the stereo and the next guest stepped in the house, a slideshow depicting his or her life appeared on a massive TV in the Riggses' candlelit living room.

"Welcome to your own funeral," it all was meant to say.

While a sign stuck to the basement door promised REINCARNA-TION THIS WAY.

When the slideshow was over, that's where each guest went. Down, down, down, to an even darker room, where the music was best described as aggressively ambient and Dylan was waiting to shush anyone who was audibly weeping and then usher them to a seat on the floor, before shooting off a text to Laura that read:

Next Victim?

In front of the befuddled guests and next to the smoking cauldron, I sat on a stool wearing a brown hooded bathrobe and wielding a large stainless-steel ladle. I did not speak.

"Is this an orgy or something?" Clint Jessup asked when he arrived, and he rubbed his hands together like he was about to get down to business.

"Where the hell did you get that idea?" Dylan replied.

"I don't know," Clint said. "That chick is wearing a robe. An orgy robe, I figured. My life flashed before my eyes, so this must be heaven."

Dylan flicked Clint's ear with a finger and said, "Sit down and be quiet. That goes for everyone."

By nine o'clock, the guests stopped arriving, so Laura locked the front door and came downstairs, bringing the total attendance to about thirty kids scrunched together on a giant rag rug and circling the cauldron like a coven frocked in Anthropologie and Uniqlo. It was enough for me to begin.

"You are all pathetic!" I hollered.

Given the raised eyebrows, this was not what they were expecting, but they were willing to hear the robed weirdo out. Not a peep from the crowd.

"That's right," I went on. "Pathetic! Think about what you saw upstairs. Is that what you want? Your entire life summed up and declared over? Because that's how you've been acting. You've been bullied into thinking it can't get any better. Meanwhile, this was supposed to be our senior year. Our senior *fucking* year! Our final shot at being young and dumb. Sure, I realize a few of you have applied early decision, but do you think any college will admit us now that we're tarnished goods? They can't discriminate because of race, religion, or gender, but how about combustibility? As far as I know, a can of gasoline has never been admitted to Princeton, let alone Rutgers. Which means this is the last gasp. And what are we doing with it? We're sitting at home and acting like we're already dead. If an asteroid was bearing down on us, we wouldn't be cooped up and alone, would we? No. We'd be spending our last days together. So let's be together, enjoy each other, make a stupid yearbook, and go to prom. Let's reopen the goddamn school!"

Go ahead and shoot a spitball at this uber-nerd if you must, but I'm not ashamed to admit I was demanding a return to academia. And wouldn't you know it? My classmates were on board.

"Huzzah!" Dylan shouted in solidarity, because apparently people shout "huzzah" from time to time.

"Fuck yeah!" Laura seconded, though I think it was mostly because she likes to swear.

While I'd love to say the rest joined in with a chorus of "damn skippy" and "amen," that isn't exactly the truth. The truth is, they nodded the sounds-a'right-to-me variety of nods, and then Gabe Carlton asked, "What's in the big pot?"

"That, my friends, is the elixir of *let's fucking live again*," I said, and I dipped the ladle in and took a sip.

"If you want to help us reopen the school, then you drink," Dylan added as he grabbed the ladle from me and gulped.

I welcomed his enthusiasm, not only because it was the first time in a while that it was directed somewhere other than my body, but also because it was the first time I'd ever seen Dylan taste the forbidden fruit of alcohol. It assured me he was dedicated to my cause, even if it worried me a bit about what sort of drunk he might turn out to be.

"If you want to be reincarnated and join our wasted squad of geeks," I said as I kissed Dylan's ear, "then you better drink."

Claire Hanlon raised a hand. "Would it be totally lame of me to ask what exactly is in the elixir of *let's fucking live again*?"

"It would," Laura said as she snatched the ladle and took her sip. "Trust me. It's delicious. And gluten free."

Becky Groves, the same girl whose scream still echoed in my ears from our pre-calc and group therapy days, stepped up to the ladle next. She closed her eyes, took a sip, and said, "I will join you. I think a return to the normalcy of school will give me some well-deserved peace."

This caused Claire to jump up and seize the ladle. "And this will give me what I deserve," she said as she dipped it in the cauldron. "I'm graduating. As valedictorian. As was always intended."

As soon as Claire sipped, a line formed behind her. Imbibing commenced and cowards were reborn as heroes, or at least as kids who were willing to give up their permanent vacation and go back to school.

The rest of the party wasn't as blatantly cultish, but it was blatantly fun. Dylan downed some more ladles of elixir and the sort of drunk he became was a . . . sleepy one. He was goofy and kissy at first—not at all scary like some boys who use numbness as an excuse to paw and punch in equal measure. He said "I love you" almost every time the alcohol touched his lips. But then, halfway through the party, he nodded off on the couch. So I sat there stroking his feet, sipping from the cauldron, and enjoying the company of my once and future classmates.

There were still many other classmates to convince, of course. The party lured mainly the extroverts and overachievers, and even some of those stayed home. Tess, for instance, didn't attend, which puzzled me more than it pissed me off. I texted her as the festivities were coming to a close.

Me: Missed you here.

Her: Sorry. Busy. What happened?

Me: Might've convinced everyone school is cool.

Her: You're kidding. Good for you.

Me: Good for all of us.

Her: I really am sorry I didn't make it. That house though. The things that have gone on there.

Me: Oh. Yeah.

Her: I hope you're not mad at me.

Fuck, fuck, fuck. I knew Tess wasn't comfortable with Laura Riggs's place and yet I had totally disregarded it during the frenzied planning stage.

Me: I'm the one who's sorry. I will never be mad at you, Tess McNulty. Never never ever.

how we got home

Asking your dad to drive your passed-out-drunk boyfriend home isn't usually the best course of action, so when I couldn't rouse Dylan, I texted Rosetti for a ride. A response arrived seconds later, as the headlights from her Tesla flicked on and shone through Laura's window.

Rosetti: Already here.

I was pretty drunk myself, so I don't remember who carried Dylan to the car, but when we were on our way, with him snoozing in the back and me riding shotgun, I raved about what a success the night had been and I thanked Rosetti for her encouragement.

"I'm sorry I haven't been much help," I said as I checked once more to make sure Dylan was asleep. "You know, with the whole fightin'-da-man thing."

"You are helping," Rosetti replied. "If you get the school open, that's a big deal. And I will be there. Staying one step ahead of them. Keeping an eye out for you, Tess, and Dylan."

"Fuck 'im," I said.

"Dylan?" she asked, her chin shooting up as she checked the rearview.

"No, no, no, of course not," I replied, and I blew a kiss over my shoulder to the backseat. "I adore my sleepy puppy boy. I'm talking about *da man*. Fuck Uncle Sam."

"Well. Easier said than done. It will require a lot of legwork. Speaking of which, have you talked to Tess lately?"

"All the time," I said, though I thought it best not to mention what we'd talked about during our bike ride. "Tess has her own stuff going on and I don't wanna pressure her into helping with this whole school thing, you know?"

"I can understand that. My only concern is that she hasn't called or texted. She said she has some theories and I'd love to hear them, but she's been incommunicado."

"She'll come around. She's always there when I need her."

"I'm sure you're right. It takes time to warm up to new social arrangements," Rosetti responded and she left it at that.

We drove in silence for a while, and the lingering effects of the elixir made me consider all sorts of things to ask Rosetti. *Are you into black licorice? Have you ever been to the Grand Canyon? If the universe is infinite, then—*

"Do you think he's dangerous?" I suddenly blurted out.

"Who? Uncle Sam?"

"No, this guy," I said, motioning with my head to the snoozing fella in the back. "You don't want him to know what we're doing.

You think he'll mess it up? Is that what worries you?"

"He's a boy," she replied. "All boys are worrisome."

It reminded me of *All the Feels*. I had never considered the hero, the hunky and yet down-to-earth Xavier Rothman, to be worrisome. Sure, he was afraid of having too many emotions, but who isn't afraid of that? The *truly* worrisome ones, that's who.

"Do you think Dylan did it?" I asked Rosetti. "I mean, did he post that whole 'burn all you fuckers to the ground' on his brother's wall?"

"You haven't asked him?"

"He said it was to help Warren. That Warren wanted to come home."

Rosetti shrugged. "Motives are strange things. But they usually make sense when all the evidence presents itself."

What I may have lacked in evidence, I made up for in imagination. I closed my eyes. I pictured a twelve-year-old Dylan sitting all by himself on a floor scattered with Transformers. I pictured him cross-legged, a laptop resting on his knees as he logged in to Warren's Facebook account and scrolled through the photos, through countless images that didn't include Dylan. I pictured him typing and retyping the post before finally hitting send.

I'm gonna blow . . . No, no, no, not explosions.

I'm gonna set fire to the office of . . . No, no, no, too specific.

I'm gonna burn all you jerks . . . No, no, no, who burns jerks?

Fuckers! Fuckers will work. The world is full of fuckers!

I'm gonna burn all you fuckers to the ground!

Perfect. Done. Send.

Oh shit, what did I just do?

I opened my eyes, turned to Rosetti, and said, "I don't think it was Warren who wanted to come home. I think it was Dylan who was lonely and wanted his brother back."

Rosetti checked the rearview again and said, "He's not lonely anymore, is he?"

I nodded. "I hope not."

We sat in silence again, the glow of streetlights splashing across our faces as we passed them. Silence is something I avoid in normal circumstances and absolutely hate when I'm drunk. Which means I opened my stupid mouth again.

"So you never went to prom?" I asked.

"Nope."

"Better things to do?"

"I thought so. I was young. Sixteen. But already focused on college and career. I was recruited into a government youth program and thought that was a better use of my time."

"You were too cool for prom," I said as I gave her a playful punch on the arm. "I know that much."

She shrugged and said, "You probably would have thought I was the opposite of cool if you had gone to school with me."

"So you've changed a lot since then?"

"Not much at all actually," she said, and the car slowed to a stop. We were in my driveway. The clock on the dash told me it was two in the morning and the charge on the Tesla's battery had fifty miles to go. "Go to bed, Mara. I know where Dylan lives. I'll take it from here."

how we got it done

The morning after the party, a group gathered at the high school with assorted tools and cleaning supplies. This was the do-tank I was talking about. Boys and girls pushing mops and swinging hammers, bringing my thoughts to fruition. Malik's parents ran the local chapter of Habitat for Humanity, so they served as the experts and told us what we were capable of fixing. Dylan was a trouper, rolling up his sleeves and doing his part, sweating off what I assumed was his first hangover. Meanwhile, I walked around offering thumbs-up and pats on the back, which was equally essential work, don't you think?

The school wasn't in terrible shape, actually. The water had been shut off after the #ForBilly riot and once we swept up the glass and debris and jerry-rigged a bathroom into working order, it seemed nicer than the sad old Shop City Mall where the youngsters were matriculating. Granted, it was water stained and stinky as hell. Black mold was a certainty, but we only needed the place for about five months. If our bodies didn't self-destruct during those months, they certainly could endure a few spores.

Next on our agenda was winning over some teachers, which was essential if we were to have any chance of convincing the school board to approve our plan. We opted for email because we figured even if the teachers had left town, they'd be checking their old accounts. Elliot Pressman did his late girlfriend, Cranberry, proud by hacking into the city records and collecting the email addresses of anyone with a teaching license in the county. Then we sent out a short blast written by our political mastermind, Skye Sanchez.

> We, the seniors of Covington High School, have seen our classmates perish. We, the seniors of Covington High School, wake up every day wondering if it is our last. We, the seniors of Covington High School, have hurt no one, and yet, everyone has hurt us by denying us the simplest and most fundamental rights and freedoms. We, the seniors of Covington High School, deserve to learn. Teach us.

Four brave souls answered the call. And after Skye presented our proposal to the school board, which had shrunken to three nothing-to-lose members, we got our wish.

"There're still a few bucks in the budget and we appreciate your sticktoitiveness," loopy octogenarian and School Board President Louise Mender said. "Can't guarantee the state will recognize any of your grades or accomplishments, but you go on and enjoy the rest of your senior year. It's the least we can do."

It *was* the least they could do. There was enough money to pay those four teachers, as well as a lunch lady and a janitor willing to pitch in. There was one bathroom, two barely refurbished classrooms, a modified cafeteria. Not much, but it would have to suffice, and we tore our way through as much red tape as possible to get things ready for a speedy return.

Not that anyone noticed. As January rolled along, bigger things happened. A jumbo jet went down over Brazil. A tsunami killed thousands in the Philippines. The cast of a new comic-book movie was announced. In other words, as we geared up to go to school, the citizens of the world shifted their attentions. Like some foreign war that people get sick of hearing about because they don't understand the politics, our plight was deemed unwinnable and no one cared about some human interest story starring plucky kids asserting their right to an education. Save that shit for NPR. There was no recent carnage, so there was no reason for most journalists to stay. Sure, a few dedicated professionals remained embedded, but the others chased after stories with fresh entrails and clear endings. As long as we, the cursed ones, stayed put, the world seemed comfortable not thinking about us.

Classes for the underclassmen started at the Shop City Mall right after Martin Luther King Jr. Day, which seemed appropriate considering the man always valued education much more than capitalism. Then, on February 6, amid very little fanfare and nearly three months since we'd last been inside its not-so-hallowed halls, Covington High reopened to welcome back its senior class.

school redux

Of the approximately two hundred seniors trapped in town, forty showed up. Not bad, considering. Rather than split up, we gathered everyone together in what we decided to call Room the First. Jocular and muscular Latin teacher Mr. Spiros greeted us. I'd never taken his class (because, come on, dead language) but I knew his reputation. Outspoken, passionate, considered swoon-worthy by the ones who appreciated beefy braininess. Tess, for instance.

"I've been in it," he said with a fist raised. "Ears deep in it. Iraq, Afghanistan. The real deal, friends. Until now, I've stayed hush-hush about my experiences as a marine because there were certain *sensitivities*. Yes, a teacher without tenure is a cowardly creature. But tenure doesn't matter much anymore, does it? They can shove their sensitivities up their keisters as far as I'm concerned. Time to get real, right?"

A chorus of "oorah!" from a few lacrosse players in the crowd was enough to fuel him, and he started pacing around the room.

"Right on, right on," he said. "We're getting real. *Real* real. Now, let me tell you about some real things. Post-traumatic stress disorder, commonly known as PTSD, is most certainly real. I had it. Or should I say, I have it, because that SOB don't simply fly away like a sparrow on the breeze. The flashbacks, the panic attacks, the sleeplessness, the deep-deep-deep holes. I don't doubt that many of you know what I'm talking about. And I don't doubt that you're drinkin' or druggin' it away. Well, that will only take you so far. You need to talk about this stuff. You need to grab it by the cheeks and give it a good look, and I'm here to help you with that. Because I understand. Boy, do I."

"War is over for you, Spiros," Eric Chambers hollered. "We're still in the thick of it."

"True dat," Spiros said in the most earnest and adorably lame way. "But I know you can get through it and out the other side. Who here has read Michael Herr's *Dispatches*?"

No hands went up, but the never-ever-shy Greer Holloway asked, "Is that one of those dystopias?"

"If you're asking, 'Was the Vietnam War a dystopia?' then you better believe it was, sister," Spiros said. "I first read that book when I was twelve and my dad, who did three tours in 'Nam, dropped it in my lap and said, 'Now you don't have to bug me with questions.' There's a quote in those pages that I think is especially appropriate for your situation. Herr says, 'All the wrong people remember Vietnam. I think all the people who remember it should forget it, and all the people who forgot it should remember it.'"

"Hits home, homey," Greer said.

Spiros blasted Greer with finger guns and said, "That's what we're gonna work on. Honoring the ones we lost and making sure you aren't forgotten by the ones who haven't done right by you. And how are we gonna do that? By broadening our minds."

"Can we read that book?" Greer asked. "Sounds rad."

"It is most definitely rad, Miss Holloway," Spiros said. "And I think reading it is an excellent idea. It will be your first assignment for my class, which we will be calling Livin' 101."

He wrote it on the whiteboard, replacing the *g* with an apostrophe and everything.

Livin' 101 turned out to be a mishmash of history, philosophy, psychology, and good old-fashioned arguments. Had she lived to experience it, debate-team queen Gayle Heatherton would have adored it. It was, I imagine, what school used to be like way back in the day. A safe space to share ideas and challenge peers on common assumptions.

Since we had only four teachers, we decided to have four classes, running an hour and a half each, with a break for lunch. Our next class that day wasn't as intense, but it was equally, if not more, fun.

Essentials of Filmmaking was held in the other room, Room the Second. We'd never had a filmmaking class in school, which had always flummoxed Ms. Felson, an English teacher well liked during her time at Covington High, though her time here didn't last. She had been "let go" the previous year when someone found compromising pictures of her and those pictures made their way onto every kid's phone in about fifteen seconds. Never mind that the images were relatively tame—boobs, basically—and more than thirty years old. There was instant concern that she was some crafty cougar, a GILF ready to pounce on any unsuspecting, thin-mustachioed Romeo. She was quickly and thoroughly canned.

As for those pictures, they were screenshots from Ms. Felson's brief stint in Hollywood, most notably as a topless bit player in a series of early eighties "boobie movies" with such awesome titles as *G-String Commandos, Follow that Virgin!,* and *T&A A&M.* Good for her, I say, because she looked smoking hot—at least she did in the blurry stills I saw—and, it would seem, she learned a thing or two about framing, lighting, and editing while she was at it.

"You're all carrying movie cameras with you every moment of your lives," she told us. "That's a distinct privilege. Yet you're pointing the lenses at yourselves. Which can be fine. Which can be lovely. Some of the time. How about we use the rest of the time to turn them around? Create the narratives you all deserve, not the ones the world is foisting upon you."

Next up was Ashtanga yoga with former driver's ed instructor Mr. Harmsa. Why Ashtanga yoga? Because Mr. Harmsa always wanted to teach Ashtanga yoga, and this was the only place he could teach it without certification. While I grumbled at first that it was a waste of time, I will admit that I felt more relaxed and focused after twisting around on the cold floor of Room the First. Becky Groves told me that it was the only time since Katelyn's death she'd felt "at one with the world." A bit of a stretch for a bit of stretching, perhaps. But hey, if it calmed Becky's nerves, we could all be thankful. No one ever needed to hear that girl scream again.

After yoga, we were treated to a lunch prepared by Kiki Barnett, a Food Network–obsessed junior lunch lady who had aspirations beyond chicken cutlets and taco bars. She whipped up braised short ribs, a black bean and quinoa salad, and key lime pie. Fortified behind the sneeze guard, she passed us our trays and her sorrowful looks, the kind reserved for incontinent pit bulls at dog shelters. When Tess thanked her for the meal, Kiki said, "If a guy on death row gets to eat like royalty, then so should you."

Right on, Kiki. We'll all be sure to pass our parents your card in case they need someone to cater our wakes.

Finally, it was back to Room the Second, where a teacher who'd never actually taught in Covington greeted us. This was Mrs. Dodd, a kind-faced woman who'd arrived in town with the initial wave of Bible thumpers. She wasn't on the email blast, but once word of our plan reached her, she was determined to be involved. Her first order of business was to nail a carved slab of wood to the wall. The Ten Commandments. Next to it, on the whiteboard, she wrote, "The Old Testament."

"Separation of church and state, lady," Claire said. "Separation. Of church. And state."

"The state has abandoned you, dear," Dodd replied. "The Lord has not."

Then the willow-voiced firebrand treated us to an hour-and-a-half-long reading from Ecclesiastes.

"'Vanity of vanities, vanity of vanities. All is vanity!'" she began, which sounded like a condemnation of our selfie-happy generation. Ecclesiastes was also particularly self-serving for Mrs. Dodd, seeing that it's told from the perspective of a wise teacher. But wouldn't you know it? We dug it. Most of us, at least, because it ended up being about the importance of living in the moment and how we're all powerless to our fates. In other words, ancient and yet timely. More than relatable. We all went home humming the old folk tune that was inspired by those biblical verses.

> *To everything, turn, turn, turn. There is a season, turn, turn, turn...*

The season was winter. It was cold, cold, cold. But good God, was it something. Not all my classmates agreed, but I thought school was more interesting than it had ever been. In the morning, we had rousing bitch sessions and discussions about life, the universe, and everything led by Mr. Spiros. Then we'd share the highlights of our collected video footage, and Ms. Felson would load it into Final Cut Pro, where we could edit and add music and narration.

Within a week, I could do the variety of yoga poses that made sex with Dylan less taxing on the lungs. We were toning our bodies, expanding our minds, pushing our boundaries. Many of us had our first taste of offal, for instance, thanks to the killer mushroom-stuffed cow's heart Kiki served us for lunch on Valentine's Day. Which might've seemed wildly inappropriate if it didn't taste so damn good.

By the time daylight saving time kicked in and the first whiffs of spring were in the air, we'd heard a big chunk of the Bible and we knew more than most about begetting and bloodletting. Plenty of boring stuff in that book, but when you strip away the filler, there are some inspiring stories too. At the risk of sounding entirely full of myself, I was like Noah. I had called all the students to school and—like the ark—it was carrying us across the floodwaters to safety.

Because you guessed it, during those wonderful first six weeks, no one—not a single person—blew up.

evolution

Rosetti made good on her promise. Every day, she was there, patrolling the halls and parking lot, occasionally popping into classes. Which, I'll admit, was weird at first, but after a while it made me feel more secure. Like she was a big sister who was keeping an eye on me. And packing heat. We didn't discuss anything about government conspiracies in the building, but we did trade knowing glances whenever we passed each other, and I always texted her the latest gossip.

Kids were apprehensive at first, but I spread a rumor that Rosetti was once a consultant on the set of a *Fast & Furious* movie, and soon she was garnering tons of attention. Which she seemed to enjoy. I'd notice her smiling when she was bullshitting with students and her wardrobe gradually shifted from pantsuits to outfits that could have, in certain lights, been mistaken for youthful and fashionable.

Dylan obviously wasn't thrilled by Rosetti's constant presence, and I never told him about the burner and what it meant. In simple terms, it meant I had connections to a world he wasn't a part of. And that was okay. That was a good thing, actually.

"I don't understand what you see in her," he said to me one morning as Rosetti's Tesla glided through the late March rain and into the parking lot.

"I see a badass chick who cares about the future," I responded.

"This is a job to her," Dylan said. "That's all. Like it was a job when she nearly ruined my family. She doesn't care about people. She's an opportunist."

"What's wrong with doing your job?" I asked. "What's wrong with being an opportunist? If I wasn't an opportunist then this whole school thing wouldn't be happening, would it?"

Dylan conceded with a wink. "The difference is I love you."

I kissed him on the cheek. "I'm sorry she brings back bad memories, but she's keeping us safe now, making sure we only get good memories."

"Well, these memories, this *school thing*, it's great and all . . ." Dylan's voice trailed off.

"But?"

"But wouldn't it be nice to get away from her and everyone else?" Dylan said. "To have the option, at least. I heard the Shop City kids are having spring break. Jetting off to the Bahamas or whatever. That sounds nice, doesn't it?"

"It does. But I never pictured you as a beach bum."

"I'm not. It's what it represents. The freedom to come and go."

I knew exactly what he meant. My first taste of freedom had

been at the beach, sharing adventures with Tess.

"We may not be able to get away from everyone," I told him. "But we still can have a spring break. All we have to do is bring the beach here."

"Ha-ha. Hilarious. So I was fantasizing. No need to make fun of it."

"I'm serious. Opportunism, my boy. There's sand to be had somewhere, right? I mean, people have sandboxes. And we've got an entire pool that isn't being used."

It was another fine thought from the old Mara Carlyle think tank, and wouldn't you know it, there was some extra-fine follow-up from the brand-new Covington High do-tank. Our always-scheming classmate Dougie O'Shea took the lead, and a few days after I proposed the idea, his father and a few marble-mouthed construction compatriots backed a convoy of sand-filled trucks up to the entrance near the pool. Spring break arrived right on schedule.

"Where'd they get it?" Dylan asked, watching in awe as the men attached hoses that would blow the sand halfway up the bleachers and all over the deck.

"Down the shore," Dougie said. "Sea Girt has plenty to share."

Maybe, though I doubted *share* was the right word.

"Exactly how much sand is that?" Dylan asked.

"I believe that is a shit-ton," I said.

"A *metric* shit-ton," Dougie corrected us. "We're Irish, son. Respect!"

Respect was given. After all, by the end of the day, the O'Shea crew had created an indoor beach that surrounded the pool and spilled into the adjacent gym. Bonus: We didn't have to worry about permanent damage.

"They're gonna demo this place once we graduate," Dougie explained. "Dad wrapped that contract up quick as shit. The town isn't ever gonna be down with this school again. Might as well fill the bitch with dirt, amirite?"

As dirty as *the bitch* was, some kids were definitely still down with it. When word got out that school was a whole lot better than sitting home and moping, more seniors began showing up. And when the final holdouts discovered that we were spending spring break lounging and swimming in addition to broadening our minds, they poured in as well.

How did they find out about the glories of our education experiment, you wonder? The handful of reporters and documentary filmmakers who remained in town still stopped by on occasion, but we were the ones who spread the word through our videos.

It's amazing what a little crowdsourcing and free time can do. Every week, the seniors cobbled together a thirty-minute video of interviews and candid footage of our days, which we then posted to YouTube. And people watched. Boy, did they watch. Basically overnight, we had an audience that was hundreds of times as big as Billy Harmon's. Millions and millions of views.

They came for obvious reasons—gore and explanations. When they didn't get those things, they stayed for the characters. Because, come on, we were interesting kids. Our videos premiered on Monday mornings and became water-cooler fodder, more talked about than any movie or TV show. We expressed our fears, our dreams.

We detailed our little annoyances and cosmic questions. There was joy too—laughing and hanging out at the beach and whatnot. But most of all, we were honest. Sometimes honesty is enough.

One of the viewers' favorite pastimes was *shipping* my various classmates. That is, making up imaginary love connections, or relation*ships*.

> I ship Malik and Greer.

> I realize Clint's not gay but I totally ship Kylton and Clint.

> I ship Dylan and Jane so friggin much. Awww!

Yes, "awww!" Because, yes, "Jane!" She showed up right after spring break, when there was a sudden influx of cash. The subscribers who saw the sad state of our school started donating money to help make the facilities cleaner and safer.

Jane would have been content earning her GED, but her dad pressured her into returning to school for the sake of "establishing valuable credentials and contacts by letting people see you for the wonderful student and mother you are."

At least that's what she said on the first video she appeared in, which is where I primarily saw her. I avoided Jane as much as I could. Which wasn't too hard. We still had only four teachers, but our numbers had swelled to 160 students by the beginning of April, so we split into four groups of 40. Each teacher taught each group one of the four periods. Luckily, Tess and Dylan were still in my group, the original forty "Pioneers," as we liked to call ourselves. We'd see the other students at lunch, or after school, when representatives from each group would get together to cull and edit video footage.

Like everyone else, I had only a partial say in how I was depicted in the videos. The mantra was, "If it's interesting, it goes in." Which meant my lunchtime PDA with Dylan was left on the cutting room floor, but Jane quickly became a star.

Hardly surprising. A mother of three, trying to make good— that's damn compelling. Not to mention she was a fountain of weepy sound bites like, "Three smiling faces are all that matter to me" and "When it gets to the point that I am nothing but a memory to my boys, I want them to remember that I tried."

To make sure that Dylan wasn't seen as some deadbeat dad, I let it slip that his brother was the father of Jane's triplets, one of my few comments to make a video's final cut. Nevertheless, the public preferred a Dylan-and-Jane pairing to a Dylan-and-me pairing, which was more than a little disheartening.

I set up a Google Alert for my name, which I know is basically the corner where masochism meets narcissism, but I couldn't help it. It should come as no surprise that it was upsetting to check my email every morning and see what the world was saying about Mara Carlyle. However, it wasn't that people were calling me an evil harpy or anything. It was that they were hardly talking about me at all.

Jane, on the other hand, had countless Tumblrs and Pinterest boards dedicated to her quotes and "Rolling in the Deep" became something more than just the title of an Adele song. Since Jane's last name was Rolling and she was perceived as being "deep," this tired pun—shortened into the hashtag #RITD—became a way to share the wisdom of the world's favorite teen mom.

Even Tess wasn't immune. On Picture Day, she wore a T-shirt with a quote from Jane on it:

GO PET A DOG ALREADY. #RITD.

I know. I didn't understand it either.

picture day

Remember those yearbooks I had hoped for? Oh, we were getting them all right. A newly formed committee was soliciting candids so that they could create something bound and printed to celebrate our resurrected senior year. Still, we all knew it wouldn't feel like an *official* yearbook without formal shots against the standard blue backgrounds. So we had Picture Day, a Tuesday in early April set aside for senior portraits. It was normally something kids did on their own time and dime, but the only photographers who interacted with us were journalists who had little interest in snapping the same boring shot over and over again. So we set up a makeshift studio in an art room and everyone shuffled in to model for Kylton Connors. Rather than submitting senior quotes, members of the yearbook committee decided to wear T-shirts with witty sayings on them. There were a few WRAP IT UP, SHORT STUFFs in honor of Brian, but most of the witticisms had come out of the mouth of Jane Rolling.

Tess's GO PET A DOG ALREADY #RITD, for instance.

"What does that even mean?" I asked her when she walked out of the art room after her photo shoot.

"It means people should do something kind that makes them feel good and makes someone else feel good," Tess said. "It means take a breath, calm down, connect with yourself and others."

"Jane Rolling, the Rumi of our generation."

"I think she's quite witty and charming. A real inspiration."

"If you say so. But then again you're not the best judge of character. You think Mr. Spiros is hot."

"I think he's *fascinating*. It's different."

"You adore that tuft of hair that peeks out from his polo."

"He's a man," Tess said, blushing. "Men have chest hair."

"And back hair," I said, scrunching up my face in disgust. "Admit it, you want to have his babies. You want to be his little Jane Rolling."

"I don't."

"You want his quadruplets. You want four of his little gyros popping out of your hoodilly. Opa! Opa! Opa! Opa!"

"Did you just call my theoretical babies gyros?"

"I did."

"Did you just call my hoodilly a hoodilly?"

"I did."

"Get help, dear."

It was conversations like this that I missed the most. They used to be all day, every day with Tess. But by this point, I was lucky to have them once a week. Tess was consumed. "By school," I told Dylan and Rosetti, but the truth was, she wasn't there too much.

She showed up for yearbook committee meetings, but it seemed the only reasons she ever attended classes were to occasionally gawk at Mr. Spiros and to humor me. She didn't even visit the beach, which seemed like sacrilege for a girl who understood the spiritual value of sand between the toes.

"I think she's almost got the case cracked," I said to Tess as we rounded the corner and headed toward the cafeteria.

"Excuse me?" she replied.

"*Lady Nightshade*," I whispered, and I checked my flanks for witnesses. "*She's here all the time now and I've been providing her with tons of intel.*"

Tess stopped, grabbed my shoulders, and did her own check for spies. "She's here all the time because she likes it. You vouch for her, so people think she's cool. Then she gobbles up the gossip you send. If her phone is on vibrate, then she's probably in a constant state of orgasm because of all your texts."

"I *provide* her with *intel*," I said, pulling away and starting to walk.

"For instance?"

"Um, this morning I told her that Ijichi Benjiro thinks American iodine deficiencies are to blame for everything. Also that Cole Hooper is building a suit of armor out of duct tape. You know, to make sure his body stays together?"

"Really? Really?"

"Okay, it's not primo stuff, but she's a pro. Things that seem inconsequential to us might be a big deal to her. Besides, you told me to keep the burner, so you must believe it's useful."

Tess tapped my noggin with a finger. "Remember, I told you it's useful because at some point we might have to use it to contact *each other*. Not Rosetti. That woman has nothing to do with it. You're the only person I trust, Mara, and if my theories—"

"Your theories?" I barked at her. "You shit on everyone else's ideas but you aren't exactly sharing yours."

Tess took a breath and said, "I'm not sharing because I don't have it entirely figured out. And what I have figured out is . . . difficult."

"Difficult like I won't get it?" I said with a huff.

"Of course not," she said with genuine concern in her voice. "You're brilliant, honey. I mean difficult in that it will be hard to accept."

"As if anything these days has been easy to accept. Try me."

We'd reached the cafeteria, where Kiki had promised a "farm-to-table luncheon in celebration of the spring harvest." From a distance, it didn't look like much more than a big old pile of kale but, nevertheless, the line to get a plateful was wrapped around the room.

"Have you heard of the infinite monkey theorem?" Tess asked me as we took our place behind Jared Jarowski, who was as oblivious to us as he was to personal hygiene.

"Is that the one about how a monkey in a tuxedo will always be funny?" I asked.

"Don't be dumb," Tess replied. "You know what I mean. Put infinite monkeys at infinite typewriters and one will eventually come up with Shakespeare."

"Oh, you need *infinite* monkeys and typewriters," I said, slapping my forehead. "That's why my novel never came together! Back to the laboratory."

"Hilarious," Tess said with a groan. "I'm being serious. Think about the whole infinite monkey theorem and the whole Murphy's Law concept of anything that can go wrong *will* go wrong, and you might start to believe that we live in the one particular universe among infinite universes where the monkeys and Murphy's Law have conspired to make a bunch of us blow up."

"Okay. I get about nine percent of what you're saying."

"What I'm saying is that it's a load of crap. Randomness is a lazy explanation. Universes aren't random. They have laws. Carla is right to think there's something inside of us, but how it got there is not important, because maybe it's always been in there. Maybe our problem is that a genetic switch has been flipped. It's more complicated than an on/off button, obviously, but the important thing to focus on is how to switch it off. Before we go off. Because, seriously, I doubt some general in a war room is determining our fate."

"So what's happening to us then?"

"The Dalton twins blew up within minutes of each other. Well, they were born within minutes of each other, right?"

"So it's associated with our birthdays? Because Dylan turns eighteen in like fifteen days and—"

"Yes, but it's not like we're all on the same clock. It's like milk going sour or bread going moldy. Buy a bunch of loaves of bread and cartons of milk and leave them in the refrigerator or on the counter or out in the sun and they'll all go bad on different timelines. Like us. Since we've had different experiences, diets, and so on, our bodies have aged differently. The Daltons were born the same time and had as similar an upbringing as two people could possibly have. Therefore, they exploded at essentially the same moment. As for the rest of us, like milk or bread, it's only a matter of time, but it's different times."

"It hasn't happened for months. Don't you think it's possible they did something back in the tents to fix us."

"If they fixed us, they'd let us know. Trust me. It's possible that they accidentally did something to slow things down, but I guarantee this thing isn't over."

"And there's no way to check our sell-by date? Assuming Doc Ramirez and that gang were on the up-and-up, why didn't they see this in our platelets and whatnot?"

"Because they didn't know what to look for. And that's what I've been working on. Finding a specialist, possibly a geneticist, who does know what to look for."

"Any leads?"

"Actually, I heard someone else might have already beaten me to the punch."

"Who?"

Tess pointed across the cafeteria to a circle of kids who had their phones poised on, you guessed it, Jane Rolling.

"Christ," I said. "What'd she do now?"

"It's not what she did," Tess said as she pulled up a Wikipedia entry on her phone. "It's who she brought."

Tess raised the screen. There was a portrait of a woman with a deeply tan and round face, sparkling eyes, and a popped collar. Below the image was one word:

Krook.

a stranger comes to town

Dr. Rolanda Krook arrived on Wednesday morning adorned in khaki and sporting mirrored aviators. I first noticed her standing at the door to Room the First, her face framed in the little window. When Mr. Spiros spotted her, he opened the door and asked, "May I help you?"

"Don't let me be a bother. Go on with your class, go on," Krook said in a soft but indeterminate accent, the type that revealed she either came from money or wanted us to think she did.

"And who might you be?" Spiros asked.

Jane Rolling stepped out from behind Krook, slipped into the room, and announced, "This is Dr. Krook of the Farthing Institute. She flew in on a red-eye this morning and she wanted to come immediately and observe our class."

"Well, that is some dedication," Spiros said. "Welcome, Doctor. Have a seat in the back if you like. We were just discussing Cartesian philosophy and the ontological argument. Are you a fan of Descartes, Dr. Krook?"

"I am a fan of all who question the nature of the world," Krook said as she floated between the rows of desks. She was not a small woman, but she moved like a dancer. She slid into one of the few available chairs and sat in the corner with her legs crossed. Jane sat next to her, sporting a grin boisterous enough to be kicked out of church.

"Okay then," Spiros said. "Where were we? Oh yes, perfect islands. What constitutes perfection in an island? If God is omnipotent, as Descartes says, then he could create a perfect island, right? But an island has certain restrictions, does it not? It needs to have a body of water around it. Would a perfect island be infinitely large? If so, then how could it have water around it?"

"You could say that about anything," Claire remarked. "Everything has restrictions."

"Exactly," Spiros said. "Descartes believed that if you can imagine a perfect God, then that God had to exist, because existence is part of perfection. But you are courting contradictions when you argue perfection."

"There's no arguing with this perfection," Clint Jessup said, flexing his muscles and pointing at himself with his thumbs. It elicited a respectable number of laughs.

"True enough, Clint," Spiros said. "You are the one thing philosophers can all agree on."

"I happen to know that Dr. Krook has some theories on perfection," Jane added.

Spiros's eyes widened. "I'm intrigued. Enlighten us, Dr. Krook."

Krook chuckled—a real belly rumbler—and uncrossed and recrossed her legs. "Miss Rolling has undoubtedly read some of my work on cellular perfection."

"So you're a biologist?" Spiros asked.

"I have a PhD in molecular biology, as well as an MD with a residency in oncology and hematology," Krook said. "But that's neither here nor there. It has been my studies with the Wooli tribe of Papua New Guinea that has been most vital to my work."

"Even more intrigued," Spiros said. "Go on. Who are the Wooli?"

"The Wooli are the world's last group of endocannibals," Krook said with a smug smile. "Meaning that when someone in their tribe dies, they consume the ashes. In a beverage, usually. Sometimes in a stew. They call this 'drinking the dead.' What few people know, however, is that this practice has its origins in the phenomenon of spontaneous combustion."

Spiros folded his arms, thumbed his chin, and said, "News to me. And I've actually read a bit on New Guinea."

"Then you know that the diversity of languages and tribes there is astounding," Krook said. "And the Wooli is probably one of the least known, but most fascinating, among those tribes. Spontaneous combustion is actually common in their villages. Their bodies burn rather than explode, but I suspect what happens to them is not that dissimilar to what is happening here."

"And yet have any of us heard of this?" Spiros said to the class.

Jane's hand shot up. Tess started to raise her hand, but reconsidered.

"Okay, one remarkably studious young woman has heard of it,"

Spiros said with a nod to Jane that surely made Tess a little jealous. "And yet you'd think this would be international news. You've seen the circus we've had to endure."

"I hardly think the same reporters would be willing to take the treacherous ten-day journey into the jungle to find the Wooli," Krook said. "And when they got there, they'd hardly be welcomed as guests."

"But you have made this journey?" Spiros asked.

"Many times. I have been there for the last six months. I only learned about your town's predicament when I made a provisions trip to Port Moresby and saw a video clip some local children were sharing. It featured young Jane here. She's quite popular in the capital."

Jane was absolutely beaming. I know "Big in Japan" is a thing, but I guess so too is "Big in Papua New Guinea." I turned to Dylan to see his reaction and he was as enthralled as the rest of the room, clinging to every word.

"Surely you brought a camera with you to document this *phenomenon*?" Spiros asked Krook.

Krook shook her head. "We are all aware that camera footage can be manipulated and the Wooli would never agree to being filmed in the first place. That is all besides the point."

"What's the point then?" Spiros asked.

"The point is that I have seen this happen," Krook said, and she finally removed her shades to reveal a pair of brilliant green eyes that popped from her olive skin. "It seems inexplicable, but there is an explanation. This is evolution in progress. In a quest for cellular perfection, the cells are self-destructing."

"Cellular perfection?" Spiros said with a cocked eyebrow. "Can't say I've ever heard of that, either."

"Ah, but, Mr. Spiros," Krook said with a finger wag. "I have no doubt you have also never heard of my mother, and yet she exists. I am proof of that. As educated as you are, sir, I'm sure you will admit there are some things that are out of your purview."

"Guilty as charged," Spiros said with a sly smile. "I have yet to uncover the secrets of a woman's heart."

I turned to Tess, who was shifting in her seat and trying to hide her face behind her bangs. I mouthed, *Bullshit?* She shrugged, and then slowly raised her hand. Man oh man, I was hoping she'd blow the lid off this sucker.

But Jane stole the spotlight again, blurting out, "Tell him about the snooze button, Dr. Krook."

"Ah," Krook said. "Thank you, Miss Rolling, for reminding me of my reason for being here. Assuming they don't die from other causes first, spontaneous combustion is an inevitability in the Wooli tribe. But it can be delayed. I have created a treatment that my husband has given the delightful moniker 'snooze button.'"

You couldn't hear much over the din of questions that were suddenly shouted. Though I'm pretty sure I could hear Tess sigh as she lowered her hand. Well played, Krook's husband. Well played.

After all, what teenager doesn't love a snooze button?

the benefits of
cyberstalking, part 2

That evening, Tess, Dylan, and I gathered on my back deck, fired up the laptop, and easily located some scholarly articles Krook had written. There were lots of charts and diagrams and it looked sciency enough, but even Tess couldn't understand half the vocabulary. A much better introduction to the good doctor appeared at a seemingly legit site called FieldWorkHeroes.com, which had photo-heavy profiles of globetrotting scientists and was endorsed by none other than Neil deGrasse Tyson, who compared it to "*Vanity Fair*, but with hadron colliders."

Krook's profile included a few shots of the scientist with her children (of which she had eight—four biologically and four by adoption), but most of the images came from her expeditions into the jungle. They showed her on a raft, at the edge of a cliff, pointing to a snake—always in khaki. There wasn't, of course, any evidence of the Wooli other than some artist's interpretation: a charcoal sketch of a tribesman in flames.

"'All humans are wired to spontaneously combust,'" Tess read aloud, which was a direct quotation from Krook. "'It's part of their cells' natural evolution into cellular perfection.'"

"Cellular perfection?" I said. "Is that sort of like the genetic switch you were talking about? Did you hear about this before Krook showed up?"

"Inklings, but I was skeptical," she admitted. "From what I can gather, cellular perfection has to do with cells freeing themselves from the organisms they are bound to, then quickly returning to a subatomic state similar to what was found shortly after the Big Bang. Purely theoretical and usually not observable in humans, because the process is supposed to take thousands of years."

"What does that have to do with some tribe in the middle of some jungle?" I asked.

"Well," Tess said. "According to Krook, the difference with the Wooli is that many generations ago some environmental factor mutated their genes and sped this process up. So they were reaching cellular perfection and spontaneously combusting after twenty to thirty years of life. The whole cannibalism thing was their solution to delay the process. Krook says the Wooli discovered that consuming the ashes of the dead put the spontaneous combustion off for a few decades."

"O. M. Gag me," I said. "This lady better not be suggesting that we lick up the remains of our classmates to live a long and fruitful life."

Dylan, who had been digesting all the talk, snagged the laptop from the table. "Let's not forget about the snooze button," he said as he clicked the image of an alarm clock featured on a banner ad at the top of the page. It launched a pop-up with a screen-busting pic of a green pill bottle. Below it, the text read:

> Dr. Krook and her husband, chemist G. W. Barlow, developed SnoozeButton™ by naturally re-creating the genetic sequences found in the ashes of deceased members of the Wooli tribe. For the Wooli tribe, it means an extended life expectancy without having to resort to the unpleasantness of endocannibalism. For the rest of the world, it may be the antiaging therapy we've sought for millennia.

I didn't need to see anymore. "So Krook is a crook, right?" I asked as I leaned back in my chair.

"There's some solid science here, and it's not far off from some other theories, but there are holes," Tess replied. "Many, many holes. And the timing of her arrival does raise some concerns."

"Some?" I said. "One. She's here to sell pills. That's it and that's all. That article is clearly sponsored content. Because, really, the Wooli tribe? Why didn't she go entirely racist and xenophobic and call them the Unga Bungas or something?"

"Jane believes her," Dylan said. "And Jane isn't stupid."

"Krook has a litter of kids and terrible fashion sense," I said. "Jane sees her as a mentor."

Dylan rolled his eyes, which, I'll admit, my comment deserved. "She's the mother of my nephews and a good person," he said.

"Maybe taking it will at least provide her with some hope."

"Wait," Tess said. "What's happening?"

"Well, maybe you two aren't quite Rosetti-level detectives," he said as his fingers raced over the keyboard, "but I figured you at least checked social media."

He turned the laptop and showed us a picture of Krook, Jane, and the triplets, who were holding a cardboard sign that read:

SHARE THIS IF YOU WANT OUR MOMMY

TO BE THE FIRST ONE TO TAKE SNOOZEBUTTON™.

It was posted that afternoon and had already been shared 258,349 times.

infotainment

Thankfully, Spiros wasn't buying into Dr. Krook either. While our peers and their parents were saying things like "How will it hurt?" he was replying, "How will it help? Putting poison in their bodies?" and they were countering, "At worst, it's probably a sugar pill and what about the placebo effect?" and he was shooting back, "False hope is the provenance of politicians and every variety of con man and I won't have my students led astray by some charlatan."

In short: Krook was not welcome in Livin' 101 anymore.

However, our Ashtanga yoga teacher, Mr. Harmsa, was more than willing to humor the woman. And he did. The very next night.

"The secrets to health are not found in your corporate laboratories but in the oral histories and nearly forgotten medicinal practices of the world's indigenous peoples," he told us as he introduced Dr. Krook on the stage of our recently refurbished auditorium (now known as the Tinder Theater, thanks to a generous cash infusion from everybody's favorite hookup site).

Yes, Dr. Krook was there to administer the first dose of Snooze-Button™, and she was decked out in her formal khaki, all pleats and button-down. Of course, the democratically elected first recipient of the pill was there too. Jane Rolling was sitting in a plush, white armchair and weeping from happiness. The entire senior class, as well as many parents, filled the auditorium seats, eager to watch and record the historic moment.

After Harmsa bowed to Krook approximately 168 times, he shuffled backward offstage, leaving Krook to run the show. Because that's what it was, a show, an even better show than my reincarnation celebration at Laura Riggs's house. It was a medicine show, as they say, with a hulking yet elegant woman pacing back and forth and holding a bottle of her wares aloft.

"I do not promise a cure," Krook said. "Anyone promising a cure is a liar. What I am promising is a treatment. I am promising that three little boys will have a bit more time with their mother. Thanks to SnoozeButton™."

Under the harsh stage lights, the tears on Jane's face looked like pearls and even my dark heart ached for the girl. Boy oh boy, did she want this more than any of us.

"You are not interested in my promises, though," Krook continued. "My words are empty vessels unless they are filled with results. So I will be brief. I want it on record that Ms. Rolling has chosen this therapy under her own volition and I will be administering it free of charge. Is that so, Ms. Rolling?"

"It is so," Jane squeaked, her eyes squinting and tearing. Pearls, all over her ruddy face.

"Excellent," Krook said. "I will apologize to those who came here expecting a big production. There isn't much pomp and circumstance to swallowing a pill. But make no mistake, this may be the most significant moment in this young woman's life."

"Besides the birth of my boys," Jane remarked.

"Of course," Krook said. "Who could forget your prides and joys?"

Then Krook winked to the front row, where those sweet little guys were sitting. Goddamn their tiny blue suits. Like cutting onions.

Jane blew a kiss to them and they each started clapping. Which was adorable, obviously. Then Krook nodded offstage and Harmsa returned with a glass of water. As he handed Krook the glass, Harmsa announced, "I will be meditating during the treatment and everyone is welcome to join me."

He sat cross-legged on the stage, made a temple of his hands, and closed his eyes. "*Ommmm*," he chanted, and his chant was echoed by Becky Groves, and then by small pockets throughout the auditorium.

Krook nodded respectfully and did not interrupt the chant with her voice. Instead, she handed Jane the glass, then took a pill from the green bottle and held it up to show the crowd. It wasn't much bigger than a vitamin, but from my seat in the fifth row, I could still see its lime sheen.

"*Ommmm*," went Harmsa and the ever-growing chorus of yoga enthusiasts. Rosetti, who was standing by the emergency exit with her arms crossed, was clearly not among them. I hadn't spoken to her since Krook's arrival, but I had texted her the night before.

Me: So what do you think of Krook?

Her: False flag, phase four. Be ready.

I didn't know what that meant. All I knew was Rosetti meant business. She was watching the stage with the intensity of a predator. I want to say she was like a jackal, but I'm not sure what a jackal is. If it's a stone-cold killer with eyes of fury and a hand close to its holster, then she was a jackal all right. Either that or a wolf with a concealed carry permit.

Up onstage, Jane's hand shook and water spilled from the glass and onto her lap as she moved it to her lips. As nervous as she was, she still managed to fill her cheeks with water and hand the glass back to Krook.

"*Ommmm.*"

Krook passed her the pill and rather than examine it, Jane jammed it in her mouth, like a kid enduring the last vegetable on the plate in order to get an ice-cream reward.

"*Ommmm.*"

Then Jane swallowed. And squinted up at the lights above her. Then gazed down to the crowd. She smiled and mouthed, *I love you*, to her three little boys.

There was an explosion of clapping and cheers. Jane stood, thrust her hands in the air. Krook grabbed one of the wrists and held it like Jane was a prizefighter. Together, they walked offstage.

Namaste, motherfuckers.

the next morning

School on Friday was full of an apprehensive excitement. At the end of the previous night's presentation, Krook had come back onstage and announced that she'd be providing Snooze-Button™ free of charge for a thirty-day trial to any student who wanted it. The Daltons would have been proud of this typical drug-dealer move. Get 'em hooked and then gouge the price. Make boom-boom-bonkers bucks.

Clearly, she was playing the odds. The last spontaneous combustion was Gayle Heatherton, all the way back in November. Nearly five months had passed, our longest stint without an incident. It was possible that the threat was over, even though there was no obvious reason. Krook was trying to fill the reason void. Because if this never happened again, she would receive credit and not only would she have two hundred customers who'd be paying her for the rest of their lives, she'd also have the world's attention. FDA approval would quickly follow. She'd be hailed as the next Jonas Salk.

Or that's what I assumed she was thinking. The satisfied smile she wore that morning when she arrived at school with Jane spoke volumes. The two walked the hall together like they were the friggin' homecoming court. And yes, there was applause. For what? Because Jane had taken a pill and survived one more day on earth, I guess.

Now, I wasn't a total monster. I could sympathize with the girl's predicament. I certainly hoped that I was wrong, that Krook was not a crook and that the pill was our salvation, but we'd been down so many dead-end roads already. I was tired of it and I couldn't believe I was the only one.

Dylan and I were on our way to Livin' 101 during Jane and Krook's triumphant procession. Seeing Jane so happy made him so happy and I loved his capacity to love, but I wasn't thrilled about his capacity to be public about it. Still, he tolerated my admiration of Rosetti, so it was only fair that I extend an olive branch to Jane.

"Go congratulate her," I said. "Or whatever."

"I should," he replied, and he ducked under a few arms that were distributing high fives and he approached Jane. He gave her a big hug and she whispered something to him. Krook could obviously hear what she said, because it made that shit-eating grin even wider. Dylan whispered something back. And then she was gone.

Pop. Blood. Gone.

No more Jane.

Only one person made a sound: Krook. It was one of those primal, horror-movie shrieks. She jumped backward, slammed into the lockers, and flailed like she was walking through spiderwebs. The rest of us stood there, stunned, but not exactly surprised.

Dylan's arms were still curled in embrace but he was embracing nothing but air and the blood that dripped from his clothes.

As Krook's racket faded to a whimper and she cowered on the floor, Becky Groves, our former scream queen turned yoga junkie, stepped from the crowd with arms outstretched, offering a hug of comfort. But instead of giving it to Krook, she gave it to Dylan.

"There, there, kiddo," she said. "We all—"

Then Becky was gone too, splattering all over Dylan and commingling with the remnants of Jane.

That was more than enough for Krook. That was plenty. She leapt to her feet and tried to haul ass out of there, but she slipped on the blood, hit her head on the floor, and knocked herself unconscious. Or she pretended to be unconscious. She lay motionless on the ground, in any case.

"What the hell is wrong with you!" Claire screamed at Dylan. "You did this! You brought this back!"

Dylan didn't respond. He hardly moved at all. His face was bathed in blood and regret. These were the only explosions he'd actually witnessed, and I instantly thought back to the original texts that had brought us together.

Invigorating. Invigorating. Invigorating.

Was this invigorating for him? Not by a long shot.

"*Let's get out of here, sweetie,*" I said softly. "*There's nothing—*"

"Take him down," Clint called out.

"No," Steve Cox replied. "Don't touch him. It's touching him that did it."

I spun and stuck out a finger at Steve and said, "If touching him did it then I would have been dead a long—"

Then Steve was gone too, his splatter shooting down the hallway like a burst of confetti from a party popper. Now there were screams. Now there were swears. Now there was slipping, grasping at the lockers and walls for support, like novice ice skaters at a rink. Now hell was upon us.

Krook's body shot up like a reanimated corpse and she bulldozed down the hall through the pack of students. I desperately needed someone to blame, so I abandoned Dylan and started my chase. I slid across the slick terrazzo floors like a socked kid on hardwood. When I reached a dry patch, I broke into a sprint.

Boom! More screams.

It was another one, behind me, so I didn't see it. I'd find out later it was Taylor Ventner, a guy with a Broadway-quality voice and kennel-quality BO. RIP and so sorry, Taylor. I wish I knew you better. I wish that day didn't go down the way it did. But it did, and I was too furious to think of anything but my fury.

I kept moving, focusing on the blur of khaki. Yoga had made me nimble, so I caught up quickly.

"You're the one who brought it back!" I screamed as I plowed into Krook, slamming her into the lockers.

"What in the—who in the—how in the—?" Krook said, her face spasming in confusion.

"She had kids," I shouted, my nose pressed to hers. "She *was* a kid!"

Krook tried to push me away, so I grabbed her shoulders to hold myself in place, but then suddenly someone was tearing us apart.

It was Rosetti, fresh from the bathroom, her hands wet and her shirt half tucked in. "What the hell is going on?" she asked.

"*Who the hell is going off* is more like it," I said. "Jane, Becky, Steve. God knows who else."

Around the corner came a mob of blood-drenched kids. They streamed past us like they were at a Black Friday sale. Mad eyed, taking no prisoners. Rosetti tried to shield us from the stampede, wrapping her arms around us and pressing us against the lockers until they passed, but Krook slipped away from her and into the crowd. When the pack was gone, so was the doctor.

"Are you okay?" Rosetti asked.

"We have to go," I said, breaking free. "We have to arrest her. We can't—"

"To my vehicle, now!" Rosetti commanded as she grabbed my wrist.

No amount of yoga could have helped me out of her iron grip and she started dragging me like a delinquent to juvie. Before I knew it, we were in the parking lot and at her Tesla. She pushed me into the backseat and climbed up front. The motor automatically hummed as soon as she sat down. She turned on the radio to drown out exterior noise. The music was thick with jangly guitars.

Leaning back over the center console, she whispered to me, "*Gordon Laramie basically predicted this in his manifesto. This is the next stage in the false flag operation. Don't be surprised if the executive orders that follow make a mockery of the Constitution. We were at a precipice here. Krook pushed us off. Don't touch her. Don't even talk to her. You do not want the attention of her superiors.*"

"Wait," I said. "You think she's . . . ? What exactly do you think is happening here?"

Rosetti shook her head, as if pitying me. "This woman's work with the Wooli? You really think it was observation? No. It was experimentation. Of course SnoozeButton doesn't work. It's a smokescreen. Build up hope in private enterprise, then strip it away. So that trust turns back to the government."

"That's not what it seems like to me at all. To me, it—"

Rosetti put up a finger. "Phase One of the false flag was most likely instituted decades back, during World War II, deep in the jungles where the human experimentation wouldn't be noticed. Phase Two was set into motion four years ago in Washington, DC, when they secretly implanted their detonators in our country's most prized and privileged resources: upper-middle-class, north-eastern, liberal-leaning, suburban adolescents. Phase Three occurred in the tents when they added tracking devices to make sure none of you could escape and seek out the truth. Now we're in the thick of Phase Four, where all hope is lost and all rights are surrendered to the government. Before you know it, we'll be in Phase Five, and everyone you know will be implanted with detonators and trackers and there will be two countries: one with the people who can afford to stay whole and one that is a wasteland of death. If you don't believe in the power of the Illuminati, then—"

"Slow down!" I yelped. "I can't follow any of this."

Rosetti gulped, as if swallowing her vomit of words. Her eyes settled and she whispered, *"First thing that will happen is they'll close it down. And then where will we go? Then what will we do?"*

"Close what down?"

Rosetti reached into the back and opened my door. "You should go. So should I. It was a failure. They're coming. They're coming."

I still wasn't sure what she was talking about, but I knew it made me uncomfortable. And I agreed with her on one thing: I didn't want to be in that car. I slipped out without uttering a word and took a few paces across the lot. The car moved slowly past me as Rosetti mouthed a wide-mouthed *go!* And then she was gone, sliding silently away without giving me a chance to ask her anything else.

Since students weren't allowed to drive, the only vehicles left belonged to Krook and the four teachers, but the lot was now full of kids who'd fled the building. It was like that first time with Katelyn, only this time was much, much bloodier.

Dylan was part of the crowd, stumbling toward me in a daze. He was like an oasis in this endless expanse of horror. I ran to intercept him, and when I hugged him, he basically fell into my arms.

"*I love you,*" he whispered.

"I'm so glad to see you," I replied as I held him up.

"Jane is gone. I'll never see her again. They're gone too. I'll never see them again either."

Thank you very much, Captain Obvious. I know these should have hardly been revelations, but it really did take all that death for the implications to sink in. With Dylan, at least. At that point, I wasn't sure if they'd sunk in with me. Because as much as I'd wept and hurt and shivered and worried and tried to bury my feelings in all varieties of bullshit, I had never really gotten to the point of feeling bad for the ones who'd lost someone they loved.

"You'll get through this," I told Dylan. "I promise."

"They need . . . someone needs to tell their stories," he said. "Honest stories. The good and the bad. Or else, they'll be forgotten. Or worse. Remembered for the wrong things."

"Of course," I said as I stepped back and put my hands firmly on his shoulders. "We can do that. Me and you. We'll be like historians. We'll chronicle their lives. We'll honor Jane and all of them and we'll be good people. Both of us. Heroes."

"I'm not a hero. I'm not anybody. I'm nothing."

It was an interesting choice of words. As I stared into Dylan's lost eyes, did I see "nothing"? Is this the moment when I reveal that Dylan was merely a figment of my imagination, the moment when you rethink everything I've told you and you say, "Holy shit! She's right! He never had a conversation with anyone but her! He didn't even touch any objects!" Is this the moment when I admit that Dylan wasn't real, and never was?

No. This is the moment when I tell you he was realer than he'd ever been. When I tell you I saw *everything*. Holding him, staring at him, I could hardly remember what I used to think of Dylan all the way back in the fall. When he was a redneck, a hardened soul, an arsonist, a father. A mystery.

He wasn't a mystery anymore. I *knew* him. Which was, I'm ashamed to admit, rather heartbreaking. Though not as heartbreaking as what happened next. For as I was touching him, thinking about who he was and what he meant to me, and feeling all the feelings that such thoughts inspire, Dylan disintegrated. He blew up right before my very eyes. Exactly as I always feared he would.

this is what happens

Yes, *this* is what happens when your boyfriend spontaneously combusts in front of you.

You fall to your knees. You press your face into the pavement as the blood drips, thick and languorous, off you, as if it were ice cream in the sunlight. You howl like you've never howled before, and the howl confirms that there are things deep inside you. Things darker than the darkest things you've ever imagined. And you believe in those things. Entirely, without question.

You send a three-letter text—*SOS*—and your parents come to fetch you and you sit on plastic bags in the back of their Durango and you stare out the window at the apple blossoms. You wear nothing but your bra and panties because you can't possibly keep those bloody clothes on your body. When you get home, you rush to the bathroom and lock the door. You shower sitting down and you cry. When the hot water becomes cold water, you shiver and you know you deserve to shiver. When you can't bear the shivering anymore, you put on pajamas and you crawl into bed.

You pull the shades on the window that your boyfriend once crawled through. You smell the sheets that haven't been washed in at least a week, that hold his scent. You cradle your phone in your hand. You open the novel you started once upon a time, the one called *All the Feels*. You read a passage from it:

> Ever since his seventeenth birthday, Xavier had a power. Whenever he touched someone, he took all their feelings. He absorbed them, sopped them up like he was a paper towel and their feelings were a spilled beverage. Then the people died. Because you can't live without any feelings.

You rewrite the passage:

> Ever since her seventeenth birthday, Mara had a power. Whenever she felt something, she gave her feelings away. Her feelings leaked out of her like propane from a furnace and people inhaled her feelings. Then the people exploded. Because no one's body can handle such noxious shit.

Then you look at what you've written and you realize something you should have known all along. You're not a hero. You'll never be a hero, or even a good person. You're a villain, always have been. You know now that *All the Feels* was never about a boy who's afraid of his own *feels*. It has always been about you and how the world should be afraid of yours. That's right. Because all your fucking feels are tearing the world apart.

Like any villain worth a damn, you delete every trace of evidence. You wipe your cloud, your hard drive, your phone. You destroy that book. And you vow to keep your secrets to your grave. You decide that you will never tell anyone, not even Tess, that you killed your own boyfriend, that you killed all of them. That you, Mara Carlyle, are the Covington Curse.

fallout

No one blamed me for that particular patch of madness. They pitied me, just as they pitied the friends and families of the day's other victims: Jane, Becky, Steve, Taylor, plus two kids I haven't mentioned yet because I didn't witness their demises.

Karl Gunderson, a bony guy who ran cross-country and seemed to have an endless supply of egg-salad sandwiches on his person, blew up while he hid in Room the First. And Teresa Thompson, class treasurer and the only black girl I'd ever known who was a card-carrying member of the Young Republicans, blew up while heading to a back exit of the school, carrying her friend Kacey Neilson, who'd broken her ankle during the melee.

Scientists didn't visit and take samples. Rosetti didn't investigate, though apparently her partner, Demetri Meadows, walked the halls and jotted some notes. Then he passed the baton to Sheriff Tibble, who gave things a cursory look and told our janitor, the affable and always-available widower Mr. Garvin, to "go about his work." As Garvin mopped up our seven dead classmates and hosed down the halls and parking lot, Tibble informed the victims' families that they could each collect a bucket of assorted remains. If they were so inclined.

The nearly empty middle and elementary schools cleared out completely. Across town at the Shop City Mall, they canceled classes. Even though we had very little contact with the other students, our predicament was still a "major distraction" to them and the school board decided to, in the words of President Mender, "take a mulligan." They'd start over next year when the legacy of the senior class could be forgotten.

Meanwhile, the legacy of the senior class was determined to soak itself into the architecture.

That's right, we didn't cancel a single day of school. We returned the Monday after the bloodbath. What other choice did we have? Nowhere else to go, we could hardly give up now. Even though things were destined to change.

It won't surprise you that I was a wreck. I didn't attend any classes that first day back. I sat in the hall, leaning against a locker and I watched my classmates come and go. Their eyes were sympathetic, but the only person who chose to talk to me was Elliot Pressman, Cranberry Bollinger's former flame.

"It'll get better," he said, putting an arm around me. "And these help."

He placed two pills in my hand. I didn't even look at what they were. I popped them in my mouth, chewed them, and let their bitterness burn the sides of my tongue.

"You loved Cranberry?" I asked him.

He shrugged. "I used to stare at pictures of her on my phone, but I deleted them because that wasn't helping. I've already sorta forgotten what she looked like."

Whatever the pills were, they did the trick. For a little while at least. I felt a rush of numbness, then I passed out. Next thing I remember, Elliot was gone and Tess was in his place.

"Honey, honey, honey," she said.

I stuck up my middle finger.

"What's that for?" she asked.

"I want you to stay away from me. You shouldn't be around someone like me."

"Honey, honey, honey," she said again.

There were other kids in the hall and I stumbled up to my feet and pointed at them one by one. "You will die, you will die, and you will die," I said.

Skye Sanchez shook her head. "We've got AP tests to take and then we will graduate and this will all be behind us."

"You still believe in a finish line?" I asked. "Fine. Then I'm crawling to it, blind and numb. Who's with me?"

They all stared at me like I was wearing a beard of bees, until an ally finally stepped from the crowd. Greer Holloway, who wore her affinity for drugs quite literally on her sleeve—marijuana leaf tattoos adorned both of her forearms—pulled a joint from her pocket, sparked it up, and said, "A-fuckin'-men."

Sometimes revolution starts with a single joint and a couple of pills.

Or so said a wise woman once.

Me. Right now, that is.

While I couldn't speak to each individual's state of mind, I can say that once I broke the seal, the collective attitude of the senior class transformed. It became firmly entrenched in unfettered and indulgent nihilism, in an attitude of "really, what the hell can they do to us now?" The night of #ForBilly was sort of a teaser, but fire and vandalism weren't gonna cut it anymore. Hedonism was the only answer.

On Tuesday, in Mrs. Dodd's Old Testament class, kids passed around a bottle of Jameson, compliments of Dougie O'Shea.

"Is this okay, Mrs. Dodd?" Claire asked when the bottle ended up in her hands.

Dodd lowered the Bible and said, "Wine blessed Abraham's army, so why not whiskey for yours?"

Good enough for Claire, and when Claire is swigging straight from the bottle in class, you know the worm has taken a distinct turn. The bacchanalia (a little Latin for you—hat tip to Spiros) started fast and only picked up steam. Our newest video—an hour-long edition brimming with Krook's false proclamations and seven spontaneous combustions—was rushed into postproduction thanks to stimulants and adrenaline. When it had a special premiere that Wednesday, our sideshow suddenly delivered what so many had been expecting. If the comments were any indication, people were both thrilled and disgusted.

About time! This touchy-feely shit was testing my patience.

MY EYEZ! Can someone wash my eyez please?

It goes without saying that Jane was instantly deified, deemed the most tragic loss since Billy Harmon.

I ship Jane and Billy . . . in Heaven!

Those particular words were probably typed about a billion times by frenzied tween fingers. I don't mean to make light of her death, I really don't, but I was having trouble trusting any of my emotions.

For chrissakes, I couldn't even cry for Dylan.

that's right

I didn't cry for my dead boyfriend. It's a terrible thing to say, but it's true. I shed my share of tears, of course, and people thought they were for Dylan, but they were really for myself. I grieved the loss of the girl I thought I was, which was a smart-ass but basically a good person. Turns out I was a smart-ass *and* basically an absolute and total shitstain of a person. I was a psycho who imagined people's deaths and then—guess what?—those people blew up.

Don't believe me? Let's run through the victims.

Katelyn Ogden. I hated her. Sure, we were friendly, but deep down I hated her. Her shit was always *so* together. She could be a tourist on the dark side where some of us lived, then still go back to her sunny existence. I despised that. I'd wished her dead on more than one occasion.

Brian Chen. He snubbed me once and that was enough to inspire my wrath. Then he went on to have this entirely lame catchphrase, while half the things I've said that should have gone viral never did. No love for "boom-boom bonkers" and so we got boom-boom Brian.

Still not convinced?

Consider Perry Love. I thought he was a homophobic and age-phobic douche, and I wanted him wiped off the face of the earth. Ta-da! Wiped. Same goes for his teammates Harper Wie and Steve Cox. How about Cranberry Bollinger? I was jealous of her and she suffered the consequences. The Dalton twins? I was constantly annoyed by them, so they had to go too. Kamal Patel? Don't get me started. Gayle Heatherton? I wouldn't be the first person to think the world would be a better place without mean girls like her. Um, Jane Rolling? Um, duh. Becky, Taylor, Teresa, Karl . . . you get the gist. Even Billy Harmon, I even wanted poor little Billy Harmon out of the picture. Though when it comes to him, euthanasia is the nicest word I can hang my evil thoughts on. Basically, at one point or another, I'd wished all of them dead. And now they were. Spectacularly dead.

All of which leads us to one clear and disturbing fact.

I did the same thing to Dylan.

The first night that Dylan and I slept together, he told me he loved me, and I told him the same thing. Then we did the deed, and when the deed was done, I felt spectacular. But each time we had sex after that, I didn't feel as spectacular.

I told myself it was typical, that first times are always the best. But deep down, there was more to it than that. Way down there in the darkness, I was hiding a secret:

I had imagined my boyfriend dead and that had made me feel . . . well, alive.

On the first night we had sex, it seemed quite likely that things would end very, very badly. Which sent a charge through my body. The possibility that Dylan could explode at any moment was, I hate to say it, a turn-on. But the more sex we had, the less likely that seemed. The explosions weren't happening anymore, so my heart wasn't thumping in the same way. I might not have been able to recognize it then, but I desperately wanted the spontaneous combustions to come back.

Sex on borrowed time. Plummeting plane sex. That's what I desired.

Sex on schedule. Commuter sex. That's what I got.

Now, you tell me: Which sounds more invigorating?

Okay, the latter might, that is if you're a sensible and sane person who's madly in love with your partner. But here's the other thing. The more confident I became that Dylan was going to survive, the less confident I became that our relationship would. I had told Dylan that I loved him, but I had only told him once. There's a reason for that.

I'm pretty sure I never did.

what I did next

This was my fault. I had seen firsthand what I had caused. I had watched so many people, including my boyfriend, disintegrate in front of me. Now how the hell was I supposed to get all that behind me?

What was better for me in the long run? To completely forgot the images, smells, and sounds? Or to remember them forever, like tattoos on my soul that I would notice along the cuff of my conscience whenever I got too happy with my life decisions?

Big surprise: I chose to forget. I went easy on all things popped and puffed and I dedicated myself entirely to booze, because it seemed the substance best suited to amnesia. My incessant drinking was written all over my blotchy face and telegraphed from yards away by my rank breath, but my parents didn't punish me. They consoled me. I could almost hear relief in their harmonies of "we miss him so much too." I know they feared their time with me was limited. Now that I wouldn't be spending it with some boy, they were probably a bit happier. I couldn't blame them, but I certainly couldn't tell them what I'd done.

As for Dylan's family, I didn't have a clue what depths their heads and hearts were drowning in. Though on Thursday, I was given a chance to learn. That's when I received a text from a number I didn't recognize. It was a more formal message than I was accustomed to, but the subject wasn't exactly a casual one. It read:

> Dear Mara, We know you must be going through a
> lot of pain right now, but we would be honored if you
> joined us for a short ceremony to remember Dylan.
> It will be held at noon on Saturday at the St. Francis
> Cemetery. Do not worry about dressing up. Simply
> bring your memories of my son. He loved you so. Kind
> regards, Denise Hovemeyer

Denise was Dylan's mom's name, but I didn't know it until that moment. As I've told you, in all the months we'd been together, I'd never been to Dylan's house and I'd never met his family. That's mostly on me. I'd never asked to visit, and the few times he invited me, I always told him it was easier if he came to my place. My parents were often at the deli, while his mom was always home.

To be honest, I was scared of the woman. He hardly talked about her, so I assumed she wasn't a pleasant person. I figured she was a mean old widow, a judgy old farmer's wife. I certainly didn't expect her to send such a devastatingly sweet text. I drank vodka and lemonade and read the words over and over until they were a blur. Soon, I was daydreaming about this ceremony.

I pictured Denise as a solid woman with square shoulders and thin lips and I imagined Warren standing next to her at the St. Francis Cemetery, amid countless tombstones bearing the Hovemeyer name. The triplets wouldn't be there because I figured the Rollings, in their grief, would want them far away from this cursed family. So it would be just those two, Dylan's mother and brother, in a cemetery swirling with fallen apple blossoms and the odor of damp spring soil. Oh, I almost forgot! The ice-cream truck would be there too, parked in the grass—a rusty monument to bygone happiness.

Then I pictured what would happen if I showed up to offer my condolences and crocodile tears. Denise would hug me, maybe ask me to call her some nickname, like Ducky or something. I'd sneak a sip from a flask and as all the remembrances were being remembered, I'd have to confess.

"I remember the beginning," I'd say. "Life was crazy and he seemed crazy and that seemed to fit. But seeming to fit and actually fitting are two different things, aren't they? That's why stores have dressing rooms, right? Dylan turned out to be a special boy, a sensitive soul. But he didn't fit. And I didn't love him. Don't get me wrong. I miss him, I really do, but I also like having only myself to worry about. Now, I can't exactly tell people that, so it's better to drink and cry and appear heartbroken. Which is cowardly, I know. If only I had realized that my dark thoughts about Dylan were there for a reason and that they were dangerous. If only he had lived long enough for me to break up with him. If only in the throes of passion, when he was inside of me—"

Whack.

I pictured Denise "Ducky" Hovemeyer slapping me across my stupid face because that's what my stupid face deserved. Then I pictured myself stumbling off, guilty of adding one more messed-up thing to the pile of messed-up things this poor widow has had to endure on a daily basis. And finally, being a villain and all, I'd be obliged to steal the ice-cream truck, to drive away in a cloud of dust, chewing gum, blowing bubbles, giving not a single fuck—all my fucks, in fact, flying straight out the window.

It was better for everyone if what I pictured couldn't ever possibly come to be. So I deleted the text and I blocked Denise Hovemeyer's number from my cell. I drank more vodka until I passed out on my bed.

out of hand

What I had started the week before took a firm hold. Half the kids showed up to school drunk or stoned the following Monday morning. Dr. Wonderman had been out on bail for months and, while he was no longer facing murder charges, he wasn't going to be straightening any teeth or tilting any minds anytime soon. So someone else swooped in and scooped up his business. Who? I don't know and I don't care. All I can say is that business was booming.

We came to refer to the day that Dylan, Jane, and the others died as The Event, and it marked the moment when our experiment in free-form schooling fell apart, when our little utopia crumbled.

"This isn't going to make things better," Spiros told us as the booze and dope were openly shared. "It's only delaying the inevitable nuclear fallout."

"Fallout has already happened, dude," Greer told him as she took a hit. "We're living in a postapocalyptic—"

And Greer blew up.

That was late April into May for you. Spiros's class was as spirited as ever, with blitzed teens saying whatever was on their minds. Occasionally blowing up in the process. Before long, Spiros was as battle weary as the rest of us. A splattering student became as innocuous as the bell between classes.

Phones were always poised, capturing the sex, drugs, and spontaneous combustions. It was not uncommon to hear the phrases "Is this too snuffy?" or "Is this too porny?" in the video editing bay after school. The snuffy and porny stuff got in, more often than not. We didn't even care if people were watching. We didn't care if they were thrilled or disgusted. This was simply how it was and we weren't going to sugarcoat it.

Remember those virgins I knew? Unheard of now. Of course, we weren't animals. It's not like kids were having sex in class or in the hallways. But if the sand by the pool could talk, it would ask for years of therapy. And poor, poor Kylton Connors.

"Why do I let every bi-curious future frat-boy convince me that he can give a decent BJ?" he confessed in one of the videos. "When did I become the crash-test dummy for your careening sexuality? There are other gay guys in this class, you know? Subject them to your confusion and teeth."

Careening sexuality pretty much covered it. Hunks like Clint Jessup were always conveniently shirtless, trouncing down the halls and hoping the sheen of their waxed torsos were enough to entice a few ladies behind a dune. It often worked, but not on me. As much as I craved arms around me, as much as I missed lips on me, I didn't want what they wanted, which was fast and loud and stupid. Rodeo sex.

And it should probably go without saying that there was also a lot of pent-up aggression. Consequently there were more than a few fistfights. When a brawl broke out in yoga and Jalen Howard punched Patrick McCoy and Patrick McCoy blew up and splattered all over Mr. Harmsa, Mr. Harmsa decided that maybe yoga wasn't the answer. The next day he shifted to Krav Maga, an Israeli self-defense technique that was supposed to teach us focus and discipline, but primarily became an excuse for us to toss our friends and frenemies around in a controlled environment. Didn't stop the explosions, of course, but they'd never again interrupt a nice quiet session of downward dog.

Mrs. Dodd's class was more or less the same—passionate readings from the Bible with little to no discussion—though her motives were suddenly clear. She didn't object to any of our behavior, which seemed counterintuitive at first, considering we assumed she was there to save us. It turns out saving had nothing to do with it. We were the Sodomites. She was there to watch us burn, to make sure we burned. Every last one of us.

When I use the words *we* and *us*, I'm talking about the senior class in general, obviously. There were teetotalers and prudes who refused to partake in the debauchery. Some of them had been among the most debaucherous in years past, but their conversion to priggishness didn't mean they were immune. Sure, they could pass a pee test, but the Curse blew a few of them up too.

Then there was me. One of the last things Dylan had said to me was that someone needed to tell the victims' stories. I promised I'd be that someone. It was a promise I most certainly did not keep. Because when things really went off the rails, when spontaneous combustions were so common that we hardly stopped classes for them, when my blood alcohol concentration reached whatever blood alcohol concentration is required to make blackouts a daily thing, I began to lose track of who the victims were.

In just over a month, we had

1. Greer Holloway, who I've already told you about on the account of her death in Livin' 101, her association with the crack tree house and Kamal Patel, her pot-leaf tattoos, and her general flakiness. But she wasn't a flake, not really. She loved animals. She was going to be a veterinarian someday, which I know is such a clichéd thing to say when someone loves animals, but she actually interned at a vet's office and did more than hold dogs while they got shots. She had a passion for all things fuzzy.

2. Patrick McCoy, who died during that yoga brawl and was one of the three. One of the three guys I slept with, that is, before I slept with Dylan. He was one of the inspirations for *All the Feels,* come to think of it. He had an infectious laugh and was damn good at guitar. A nice-enough guy, most of the time, though he did have a temper he bottled up and uncorked every now and again. That's why we broke it off. Because he called me a bitch. Which, obviously, I often am. Though I hardly deserve to be called one because I overslept and missed a brunch date at Houlihan's once.

3. through 19 (I think). There was Poul Dawes, a skater who wore polka-dotted shirts and slept with a lot of girls. And Helen Reedy, a girl who was sleeping with Poul Dawes when he blew up, a girl who had a full forty minutes to bask in that horror—to pick the polka-dotted fabric from her teeth—before she was gone too. Rahul Sneed, a loner who almost never made eye contact except that one time I saw him working at Rosedale Assisted Living Center, handing out ice-cream sandwiches to patients, my ailing grandma included. Stephanie Stupinksi, the captain of the volleyball team who shouted *shazam!* every time she spiked the ball. Cole Hooper, a guy who was superhot but no one else seemed to notice he was superhot, so I pretended he wasn't superhot because I didn't want to be the girl who thought a guy was superhot who was so super *not*, if you know what I mean. Oh yeah, and he's the one who made that suit of armor out of duct tape. Didn't hold him together, obviously, but thankfully it made cleanup a lot easier. Then there were like . . . eleven others? Twelve? I'm not sure.

Pathetic, right? But this is how I chose to deal. My negativity seemed to be running roughshod through the school, ripping people apart, and if I spent my time pondering who these people actually were—as Dylan might've wanted me do—then how could I possibly live with myself?

To be fair, I wasn't staring kids down in the hall, casting evil hexes, and watching them explode. I was actively trying to rid myself of every emotion I had. If this part of my life were a book, it'd be titled *None of the Feels*. Didn't change the fact that I'd already produced a surplus of bad vibes. No matter how many emotions I tried to stifle, the amount of animosity I'd already released into the world was pushing these bodies to the limit. Even the smallest annoyance was likely to set someone off.

It was impossible to predict the who and the when, even if I did understand the why. Tess's analogy about spoiling bread and milk suddenly made perfect sense. Not everyone blew up at the same moment because it was a cumulative environmental effect. I had hated some people more passionately and more often, and some bodies were more resilient than others. Their times came when their times came. There wasn't much I could do about it anymore.

So yes, I was powerful, and yet I was powerless. That fact (along with the booze) is why I stopped caring altogether. I might have been more disturbed by how easy apathy came to me, if apathy weren't so en vogue. My classmates were taking all the deaths in stride too, and the dead were doomed to be statistics to anyone who didn't truly care for them. Not everyone could have their wakes at the State Street Theater, after all, and so the victims were treated to a few RIPs that were hardly shared outside their inner circles. It was like they'd been living in the Rosedale Assisted Living Center, where the best they could have expected was an ice-cream sandwich and a kiss on the cheek before they left this mortal coil. And after they left? One could only hope the obituary writer spelled their names right.

Our janitor, poor Mr. Garvin, was tasked with cleaning them all up, but we made sure it was worth his while. The constant stream of donations coming our way meant we could pay him, Kiki, and the four teachers well into the six figures. As bad as it got—and it got bad—they stayed on.

Of course, Rosetti wasn't walking the halls anymore. I hadn't seen or heard from her since The Event, when she blabbered her accusations and slipped off right before Dylan's death. She had told me that "they" were "coming." Well, whoever *they* were—the government, I figured—they never showed up. Unless you count Rosetti's partner, Demetri Meadows. Sheriff Tibble didn't bother to investigate anymore, but Meadows poked around after every combustion.

Buoyed by vodka, I cornered him one day in the cafeteria and asked, "Where the hell is she?"

"Who?" he responded as he removed an air duct grate.

"Your partner, partna," I said.

"I haven't had a partner since November."

"Um, you forgettin' Ms. Rosetti?"

He shook his head the way Mom once did when she fired this kid from Covington Kitchen and then that kid's parents showed up a few weeks later, clueless that their little darling had been shitcanned for gross incompetence.

"Wait," I said. "She transfer or something?"

"A lot of things fell apart the night of those riots, including our theory about the dentist," Meadows said nonchalantly, as he flicked on a flashlight and peered into the air ducts. "Didn't mean Rosetti had the right to beat the piss out of the man. No matter how frustrated she was. No matter how much we'd all love to beat the piss out of a dentist."

"Wonderman? So this . . . this hasn't been her case since . . . November?"

"They took the woman's badge when you were all on your little camping trip," he said, flicking the flashlight off. "This is my case and my case alone. If you have information that'll help, feel free to share. Otherwise, move along."

I did. I moved along to the corner of the cafeteria where I pulled out the burner. I texted Rosetti:

Where you been?

The text bounced back. Rosetti's number had been disconnected.

let's not forget

Tess. Tess. Tess.

She was still around, but not really. After I had given her the finger in the hall, I had done other things to alienate her in those first few weeks following Dylan's death. When she'd text me or send me a silly Vine to cheer me up, I'd ignore her. When she'd sit with me at lunch and tell me it was okay to cry or that if I wanted a hug, I could have "the biggest hug in the universe," I'd usually shrug and sip whatever cocktail I was wielding.

She either got the message, or she got distracted, because as school became wilder, she became even more scarce, popping in for the occasional class, but rarely staying a full day. Deep down, I wanted her to keep trying, to grab me by the cheeks and yell, "Do better, Mara! Be better!" Of course, I didn't tell her that. Because then I'd be tempted to confess and I feared she'd never forgive me.

On top of it all, I worried that she was developing a drinking problem of her own. Every time I saw her, she was carrying a Nalgene bottle filled with a milky concoction that made her wince when she sipped it. Anyone who was close to Tess knew she had sworn off alcohol after a few bad experiences, so this was not a good sign.

But did I say anything? Did I try to make her laugh or offer galaxy-wide hugs?

Of course I didn't. I went about my own drinking. And I went to classes. When I could hold my head up, I participated. I wanted to be oblivious to the hell I had unleashed and continued to unleash, so my waking moments needed to be filled with distraction. Most of the time, Spiros's class took my brain down intellectual paths instead of emotional ones, and while I didn't contribute to the videos anymore, I craved Ms. Felson's calming presence as an antidote to my disillusion with Rosetti and Krook.

"If I was your age, and this happened to me, I would have done all the same things you've done," Felson told me once before class.

"You have no idea what I've done," I mumbled to her.

"Maybe not. But that hardly matters. I know what I was capable of. Which was everything."

She was right about that.

Sometimes Krav Maga let my brain off the hook and let my muscles and lungs temporarily work through whatever one feels when one feels capable of everything. Sometimes it made me collapse on the mats in the corner of the room where I'd zone out until lunch, when Kiki gave me solids to sop up all the liquids I'd been consuming. After that, it was time for more of the Good Book, which . . .

well, I usually skipped. Once Dodd's motives became clear, I didn't need to hear about how I was doomed in both the present *and* the hereafter.

I didn't go home when I skipped, though. I usually napped in the sand by the pool, in an attempt to steady my head before facing my parents. They weren't clueless. They could see me sinking deeper and deeper. They also weren't warlocks. They couldn't magically pull me out of this. The least I could do for them was pretend to be sober.

I have no idea what the official population of Covington was in May. A few hundred at best. The seniors and their families, basically, and even some of those families had jumped ship. Many of my classmates were already eighteen and it was perfectly legal for their parents to say, "Sayonara, suckas, we're moving to West Palm. Make sure to mow the grass while we're gone."

After the elementary and middle schools closed, and classes at Shop City Mall were canceled, almost every other kid who had the means had fled town. Why not, right? As far as I knew, no one was tracking them. Sure, they had a good chance of being ostracized in their new communities, but it was still better than being here.

This is all to say that the handful of people like my parents, who stuck around to watch things go from bad to worse, suffered mightily and silently. They had each other, of course, and sometimes they'd get together for drinks or dinners where they'd blow off steam. But mostly they watched over us, trying not to remind us of our predicament or trying to keep us comfortable, if not hopeful. It was like hospice. Only our parents weren't trained to deal with this nonsense.

Now I know what you might be thinking.

But, Mara, weren't you immune to the Curse? Seeing that you were the Curse? You could have spared your parents some misery by assuring them that no matter what, you'd be okay.

I considered that. I even imagined the confession.

"I've got some good news and bad news," I'd tell them.

"Bad first," Mom would say. "Always the bad shit first."

"I'm the Covington Curse. I've been causing all of this. With my big bad brain."

After the requisite ten minutes of jaw-dropping shock, Dad would say, "And . . . the . . . good news?"

"They're all going to die, but I'm going to live!" I'd shout. "Yay me! Now let's go have some ice cream!"

Only that ice cream would have to wait, because the thing was, how could I know I was immune? How could I be sure that I couldn't do this to myself? What sort of damage does a season full of self-hate do to a girl? And what would it take to push that girl over the edge?

So, no. I kept my lips zipped and my emotions dull and I tried to act sober around my parents. It was the least I could do.

what I didn't know

There were only a few weeks left before graduation when I discovered the squeaky clean underbelly of our seedy school. I was skipping Dodd's Bible-thumping session and stumbling toward the beach when I noticed a light on in a former bio lab. Donations had brought improvements to the building—refurbished theater, cafeteria, and bathrooms were the main ones—but all classes continued to be held in four rooms: Rooms the First and Second, and Rooms the Third and Fourth, which had been added in April. Other rooms were occasionally used for trysts and miscellaneous mischief, but that was always under the veil of darkness.

So when I entered the bio lab to investigate the suspicious brightness, what I found truly shocked me. A dozen students sitting at desks, hunched over test sheets. Skye Sanchez was there. So were Malik Deely and Laura Riggs. Even Dougie O'Shea was hard at work, penciling in bubbles. These weren't necessarily the smartest kids or the biggest do-gooders, but there was one quality they shared. They could all be accused of having ambition.

School Board President Louise Mender was slumped in the corner, contemplating a word search, doing the duties of a proctor. When she saw me, she put a finger to her lips, then motioned with her chin to an empty desk. At the next desk over, an unmistakable set of bangs hung over a face that was twisted up in concentration.

"Tess!" I hollered.

As Tess's head shot up, Mender's crooked finger shot out. "If you're going to cause a ruckus, then vamoose!"

Which I did. I had no other choice. Shocked by the studiousness I had witnessed, I vamoosed. Vamoosed like hell. I needed the beach more than ever. Sure, there was usually some variety of shenanigans going on there, but it was as close to tranquil as school got. There was always a dune to hide behind, always sand on my skin, always a shimmering dimness.

When I got there, I plopped down and tried to process what I'd seen. It was an AP exam, obviously, because what other exam would a senior take? What I found so mysterious was that I didn't know it was happening. Had I heard and forgotten? Or had no one bothered to tell me?

Either way, it meant I was clueless, not only about what was going on with this school, but about what was going on with my best friend. In years past, Tess and I stressed over exams together, studied together, traded texts as soon as we exited testing rooms to reassure each other that we'd done better than we feared. It seemed such an inconsequential part of our friendship back then. But now? Huge.

I lay back in the sand and I wept for entirely too long. When I finished weeping, I closed my eyes and wondered. Not about where it all went wrong—because I was pretty sure I knew where that was—but about where it could possibly, ever, conceivably go right again. I wondered and wondered and wondered . . . until I heard something. Tess's voice.

"Hey, kid," she said as she sat down next to me. "I thought you might be here."

"Well, look who finally found her way to paradise?" I grumbled as I opened my eyes, sat up, and wiped off my shoulders.

Tess kicked her shoes off and put her toes in the sand. "I'm sorry," she said.

"For what?"

"For not being there for you."

I shrugged. "You gave it a shot. But I pushed you away. Now I'm trying to figure out what I pushed you into? An AP physics exam?"

"History," she said. "Physics is tomorrow."

"So what have you been doing? Studying this whole time? This party not good enough for you?" I motioned to the mounds of sand and to the pool and its wobbly turquoise glow, to the cigarette butts and the empty bottles, to the bikini tops dangling from the graffiti-riddled lifeguard chair.

"I never judged you and the others for how you've been dealing. Some of us are simply focusing on other things. Doing all it takes to move on."

Then she handed me something. A warm, leathery book with a cover design that resembled a cereal box, but instead of pieces of cereal, it had small, square pictures of my classmates, piled together in a bowl, a breakfast of smiling faces.

Quaker Life was the title. It was our yearbook.

I knew Tess had served on the committee prior to The Event, but I didn't know the committee had actually stuck with it afterward. I flipped the book open and began to browse. The dedication at the beginning took up thirty-something pages. A page for every victim. The profiles were glossy and glowing and more or less bullshit. *A rebel with a heart of gold* was printed beneath a goofy still of Dylan that the editors had screencapped from one of the videos.

"The caption wasn't my idea," Tess said. "I wanted to ask you how you thought he should be remembered but—"

"This is fine," I said. "What I want shouldn't matter."

I kept browsing. One small section featured the portraits taken on Picture Day (back before The Event) but only a handful of candids commemorated our peaceful era of learning. Mostly it was our unhinged finale. In fact, the yearbook barely showed teachers or classes or anything that resembled school. Beer bongs beat out Bunsen burners, and to the casual viewer this would have appeared to be a meticulously documented kegger, not a tribute to our education. It was meant to seem celebratory, but to me it seemed sad, and I felt guilty about the massive part I had played in it. It also didn't help that almost all the pictures of yours truly showed me passed out or in the process of passing out, a bottle always nearby.

"They were going for a certain vibe," Tess said. "I mean, it's what people were taking pictures of and what they said they wanted to remember. Our perseverance. And I'll freely admit, I was too busy with other things to veto any inclusions."

"It's fine," I told her. "It tells the truth. It is what it is."

"Go to the end."

I flipped through the final third of the book until I saw it. A full page covered in an old snapshot of me and Tess. We were sitting on the back deck of my house brandishing smiles of pure, if temporary, happiness. The gaps in our teeth told me this was from third or fourth grade, probably not long after Tess's dad took off. Below the picture, Tess had written a message.

We made it.

I ran my hand across the image, as if I were petting these two innocent girls, imploring them to not give a single thought to their futures. "We're not quite there yet," I said.

"We will be," Tess replied.

I closed the book and tucked it under my arm. I was thankful to have it, if only just for that one picture, but I wasn't sure what it was supposed to mean. Was Tess telling me to be proud? Or embarrassed? Was I supposed to be happy or heartbroken to leave this all behind?

"So have you become like my dad and Skye and everyone else?" I asked. "Are you clinging to the hope that it's all going to stop at graduation?"

"No," she said. "Because that's not science. Science says there's a way to solve this, and I'm working on that. I've been reading about Amur leopards."

"As one does," I snarked.

"I'm serious," she said. "Amur leopards are very rare and hard to capture, but scientists have recently been keeping tabs on them, thanks to, you guessed it, tiny biological tracking devices."

"It wasn't me who guessed it, but go on."

Tess didn't even bother to roll her eyes. She just kept speaking to me in the calm cadence of a teacher. "The scientists start by putting the devices on the liver of the Manchurian wapiti, whose only predator is the Amur leopard. The Amur leopards gobble up the livers, like we gobbled up everything they gave us in the tents, and the devices implant themselves. Well, the bad news for Amur-leopard-tracking scientists is good news for us. A toxic waste spill in the Amur River, where the leopards drink from, effectively disabled the devices early last year. Stands to reason it would do the same to what's inside of us. Now, the chemical compound is hard to replicate, but I have some online friends in the Russian Far East and they've been willing to send me some jarred samples."

"So wait? You've been drinking toxic Russian river water? *That's* your solution?"

"That's *science*," she said firmly. "I've been very careful about my intake. It's gross but it's hardly a risk. Besides, it's worth a risk. Because if I disable the tracking device, then I can leave. And if I leave, then maybe—"

I cut her off because I wasn't in the mood for maybe. "You wanna know something that isn't science?"

"What?"

"Our friendship. There's no logical reason we should be friends."

Tess paused, as if this were something she'd never considered. Then she said, "Freshman year."

"What?"

"Freshman year," she repeated. "You and I sat right here. Well, not right here, but close to here, in the bleachers somewhere. We watched a swim meet. Do you remember that?"

"Vaguely," I said, which had become my go-to answer regarding memories.

"So you don't remember what you said?"

I shrugged. From over the dunes arose a gasp of pleasure. The lure of a shirtless boy had worked on someone.

"We were watching the kids swim back and forth," Tess went on. "And you said, 'That isn't a race down there. That's timed survival.'"

"So I was clever," I said as I stood and stretched my legs.

"Yes, you were, and you still are," Tess replied, and she tugged on my skirt like she wanted me to sit back down. "High school is basically *timed survival*. But you know the reason it's survival and not certain death? It's because there are edges to the pool. There are ways out. You've been an edge to my pool for as long as I can remember. Since my dad. Since . . . everything that's happened. With your humor, your devotion, your, well, just being you. You've been my way out. I hope I've been yours."

"You're terrible at metaphors," I said as I shook my leg to make her let go.

She relented, burying her hands in the sand and saying, "I'm telling you that I love you, but there's some stuff we really need to talk about. I hate to see you give up. You're destined for great things."

Those words hit me hard, because I had seen who was actually destined for great things—the kids back in the bio lab. No matter what their AP results said, these were the kids who would succeed. People like me were just standing in their way. So it was best for everyone if I came clean. But I couldn't bring myself to do that yet. Not in front of Tess.

"My destiny is to have another drink," I replied as I made a visor with my hand and scoped out the easiest route through the dunes to the exit.

"Save the drink for prom," she called out.

I paused. "What?"

"Next week. Saturday. It's happening."

"So? You want me to help you pick out a dress or something?"

"No, because I'm too busy and I'm not going. But you should. Find yourself a boy to ask. Ditch all the guilt surrounding Dylan. I know it probably feels like you could have done something to stop it, but believe me, you couldn't. It's time to move on."

I looked down, chuckled a little at how right and wrong she was, and said, "The only person's fate I can control is my own, huh?"

"Exactly," she said. "So end the year on a high note. Go out and have a blast."

No pun intended, I assume, and I'm sure she didn't realize how tragic her words could end up being.

"Thanks for the pep talk," I told her as I set off into the dunes with the yearbook under my arm. "Maybe I'll try to be there, at least for a little while."

pregame

Yes, there was going to be a prom. Kids were going to shake their butts to Beyoncé and convince themselves it was the highlight of the year. Perhaps they'd even believe it.

The planning had gone on exactly like it had with the yearbook. Behind closed doors. Or at least behind doors that I didn't open. I was coming to realize that if you don't look for something, then you rarely find it.

The chosen venue was the Hotel Covington. Skye Sanchez's parents ran the place, and while it wasn't exactly one of those grand hotels of yesteryear, it was rather nice—a white pillared behemoth perched along the edge of the Patchcong River Gorge. It was ideal for a prom, and considering that the only people staying in it were a handful of reporters and weirdos still fascinated by the carnage, there was room to spare.

"As far as my parents are concerned, money is money, and thanks to crowdfunding we have enough cash in the kitty to cover even the most exorbitant cleaning expenses," Skye told me when I asked her what they might do about a bit of blood in the ballroom. "Besides, I'll be wearing washable shoes and bringing at least two backup dresses. I suggest you do the same."

"I know I'm late to the game," I said. "But can I pitch in somehow? Make sure the night is special for everyone?"

"Bring a bunch of Oinkers and I'll fix it so that you're prom queen," Skye said. "Bring a bunch of Oinkers and a date? I'll make sure he's king. Unless you're going with Tess, that is."

I shook my head. "I think our Tessy is sitting this one out. I'm flying solo."

That's right. I wasn't taking Tess's advice about finding some new boy—I didn't want some new boy—but I was still taking her advice. I was going to prom. I had given this plenty of thought. Every time I had kept things to myself, it had ended badly. If not for me, then for the people around me. And I didn't have many people left around me. So it was time to confess. In front of the people I had terrorized. Once and for all. In formal attire. And whatever the consequences of that confession were, I was sure I deserved them.

When the evening finally came, I put on a simple green sundress, the type of thing that always inspired unsolicited compliments, which seemed preferable to rolling the dice and setting Mom and Dad back a few hundred on a frilly nightmare that would make people grimace and say "you look *amaaaaazing*," through tightly clenched teeth. I wanted to look good, but if I was going to lay myself bare, then I also wanted to look like me.

"You are so goddamn pretty," Mom said as she held her phone

up and I rocked from one foot to the other on our front steps. She was taking the standard prom shots, the ones that usually feature a tuxedoed fella, or at least a squad of chicks squealing and shouting to celebrate their singleness. But not this time.

"I'm only being myself," I replied, my eyes on the dandelions that had started their yearly invasion on our lawn.

"We're glad you... that you have your wits about you right now," Dad said.

Translation: *We're glad you're not totally obliterated at this moment.* Which I wasn't.

I looked up and told him, "I want to be sure I make the right decisions tonight."

"That's wonderful to hear," Mom said.

"We're sorry Dylan can't be here to share this special evening with you," Dad said.

Special evening? That would be a word for it. "Trust me," I said. "Dylan would not have been into this scene."

"Well, he was into you," Mom said. "And who could blame him?"

I didn't want to talk about Dylan anymore, for obvious reasons. So I kissed both of my parents on their cheeks, and said, "You know that none of this was ever your fault, right? None of this will ever be your fault. I love both of you so much, and you've got so much to look forward to in life."

Which made them cry, of course, but I wasn't going to stay around to watch that, because that's when my ride showed up. I left to go do what I had to do.

oh, what a night

Who was my ride? Obviously, no limo companies would agree to chauffeur us, and even though the police offered shuttles, it was hardly the arrangement anyone wanted for their prom. Luckily, when word got out, Google dispatched a fleet of those self-driving Priuses decorated with sparkly lights on the inside. It was clearly a promotional stunt to prove that these technical marvels were safe even when kids were exploding inside of them. We didn't care. All that mattered was that we could arrive in some semblance of style. Nerdy style, but style nevertheless.

Like I said, there was a lot of money to spend, but the idea was to keep things authentic and simple. There was talk of periscoping the proceedings, but the kids who did the planning decided on the opposite. If anyone so much as raised a phone, it would be confiscated. This would be an exclusive event. Seniors only. Music would be provided by Tick, Tick, Tick . . . , a band consisting entirely of members of our class. Dougie O'Shea—under the ridiculous moniker of ShamRockz—would DJ, but only when the band was taking a break. There would be a fully stocked bar and plenty of Covington Kitchen–cooked appetizers to go along with a mountain of Oinkers. No chaperones. No rules other than "have a kick-ass time." It was basically the prom all high school students wish they could have. Except, well, for the strong possibility of blood, blood, and more blood.

When I arrived, my classmates were already hopping, spinning, and acting like fabulous fools under paper streamers and stars made from aluminum foil. Tick, Tick, Tick . . . was not a particularly good band, but they were enthusiastic, and that counts for a lot. The drummer, Rosie Drew, was kicking the shit out of the bass drum, which was shaking the hell out of the place.

I walked across the quaking dance floor and over to the bar, where I poured soda into a champagne flute. Skye was standing there and she clinked my glass with hers, which was full of the real stuff.

"That outfit," I said. "Damn. Supercute."

She was wearing patent leather heels and a silver-sequined mini, which was a bit short for my taste, but what the hell, right? It seemed like the sort of thing you could easily wipe blood from, and Skye was so pretty that most people would ignore the obvious Christmasiness of it.

"Thanks," Skye told me. "You're wearing the hell out of that dress too."

Truth is, she'd hardly given me a glance; her eyes were locked on some sweaty dude on the dance floor—Jackson, Jayson, something like that. Still, I said, "Very nice of you to notice."

She sipped her drink and replied, "I wish Katelyn had lived to see this. She loved it when everyone got together."

"No doubt," I said. "Thanks for setting it all up. This is really nice. The perfect way for things to come to a close."

"Fully catered rites of passage. It's what we Sanchezes do best."

I nodded, motioned to our dancing classmates, and asked, "So, what do you think they'll do?"

"Get drunk, dance, hook up. Standard stuff."

"No. I mean, after graduation."

Skye sipped her drink and said, "College, I hope. Did you hear? I got a scholarship to Smith."

"Really? Hell yeah for you. How'd you manage that?"

"ACLU is putting the pressure on. Deadlines are being extended. Exceptions are being made. Maybe the world is coming around to us freaks."

"And maybe the powers-that-be will finally let us freaks run free?" I asked with my eyebrows at full mast.

Skye clinked my flute again and gulped down the rest of her champagne. "Supreme Court will never let this situation stand. Might as well get on with things. Like you so elegantly once said, 'Let's fucking live again,' right? You should apply to Harvard, you know? You're smart. Creative. Harvard could use a badass feminist like you."

"I don't know. After tonight, I doubt I'll be considered Harvard material."

"Plan on making a scene, are you?" Skye said with a wink.

"Something like that."

"Have fun with it. All my parents ask is that you keep any monkey business out of the lobby," she said, then tossed her flute over her shoulder.

I flinched, but the flute didn't break when it hit the floor.

"Plastic," she told me with a wink. "Nice plastic, but still plastic. Come on. This isn't our first rodeo." Then she sauntered onto the dance floor, waving her arms above her head as she went.

Tick, Tick, Tick . . . was still giving it their best even though their best was a bit off-tempo and off-key. The room was full, the crowd alert. Now was the moment. Now was my chance. I needed to act while I still had the courage and conviction. The booze was curling a finger at me, promising even more courage, but I knew if I started to sip, I'd eventually gulp and I'd lose that essential conviction and join the dancing throng.

So I stepped away from the bar and climbed onstage. The singer, Benji Goldsmith, thought I was looking to duet, so he was happy to slide over and make room at the microphone. But rather than belt out the chorus to "Firework" I hollered, "Cut the music!"

They may not have been talented, but they were obedient. The musicians hit it and quit it. Except, that is, for Rosie, who, head down, kept assaulting the drums. It was like gunfire and it drew every eye to the stage. When she finally looked up, she realized that now was not the time for a bitchin' solo and she set her sticks in her lap.

"Thank you," I told her with a little bow, and then I turned to the crowd. "Apologies for the interruption."

My classmates seemed peeved, but not particularly hostile. Some asshat did shout, "Show us your tits!" but I couldn't waste any anger (or nipples) on him. Because I could see myself getting worked into a frenzy and wishing people dead and pushing bodies to their breaking points, then—*splat, splat, splat*—the dance floor might end up like act 5 of *Hamlet*. When, really, the only person who deserved my anger was myself.

"I have something to say, something to confess," I announced. "Then I'll be out of your hair. Or in your hair, possibly."

Puzzled looks confronted me. There was no patience for cryptic shit.

My voice slipped into a whisper. *"What I'm trying to tell you is . . ."*

Then I froze, because goddamnit if Tess wasn't at the entrance of the ballroom. Now I'm not exaggerating when I tell you she was stinkin' gorgeous standing there in a red satin mermaid dress. Not that she usually dressed like a bag lady, but this was by far the most elegant I'd ever seen her. She was downright sexy, far hotter than Skye. She pushed back her bangs and smiled at me.

"I . . . I . . . I . . ."

Up until that moment, my intention was to lay it out there, to prove to my classmates that I was the cause of all this horror, and then await sentencing. Maybe they'd descend upon me like jackals and tear me apart. Maybe they'd grab my hair and plunge my head in the punch bowl and make me literally drown in booze. Or maybe, just maybe, they wouldn't have to do anything at all. Maybe my confession would be the final straw, the last bit of self-hate that would turn my own powers against me. Maybe I'd blow up right then and there and provide a warm and splashy end to the shitshow.

Spoiler alert: None of those things happened.

The sight of Tess in the ballroom delivered an existential jolt to my body. I hadn't spoken to her since that afternoon in the sand. I was fortunate enough to have a moment with my parents before I left for prom, to tell them I loved them and assure them they were innocent. But what was the last thing I'd said to Tess? Basically, "Screw you for believing in me."

The shock of seeing her now—she wasn't supposed to be here!—combined with what I was about to do was so overwhelming that I didn't realize it when someone wrenched the microphone from my hand.

"Worst. Confession. Ever!" boomed from the amplifiers.

livin' on a prayer

What the, what the . . . ?" I whispered to myself as I turned to find a wobbly Claire Hanlon standing next to me, all but gnawing the microphone like a turkey drumstick.

"I'm sorry, Mara," she slurred as she rubbed the felt against her cheek. "Confessions gotta have some oomph to 'em."

Oh, Claire. The debauchery had taken an especially firm grip on that girl. Like me, she had spent the last month or so in a drunken stupor. Only this way of life was new to her and she hadn't quite gotten the hang of controlling her impulses.

"*I wasn't finished,*" I whispered to her.

"Oh, you're finished all right," she bellowed, and then she turned to everyone. "All of you are *soooo* finished. Just think of standing in my way and you're done. Capital D-O-N-E done. Know why? Because I say so!"

There was silence, for probably only a second or two, but enough to send the appropriate chill through the room.

"That's right," Claire went on, pointing a thumb at her own chest, "*I* am the Covington Curse. Everyone who died, died because of me. Me! Because I deserve to be valedictorian. And these losers and their bloated GPAs stood in my way. I've got a spreadsheet, ya know? Paid that Pressman kid to hack the system and get all your grades."

"*Seriously,*" I whispered.

Claire turned, threw me some major shade, and said, "You should shut your mouth, Mara. Main reason you're still standin' is 'cause you tanked chem sophomore year. But don't you dare test me, girl. I've taken down others for less and might still need to take down one or two more of you losers. Doesn't matter what your grades are. If you challenge me, you won't survive. So there you have it. That's a confession for ya!"

Then . . . *Pow!*

It was the amplifiers again. Claire had literally dropped the mike, a punch to all of our guts. No one had been expecting this, least of all me. Claire thinks she's the curse? Getting a B in chem is considered tanking? Do people who drop microphones know how expensive those things are? I bent over to pick it up, but Clint Jessup, who was standing at the edge of the stage, beat me to the punch.

He pulled the microphone into his grasp and announced, "Actually, I'm the Curse."

Another bout of silence and then a squeaky voice called out, "No, Clint, no!"

"It's true," he said, gazing sympathetically across the crowd to the source of the voice, devoted football-team stat-keeper Marcy

Hand. "I've been so keyed up, so itching to get laid all the time that I think it's, like, my sexual energy. It's too much for people's bodies to handle."

All right . . . interesting.

And there was more. Laura Riggs sidled in and snagged the microphone next.

"Sorry, Clint, you're hot, but not that hot," she said. "It's me, actually. I'm the Curse. I've been fucking around with witchcraft for a while now. Ancient chants and things like that. I've got this class picture from eighth grade and one day I pricked my finger and dripped blood on the faces of people I don't like. That includes everyone who died. Plenty of others too. So, yeah, there's a whole lot more to look forward to. I'd like to say I'm sorry, but . . . sorry, not sorry."

There were whispers in the crowd.

"I thought it was me."

"I was sure it was me."

"I'm the Curse. I've always been the Curse. Haven't I?"

Thank you, Mr. Spiros, for the crash course in the classics, because suddenly it felt like I was being mocked by a Greek chorus. It was like I was the subject of some ancient fucking tragedy, the fool who was only now discovering how foolish I truly was, something the audience had known since the curtain had opened. I stepped offstage and put my hands over my ears.

No amount of muffling, however, could block out the sounds of Tick, Tick, Tick . . . Either in an attempt to distract us from the confessions, or in a bid to celebrate them, the band burst into another tune and Benji recaptured the microphone. It was a song everyone in the room knew by heart, that everyone in New Jersey knows by heart. It was the song Tess and I used to sing when we rode our bikes down the shore. It was the song Dylan played in the silo on a day that felt so long ago, but wasn't even nine months ago.

> *Tommy used to work on the docks,*
> *Union's been on strike, he's down on his luck . . .*
> *It's tough, so tough*

Fists began pumping and everyone was suddenly singing along and there was relief on so many faces and weight off so many shoulders, but not mine. Definitely not mine. Even in the moments following Dylan's death, I had not felt this aimless. It wasn't like I'd been waking up every morning with a plan, but I usually had a vague idea of how I would approach the day. Booze, school, booze, sleep, booze, sleep, put on a dress, and go martyr myself at prom.

Now? Well, I hardly knew how to breathe.

And I didn't breathe, at least not for a few moments. Feet stomped and the dance floor shook. Catharsis was in full effect as the singing got louder.

> *She says we've got to hold on to what we've got*
> *It doesn't make a difference if we make it or not*
> *We've got each other and that's a lot . . . for love*
> *We'll give it a shot.*

Someone placed a hand on my shoulder, to pull me into the current of the sing-along. It rebooted my lungs and I brushed off the hand without checking to see whose hand it was. My eyes locked on the bar, I fought through the crowd, and grabbed the first bottle in reach. Vermouth. Swigging from it, I slipped out the emergency exit in the back.

the weather

The sun was down and it was raining. A cold rain, but one that washed the shock from my body as I trudged up a grassy hill. When I reached the top, I sat down. The hotel and its Prius-stuffed parking lot was now below me. Beyond the hotel was the Patchcong River Gorge, cloaked in a veil of drizzle. I kicked off my shoes and they shot down the hill like it was a log flume.

I sat there drinking and feeling sorry for myself. Then I sat there drinking and feeling angry at myself. Then I sat there drinking and feeling nothing, watching the rain like every pitiful person who ever thought that rain can stand in for emotions when, really, it's only weather. Stupid fucking weather.

Still, something good came out of that weather. Tess. She emerged from the downpour like a dream within a dream—an implausibility buried in implausibility. Her makeup was streaked across her temples and her dress was bunched at the back, creating a small crimson train that followed her as she marched up the hill.

"I always know where to find you," she said when she sat down.

Cross-legged, I wedged the bottle in my lap, put my chin in my hands, and replied, "You weren't supposed to be here."

"I wanted to surprise you."

"You certainly did that," I said, and I downed another mouthful. "Please tell me you're also here because you have it figured out."

"I wish I could. The tracking device? Handled. I think. To deal with the rest I need to get out of this place."

"You know I thought I had it figured out. I thought I had it all wrapped up."

"So did everyone else, apparently," Tess said with an empathetic sigh. "I guess it's natural to look inward."

"Where else are we supposed to look?"

Tess didn't answer the question, but where she looked was at me. "I've been thinking about what you said. About our friendship and how it doesn't make sense."

"I say a lot of shit," I replied, and I took another slug from the bottle. "It doesn't make a bit of difference, obviously."

"No, it does," she said as she pushed her wet bangs out of her face. "It's something we have to consider."

"What's that mean?"

"Let's say someone figures this out? Let's say we both survive this and live to be old ladies."

"Then we get a house down the shore together and wear kimonos and smoke hookahs and do old lady shit like we've always said we would."

She embraced herself and shook her head. Her makeup had washed off entirely and now she was this soaked and shivering girl. Scratch that. She was this soaked and shivering and gorgeous

woman in this stunning red dress. Who was telling me to stop being naive.

"Let's enjoy what we have, while we have it," she said.

"That's what you're supposed to say. But that's not what I want."

"You want senior year to do over again?"

"I don't know. You wrote *We made it* in my yearbook."

"Yeah, so? We did make it."

"That's not what it's been about for me."

Tess put a hand on my knee. "I realize that, but I'm so proud of
you, Mara. For being who you are."

"What if I killed him?" I asked her softly. "What if I killed them
all? By being who I am."

Tess didn't laugh or call me silly or selfish. She simply smiled
and said, "You're a force of nature, Ms. Carlyle. That's the one
thing I know for sure and the one thing I'd never change about
you."

I took one more gulp of vermouth, tossed the bottle to the side,
and I leaned into her. I let my body slide down her body until my
head was in her lap, like I'd done so many times in the past.

"I love you," I said. "Bunches and bunches and bunches."

"We're the same," Tess told me.

I closed my eyes and replied, "You know that's not true. I'm a
fuckup and you're . . . well, Tess. Which is the opposite."

"That's not what I mean. I'm talking about this whole crazy situation. It hasn't changed us at all, has it?"

I battled to keep my eyelids open as I whispered, *"That's good,
right? Tess and Mara. BFFFs. Best fucking friends forever."*

"Yeah," Tess said with another empathetic sigh. "But *things* are changing. Even if all the terrible stuff hadn't happened, things were always going to change. There was no stopping that."

The thumping bass drum coming from the hotel sent vibrations up the hill that made the raindrops on the grass shimmy. Inside, the party raged on, and if anyone was spontaneously combusting out on the dance floor, then no one was bothered enough by it to storm the exits. The doors remained closed, the parking lot sedate.

Even if I had a response—which in this very rare moment, I did not—I still couldn't fight off the grip of the drunk. Tess's face went blurry, so I closed my eyes to refocus. They stayed closed, and the rain, as cold as it was, worked like a lullaby. Pittering, pattering, coaxing my exhausted body to sleep.

i'll come running to see you again

Do you want to know what I dreamt about? Do you want to analyze the images that flicked across my unconscious mind? Of course you don't. No one cares about anyone else's dreams because they don't matter. Not really. The only thing that matters is what comes next.

What came next was I woke with a start, exactly where I fell asleep—in the grass, on the top of that hill. Only now I was alone. I don't know what woke me. My dizziness made the possibilities as muddy as the earth. The rain was pounding and the grass was matted and brown. Maybe even a little red, like blood, but it was hard to tell in the darkness.

"Tess," I called out. There was a patch of forest behind me and I pulled myself to my feet so I could get a clear view of it. I didn't spot anyone sneaking away or crouching behind a tree for a whiz.

"Tess!" I called again, louder this time, then took a step and slipped. The wet grass sent me zipping down the hill. I had enough wits to slow my momentum by digging my bare heels into the ground and when I reached the bottom, I rolled into a patch of mulch, and lay there for a moment on my stomach, breathing in its sour earthiness. It worked like smelling salts, slapping me fully awake. I stood, but I didn't bother to wipe myself off.

"Tess!" I yelled, as loudly as I could, and I ran toward the hotel. I tried the emergency exit, but it was locked, so I circled around to the front of the building and passed through the parking lot. Amid the sea of dorky Priuses was a beacon of cool.

A Tesla.

There was only one person in Covington I knew who drove a Tesla. Sure enough, Rosetti was sitting behind the wheel, her face revealed with each pulse of the wipers.

"Tess!" I yelled once more, but I yelled it at the car, and it was the first time I noticed the similarity in the names.

The headlights flicked on and the Tesla crept toward me. I didn't budge. When it was a few feet away, it started to turn, trying to sneak around me, but I moved back in front of it and with a hand sliding along the curve of the hood, I made my way to the driver's side door and banged on the glass.

"Did you see her?" I asked. "Did Tess come this way?"

The window eased down and I got a good look at Carla. I'm calling her Carla now for a good reason. In the glow of the dashboard lights, she didn't look like Special Agent Carla Rosetti of the FBI. She looked like Carla, a woman who was wearing her hair up and had a smear of eye shadow across her lids. Lavender, to match her dress.

"What did you say?" Carla asked.

"Tess," I told her. "She was with me, and then she was gone. Did you see her leave?"

I leaned in to check if Tess was maybe a passenger in the car, and as I did, I heard music coming from the speakers. It was like a low-volume dance party in there. I didn't see my friend but I noticed that Carla wasn't looking at me. With her chin bobbing to the beat, she was staring through the windshield at the hotel.

"People have been coming and going all night," she said. "It's quite an event."

That's when I realized I'd seen the dress Carla was wearing before. When I was stalking her online, I'd noticed it in a series of wedding photos. It was the bridesmaid dress she'd worn once. To a friend's wedding. A good friend? An old friend? A former friend? I had no idea.

"What are you doing here?" I asked.

"Stakeout," Carla said. "Making sure everything is on the up-and-up."

"But you're not even an FBI agent anymore, are you? I mean, Meadows seemed to indicate that—"

I stopped short because I spotted taillights nearby, moving on the far end of the lot toward the road that snaked away from the hotel along the edge of the gorge. There was no engine roar to accompany the lights. It was one of the Priuses, carrying someone away from prom.

"That could be Tess in there!" I shouted, pointing. "We should follow her. We can't let her get away."

As I started moving toward the other side of the car, the sound of locks engaging stopped me in my tracks.

"I'm not going anywhere," Carla said. "This is where I need to be."

"There's nothing here if Tess isn't here," I explained as I stepped back toward the driver's side window. "We need to catch her. We need to make sure she doesn't leave."

"I am not. Going. Anywhere." Carla's voice was full of insolence and her eyes remained glued to the hotel.

Thirty-six. Again, that's how old I had calculated Carla to be. Which isn't old, I know, but it's twice my age. If she were the Jane Rolling of her class, she could be my mom. By that logic, she could be a grandma. Yet, in truth, I know she would never have let any poopy diapers slow down her career. It was a career full of accomplishments, of busting baddies and making the world a better place. Admirable. Incredible, even, especially for a woman in a field dominated by men. Yet here she was, sitting in a hotel parking lot, on a "stakeout" of a prom. I can't say I had her entirely figured out, but the things I was discovering scared me. For too long, I had dreamt of being like Carla. Now I legitimately feared it was my fate.

Consider this: Back when I was in elementary school, I couldn't possibly imagine what it was like to be in middle school. Then middle-school me couldn't fathom my high-school incarnation. But at that moment, staring at Carla, I was staring at my future. Which was full of anger. Suspicion. Regret.

"Tess," I pleaded.

"That's the problem with your generation," Carla said, finally turning to me. "You assume everything should be given to you simply because you want it. But when you get what you want, do you appreciate it? No. You take a selfie and move on to something else. Entitled. Little. Brats."

"Tess," I said. "Tess."

Carla stuck a finger out the window and rain dripped off the purple-polished nail. As she pointed at the taillights from the Prius that had briefly paused at the edge of the lot before turning onto the road, Carla said, "Fuck Tess."

"What?"

"Fuck. Tess."

Really? *Really?* Oh, she should have known better than that. I had suffered needles, concussions, dead boyfriends, and flip phones for this woman. Now she expected me to stand there and listen to that shit? Did she not realize I was a girl with absolutely nothing left to lose and daily training in Krav Maga?

My training had served me well. I stepped forward, swiped, and got a hold of that finger. For a moment, I felt like my uncle's dog must've felt after he caught a squirrel he'd been chasing for months around the backyard birdfeeder. As in, *Um . . . I actually did it? Can I possibly go through with this?*

When Carla tried to wiggle her hand free and grunted, "You pathetic little child," the answer became a resounding *You bet your sweet bippy I can.*

I bent the finger back with mighty force. And it worked. Man, did it work.

"You are gonna get out of that car," I told her.

Which was a foregone conclusion, given how much pain she was obviously in. "Okay, okay, o—gahhh!" she shrieked.

"Now!" I ordered.

With her free hand, she disengaged the locks. I gave her finger another push and she opened the door. One more push and Carla Rosetti, former special agent of the FBI, tumbled out onto wet pavement.

I could have kicked her. I could have stepped on her back and left a footprint on her dusty-ass bridesmaid dress. But I don't think she deserved that. And I am many things, but I am not a sadist. I am, as I told Dylan once, an opportunist, and opportunity was presenting me with a seat, a steering wheel, and an accelerator (or whatever the fuck you call a gas pedal on an electric car).

start your electric motors

Wanna guess the last time I'd driven a car? No? Okay, then I'll just tell you.

It was the day I got my license. On a bright summer morning after sophomore year, I saddled up with the evaluator guy in Mom's Subaru. I adjusted the mirrors, drove a few blocks, parallel parked, used the turn signals, pulled back into traffic, made a few left hand turns, and returned to the DMV lot. The guy checked off some boxes on a sheet and shook my hand. Twenty minutes later, some glossy-eyed lady gave me a glossy license with a glossy-eyed picture of me on it, and I told Mom, "See, I can do it. Now drive me home."

Nearly two years ago, in other words.

Goes without saying that I wasn't quite ready for NASCAR, but I figured I could at least catch up to a computer-navigated sedan that was obliged to follow all traffic laws. So I stepped on the accelerator and the Tesla's motor hummed in satisfaction. The car had been waiting its entire battery-powered life for a moment like this, and it was a real champ handling the tight curve from the parking lot onto the road that snaked away from the hotel. Like that, I was in hot pursuit of those taillights.

Now I know what you're thinking.

Oh, you poor dope. Did you really believe Tess was in that Prius? It could have been anyone in there, right? Didn't you suspect it was more likely that something else happened to your friend? That some other, more terrible fate befell her?

Maybe I did, but I was only willing to accept one scenario at that point. I was focusing on the long odds, on the possibility that Tess had slipped off without saying good-bye because good-byes are a monster. Fuck good-byes and their gripping claws and endless slobber. I never planned to say good-bye to Tess and I assumed she never planned to say good-bye to me. But maybe Tess planned to leave me behind, to set off on a quest to fix this thing that not even the *professionals* and *adults* were capable of fixing. So feel free to pity me for chasing that sliver of hope, but please understand that I wasn't chasing a good-bye. I wanted to leave with Tess. There was nothing for me in Covington without her.

The stereo was still spitting out music, a god-awful tune where some woman kept hollering, "Everybody dance now!" Like a Navy SEAL changing the clip on an assault rifle, I ripped Carla's phone from the USB jack and swapped in mine.

"Play Drive, Fucker, Drive!" I told Siri as I hugged another curve.

The playlist was on shuffle and kicked things off with a song that didn't have any swears but had the throbbing beat I needed.

It spurred me on and I drove, drove, drove. Faster than . . . well, faster than that Prius. I wasn't looking at the miles per hour or even the dash for that matter. I was laser-focused on those taillights growing brighter and wider in front of me. I didn't even roll up the window, which was letting the rain whip against my face and shoulder.

That rain! Oh, that fucking rain was pounding so hard that the wipers had trouble keeping up. I let the taillights be my guide and I had to trust that the Prius's cameras and GPS knew where the road was because I could barely see any lines. I did know there was a cliff out there somewhere, skirting the edge of the pavement, and one false move would send me and my vehicle into the Patchcong River Gorge. I was trying not to think too much about that, though, because soon I was close enough to see more than the taillights, to make out a muddy silhouette illuminated by the sparkly lights inside the car.

I lay on the horn. I would have flashed my brights but I didn't know where my brights were and all my concentration was on that passenger, on making that passenger holler to the robot chauffeur, "Prius! Prius, my boy! It appears someone is tailing us. Would you be a sport and kindly stop so that I may tell this motorist to, how shall I put this, *go suck a dong*?"

But the Prius didn't kindly stop or even slow down, and when my incessant honking didn't make the passenger turn around, lean forward, or do much of anything, I considered a more drastic measure: Some bumper-to-bumper action. A love tap, if you will.

Self-driving cars are sticklers for safety, so I figured the Prius would have to pull over if it sensed danger, and I accelerated until I was tailgating it like a world-class asshole. Only problem was, I didn't trust myself to finish the move. What if I tapped too hard? Would it send the Prius over the edge? What if I lost control? Where would that send me?

As much as I thought I was ready to accept any fate the world threw my way, I wasn't ready for death, and this moment proved it. Death was there if I wanted it. All I had to do was jerk the wheel and say "fuck this noise forever" and dive hundreds of feet down into the gorge. But I wasn't even willing to risk doing that by mistake.

I was determined to survive. So Tess was right when, after the crash with the Daltons, she had declared me a survivor. Not that I deserved to be. I couldn't understand why, of all people, I had made it this far. Why on earth was Mara Carlyle the one who was allowed to keep on going?

I took a breath, eased off the pedal, and fell back a few car lengths. Meanwhile, the singer on the stereo pleaded:

> *I'm right over here, why can't you see me? Oh-oh-oh.*
> *I'm giving it my all, but I'm not the girl you're taking home.*
>   *Oo-oo-oo.*
> *I keep dancing on my—*

I pulled the plug on my phone because those lyrics were a bit too on the nose, wouldn't you say? As I reached forward to turn the stereo off, I finally noticed the blinking lights on the dash. Even now, I'm still ashamed I didn't notice them earlier, especially the big red one that lit up a display of the battery power:

O MILES LEFT. CHARGE NOW!

On cue, the car let out an electronic sigh, an okay-I've-had-about-enough-of-this-for-the-evening-now-get-to-walking kind of noise. Then it went dark. Every light and everything else that whirred and hummed cut out. No matter how hard I pressed the pedal, the car wasn't going to go any faster. All that was left was momentum and momentum was not enough.

So the Tesla slowed down as the Prius pressed on. I had no lights of my own, or even wipers, so I stuck my head out the open window and guided the car into a parking area for a viewpoint along the road. That enigmatic silhouette, that dark shape that could have been male or female, that could have been any one of the kids who'd attended prom, got smaller and smaller, and those taillights, burning red like little flames, followed the turns in the road and escaped into the rainy night.

to be honest

Enclosed in the lifeless car, with rain drumming the roof, I knew that the silhouette I had seen was probably not my best friend. I knew the more likely scenario was that Tess never left that hill. With my head in her lap, with me sleeping soundly, with her hands on my hair, she had . . . well, she had washed away in the rain.

Maybe it was the sound of the end that woke me. Maybe it was my head hitting the ground. Maybe I slept through it all, like I'd slept through so much of my best friend's life, and when I woke up, she was already part of the earth, part of the water trickling down and past the hotel, over the cliff's edge, and into the river.

Yes, I knew that. But I wasn't ready to accept that. I lifted my phone and dialed Tess's number. It went straight to voice mail.

"Honey," I said. "Are you there? If you are, I need you to call me. I need to hear your voice. I love you, Tess. I love you so much."

The phone was my only light, and I set it in my lap and it cast its glow across my wet and mulchy dress. There were no texts, snaps, or notifications to check, nothing to indicate anyone out there was thinking of me. So my focus landed on the fluffy pink icon of the MemorEasi app. I pressed it, and when it prompted me for a name, I typed:

Tess McNulty

Why? Because if I didn't have her voice, at least I could have her face.

I filtered by geography—*Covington, NJ*—and there it was, a picture from the local paper of Tess in her field hockey gear. Half-smiling, half-serious, quintessential Tess. I eased my finger down to tap the image, but I stopped short. I closed my eyes, and sat there with them closed for a small slice of eternity.

Then I hurled my phone sideways out the window toward the gorge. The rain was pounding so hard that I couldn't hear if the phone bounced off the pavement or was deflected by the railing, but a few moments later, I did hear a voice.

"I think you dropped this."

I opened my eyes and there was light all around me.

Then there was a hand passing me back my wet, but still functional, phone.

Then there was a face next to my window.

Then there was a smile.

how things got to this point

That smiling face in my window? Sorry, no. It wasn't Tess.

It's been five days since prom and no one has found a trace of her. Google won't release any data about their Priuses—something to do driverless-car/dance-attendee confidentiality, I guess—so that's a dead end. And when Mom called the police station to say, "I think my daughter's friend might have spontaneously combusted on a hill, but the rain probably washed her away," it wasn't the best method to rally the troops. It also didn't help that when one of the troops apparently did rally and poked around the hotel grounds the next afternoon, all he found was a dude on a John Deere wiping his brow as he looked proudly over the lawn he just mowed the living shit out of.

So yes, it's been five days since prom, since I last saw my best friend. Five relatively calm days in the wildest year in this town's existence. I'd like to say *in this world's existence,* but I also want to believe at least some of that Old Testament stuff is true. As twisted as those stories are, they always feature survivors. That God is a wrathful one, all right, but the human race goes on. So too will Covington.

Why have the last five days been relatively calm? Well, I haven't heard of anyone blowing up, for one. And I've stayed home, where my parents have emptied their stash of liquor, removed the sharp objects, and disabled all data plans and Wi-Fi (though we're not savages over here; we can still text and call people on our phones).

I can't blame them. When they found me drenched, barefoot, and bawling at the front door on prom night, they knew something was wrong. I told them about Tess and they worried about what I might do to myself.

Of course, I haven't done anything to myself. I've spent most of my time in the Mara Carlyle think tank. I've been pondering all the theories. Exactly as, I suspect, you have.

So let me ask me you: Are you Team Tess? Do you think our genetics got flipped-turned upside down? Or is it a government conspiracy like that sad-sack Carla Rosetti believes? Could it be possible that Laura Riggs and a bit of witchcraft caused it all? How about the sex tornado known as Clint Jessup? Do we count out Claire Hanlon and her unstoppable quest for the top of the class order? What about all of the seniors who've survived? Should we shoulder the blame together? Or should we simply accept this as a phase we had to go through, the worst growing pains imaginable? And what about me? By unveiling the mystery that is Mara Carlyle, have I satisfied your curiosity about the Covington Curse? Are you happy blaming me for the parade of death?

Do you really fucking care?

You do? Well, bless your heart, because I don't anymore.

I've given up theorizing and I'm focusing on one of the last things Tess told me. She said that we were "the same." As always, she was right. I *am* the same. Through all this shit, I haven't changed. Not really. I love my parents. I love my best friend. I am capable of so much love. Even if I am capable of so many other dark and strange feelings. Maybe *because* of that fact. I have thoughts. I have opinions. I have emotions that run the gamut. They come on all of a sudden, and I will feel guilty about some of them, sure. I will try to be better, of course. But I can't will it all away. These things are me.

And tomorrow, I—along with the rest of Covington High's seniors—will either go *wa-bam* or graduate. As much as I've mocked the assumption, I do sincerely hope Dad is right, and the dark cloud will pass and everything will be peachy for us as we head out into the world. However, if that's the case, then I worry a bit about the next crop of seniors. Because there's always a next crop.

Which brings us to the face. You've been wondering about the smiling face in my window, haven't you? The noble person who saved my phone from the certain void of warranty? Who was it and what happened?

Her name was Lucia Watson and she drove me home from prom. In a car of her own, a black Mustang with red leather seats and an engine that sounded like it was chewing on pebbles. As I rested my head against the passenger-side window, she asked me questions.

"Did you have fun?"

"Not exactly."

"Are you scared?"

"Of what?"

"That it's going to happen to you?"

"You're really asking me that? What do you think?"

"I'm curious about how you've been dealing with it. That's why I asked."

"Is that why you crashed the prom?"

"Well, I never had a chance to crash it because I never actually made it there. I found you, remember? At the side of the road? Ditching your phone?"

"Okay, then is that why you were *going* to crash it?"

"I wanted to make sure you were all having fun, that things were ending well for you. This was your last hurrah and then it's our turn."

That idea of turns is an important one. Especially when you find out who Lucia Watson was, and still is. For one more day, she is a junior at Covington High. Well, it's hard to say whether Covington High actually exists anymore. Classes are officially over. The building will soon be leveled. The Vatican will probably send in someone to sprinkle holy water on the campus and the town will let it run fallow. Maybe they'll erect a memorial someday, but shit like that gets so mired in controversy that I doubt it'll happen anytime soon.

Still, the kids who are juniors are going to be seniors in no time at all. I can guarantee that. Okay, some will drop out and others will homeschool or go the GED route, but come September, the majority will walk down a hall and step into a classroom. Maybe not in Covington—and hopefully not in a converted Lens-Crafters—but somewhere.

Lucia Watson is part of that majority. She and her parents believe in the power of a public education and I'm sure they've got the tax receipts to prove it. You might even remember her dad as the hard-hatted gentleman who helped reconfigure the Shop City Mall and treated me and Tess like we were a couple of plague rats. Well here's hoping he treats his daughter a bit better should his daughter have to face what we faced.

"Will you walk me through it?" Lucia asked me when she pulled her Mustang into my driveway on prom night.

"What do you mean?" I responded as I opened the passenger side.

"Tell me how you made it this far. What did you do to deal with it?"

I stepped onto the pavement and back into the rain. Without looking over my shoulder, I said, "Thanks for the ride."

I trudged up the walkway and sat on the front steps with my back to the door. When my parents opened the door, the car coughed away into the night. Dad stepped forward and reached out his hand as Mom asked, "Who was that?"

"Nobody who matters," was all I said before grabbing Dad's fingers, pressing them to my face, and completely breaking down.

Well, "Nobody who matters" has been texting me all day for the last five days. I don't know how she got my number. She's called too, but I haven't answered. Sure, I could block her cell, but she's been keeping me abreast of what's been happening (the search for Tess) and what hasn't been happening (finding Tess) since prom. That's valuable information for a housebound girl with no internet.

Besides, her curiosity has inspired a rare bit of magic. It has spontaneously transformed me into a stark-raving optimist. I'm not kidding. You see, Lucia was there at perhaps the lowest moment in my life, and yet she's still in awe of me. Weird, right? Like I'm some wise sage who has everything figured out. Like I've got my shit together or something. Lucia likes me. She trusts me. She asks me things, which is a sure sign that she's interested in me.

What was your strategy for finding humor in your predicament?

Which books might you have read that helped contextualize this moment in your development?

What detergent did you use to wash your clothes? You know, after?

I didn't respond to her initial questions for fear it would seem like I had nothing better to do. It didn't stop the barrage, though, and her persistence eventually paid off. Which is to say that this morning, there was finally something I was prepared to answer.

What comes next for Mara Carlyle?

this. this. this!

I will do more with the time I have, but not because I'm afraid that the time I have is limited. It may be a lot longer than I could ever expect, and I sure as hell don't want to waste it brooding and worrying about my every little thought.

Assuming I don't blow up during this next cycle of the sun, I will go ahead and I will graduate. At graduation, I will whistle for my classmates and cry a little. Maybe I will cheer Claire Hanlon's speech or maybe I will boo it. Depends on what she says. I will definitely collect my diploma and throw my cap to the heavens.

Then I will keep going, as long as my body keeps itself together. I will kick down the door to Tess McNulty's room—sorry, Paula— and I will decipher her notes and scribblings and I will drink Russian river water and disable this goddamn tracking device in my body, because Tess said it's possible, and Tess is always right. I will blast the Drive, Fucker, Drive! playlist and search far and wide for my best friend, because no one has found her yet and as far as I'm concerned that means she's still out there, *Veronica Mars*–ing this mystery into submission.

I will apologize to Jennifer Lawrence, to anyone I have intentionally hurt, but I will never promise to stop hurting people, because I don't believe that's a promise I can keep. Maybe Skye Sanchez was on to something, and I will end up at Harvard for a while—or some other school that's less enamored of itself and more enamored of me—but I will always come home to Covington, because Covington will always be my home, and my parents will always be my parents, and Oinkers will always be the best goddamn sandwiches in the world.

Maybe I will try to write another novel, something with a one-word title that would make Tess squirm—*Awesomesauce* or *Amazeballs* might work—but I will try not to read too deeply into whether it's a metaphor for something, or an allegory or whatever, because that doesn't matter, and no one buying a book cares about that crap. All they want to do is cry.

Which is something I will also do. I will cry. For myself, for other people, for the loves I lose. Because I will have loves. And I will lose at least a few of them.

No matter what, I will act like a grown-up, because I am one, along with many other things, including a time bomb, perhaps, or even weapon of mass destruction. Without a doubt, I will continue to be a woman who makes a metric shit-ton of mistakes.

I will be the same, because I am the same.

I will be the same.

wrap it up, short stuff

I repeated that last part because, if Dad is right, saying something twice makes it more likely to come true. Superstitious? Um, yeah. Wouldn't you be if you were me?

Of course, I know it's impossible to say with any certainty what comes next. I could die in a few minutes. Hell, so could you. Leaving a whole lot of "if only" in our wakes. The single truth that I can offer you with full confidence concerns what just happened.

So? What just happened?

Well, I texted Dougie O'Shea, for one, and I asked:

Did your dad demolish the school yet?

Him: Few more days.

Me: I need sand. ASAP. What does he charge to haul a load in his truck?

Him: ShamRockz drives a truck, ya know?

Me: OK. What do you charge?

Him: For you, baby girl? Nothin.

That was this morning.

Now it's the evening, a breezy end to a June day and I'm sitting in a beach chair at the edge of my deck, dipping my toes in a pile of sand that used to sit next to the Covington High pool. Mom and Dad were a bit perplexed when Dougie backed the truck past the house and dumped a small beach in our backyard. To their credit, they didn't say shit about it, simply stood at the window watching, no doubt thinking about how their only child would be graduating high school tomorrow. Even when Laura Riggs showed up to lend me her hookah, they hardly blinked. I was whole. I was home. For the time being. That's all they cared about.

I don't own a kimono, so I had to settle for a paisley terrycloth robe Dad owns. Doesn't fit me, but that's a minor detail. It's the symbolism of the thing that matters.

I do have second robe, Mom's pink silk one, but I'm saving that for someone else. It's draped over the empty beach chair that's sitting next to me. You might think that's a little pathetic, that I'm in major denial, but hear me out for a second. Because I have one more thing with me.

The burner.

I noticed it this morning, collecting dust on a shelf in my closet above where I store the beach chairs. I had set it there after Carla's line was disconnected. Figured it was useless. Seeing it again, I suddenly remembered what else I had programmed into the thing. I had the number of the matching burner, the untraceable connection to my bestie. My BFF. My Tess.

You know, just in case.

It's no surprise that the battery was dead, so I snaked an extension cord to the deck. The burner is now sitting in my lap, straining to fill itself with enough charge to find a signal so it can skip across the earth from cell tower to cell tower and locate a text or, I hope, a voice.

It's not there yet, so I will puff on this hookah and wait a bit longer.

My beach faces west, toward the farmlands at the edge of Covington. A perfect spot to watch a sunset. Remember when I said I was the same person I've always been? Well, that's not entirely true. I used to think that sunsets were cheesy, that they were images of uninspired sentimentality. But let's be honest, because we should always be honest. If a person invites you to watch a sunset, you go, don't you? You don't say jackshit about what's cheesy or uninspired. So neither will I. I know now that sunsets are glorious things. And this one—this one!—is absolutely invigorating, a fucking gorgeous splash of red on the horizon that marks an end, one I always knew was coming.

epilogue – 4 years later

I didn't blow up.

You might've been wondering if I did. But I didn't. I simply watched the sun set and smoked my hookah. Sorry. Anticlimactic, to say the least.

It's been four years since all that shit went down. I've had plenty of time to reflect, so I could drop some serious wisdom on you right now, and you could tattoo my pithy quotes across your midriff, and then they'd always be there for you, to comfort you in your times of need. But let's be honest. No one really wants that. You just want to know what happened next. I'd tell you to Google it, but we're friends now, aren't we? It's so much nicer if you hear it from me.

Graduation happened next. No big surprise there.

It's possible that you already know what went down at graduation, but chances are you don't. Either you stopped paying attention, or you didn't catch that chyron, or you're an alien reading my account one million years from now and you're scratching your antennae and thinking, *This? This book is the tome that all of humanity's religions were based on for its final fifty thousand years, before the world's dogs got fed up and said, "We're sick of being called puppers and doggos!" and then ate every last person? Okay. Sure.*

So in case you didn't know, our graduation ceremony was perfectly lovely . . . until it wasn't. At the beginning, we laughed and hugged. We told people that we loved them, even though we didn't really love them. A drunk-off-her-ass Claire Hanlon gave a speech about how spontaneous combustion was a metaphor for . . . something. Or maybe it was an allegory. I don't remember. I zoned out after a while. It doesn't really matter anyway. That part wasn't important.

The important part was when the diplomas were handed out. Mr. Spiros and Ms. Felson did the honors. Thanks to my alphabetical excellence—*Gimme a C for Carlyle!*—my shining moment was early in the process, which meant I had to spend the rest of the ceremony tapping my toe and waiting for a chance to toss my cap sky-high.

Finally, Cassie Zabriskie grabbed her rolled-up ticket to adulthood, and we were seniors no more. I moved my tassel to the other side of my cap and that's when it happened. The sky cracked open, the golden light enveloped us, and the voice of God echoed through—

I'm fucking with you. Though that would've been pretty cool.

No, what actually happened was—*BOOM!*—Lucia Watson blew up.

The former junior had been in the front row of the audience, wishing us all well, and she became a senior at the exact moment the rest of us weren't anymore. Her newly minted status meant she did that disgusting and horrible thing that Covington seniors tend to do, which is go bye-bye in a glorious splatter of blood.

It took a few seconds to wipe off our faces and assess the situation. But when we did, Laura Riggs shouted, "Oh, fuck yes! It was only Lucia!"

I assume that Lucia's parents gave their daughter a solemn, loving funeral, and the girl certainly deserved one—she was a total sweetheart. But I have to admit that the moment after she died was a glorious and transcendent one for the rest of us. The torch had been passed, so you better believe we cheered our asses off and threw our caps so goddamn high that the tassels got tangled in the angel wings of our former classmates.

#ForBilly #RITD #ThankYouLucia

It's too bad you weren't there to witness it, but hardly anyone other than us attended. Our graduating class was, and still is, a pack of pariahs. And so were the Covington High graduating classes that came after us. Many of Lucia's classmates moved away, but that didn't spare them a bloody fate. They weren't contagious, but they were susceptible. As soon as a few of them popped, the rest of the country agreed to return them home posthaste. Laws were passed. If you attended Covington schools at some point in your life, then Covington is where you were condemned to live, at least until you made it to graduation.

Since spontaneous combustion affected such an insignificant

portion of the population, the rest of the country was cool with restricting our constitutional rights, and essentially ignored the events. "Not my kid, not my problem." And some people even considered us lucky, because the federal government tossed our town a few hundred million dollars to build a state-of-the-art high school with slick surfaces and drains in the floor. Easier to hose down after the last bell.

All told, there have been 134 senior deaths by spontaneous combustion in Covington over the last four years. Across the country during the same time period, approximately the same number of kids have died from TVs falling on them.

Ah, statistics. So much fun.

I'd like to update you on what Skye Sanchez and Dougie O'Shea and the rest of my graduating class are doing with their lives. You know, give you some one-sentence summaries, like, "Skye became the youngest member of the Supreme Court in history" and "Dougie O'Shea lost both arms in a punkin chunkin accident." But honestly, I've lost touch with most of them. A bunch of them have even changed their names. Shared tragedies sometimes bring people together. But sometimes they push people way the fuck apart.

I can at least tell you what I know about Carla Rosetti.

She lives with her parents these days, somewhere in upstate New York. She has an Instagram account featuring super high-def close-up photos of insects and flowers and things that reveal even more beauty when you look at the intricate details. They're quite stunning.

Sometimes she posts short poems that she's written, free verse about her heart being "a bald eagle yearning for infinite horizons." They're quite terrible. But they get more likes than the photos, so what do I know?

I can't tell you whether she's happier now. That's the trick of Instagram. Everyone on it appears to be living their best life. I hope she's living her best life. Not because she personally deserves that. But because we all do. That's not what all of us get, unfortunately.

So what did I get? Where did I end up? College? A job? A fulfilling relationship?

For some reason, I suspect you don't actually care too much about any of that. I survived, and that's all that matters in a tale like this. Spontaneous combustions and falling TVs didn't get me, so it's time to focus your attention elsewhere.

Just in case you missed it, they made a movie about me. A goddamn major motion picture! That's certainly something to put on my résumé. I'm superhot in it. So is Dylan. Tess too. I mean, everyone is hot in it. My dad? Hot. My mom? So hot. That's the thing about movie stars. They tend to be hot.

But invariably, people who watch the movie say to me, "It took so many liberties with your story. For one, the president isn't even a woman in it. It's another insufferable old white dude. It's not the same, Mara. IT'S NOT THE SAME!"

Duh. It's a movie. Movies are their own beasts, and God bless them for it. I personally love the movie (my wardrobe is on point!), but I certainly don't mind when someone proclaims that my version of events is "soooo much better." My version of events still has some holes in it, of course. One big best-friend-shaped hole in particular.

I'm talking, of course, about Tess, Tess, TESS!

Did she join me at graduation? Did we get to smoke a hookah together? Did we cash in our story for a few million bucks and buy our dream beach house? Did my finest and truest friend abandon me? And if she did, did I deserve it? Or did she combust on that hill, and trickle down the wet grass to become one with the earth.

I'm not going to tell you. I've given you so much, for better or worse, but I'm not giving you this. And the reason is simple.

I don't want to.

Saying something out loud, writing it down, committing it to record, is what ultimately makes it true. So that's why you get nothing about Tess. It's not because you deserve nothing. It's because she deserves *everything*. All the possibilities. All the fates. All the feels. She is Schrödinger's cat, and I'm not about to open that box for you.

But I will let you in on a secret.

When Tess and I were younger, long before the shitshow of senior year, I would dream about the beach house. And my dream always ended the same way. With both of us dying of old age, at the exact same moment, reclined in our beach chairs, our arms draped over the sides, knuckles in the sand. It comforted me to imagine this future, because I was sparing each of us the pain of losing the other.

I think differently about things these days. Call it a spontaneous combustion of self-awareness. I know now that it was a selfish vision of the future, because I didn't ask Tess if it was a future that would comfort her as well.

Okay, clear some space on your midriff. Wisdom is on its way. What I'm trying to say is this.

Ask.

If you love someone, ask them what will give them comfort. Some people—such as yours truly—might be totally unreasonable in their requests. But it's likely that most people will list off simple things you can do. Or they'll tell you to just keep doing what you're doing. Or they'll request that you do nothing, which can be heart-breaking, I know.

You have to start by asking, though. Then you have to do what you can, for as long as you can, and when the future you get is not the future you imagined, you're more than welcome to tell the cruel hand of fate to fuck off. But please rest easy in knowing that the things you did mattered to someone. And that someone mattered to you.

acknowledgments

As much as I'd like to claim I came up with the concept of spontaneous human combustion, I am not that clever or, arguably, that strange. The idea has been a part of the cultural consciousness for centuries, if not longer. Dickens and Melville wrote about it. One of Spinal Tap's drummers died from it (as did Kenny on *South Park*). I probably first encountered it on *Monty Python's Flying Circus*, when an elderly woman played by Michael Palin spontaneously combusted and John Cleese told his grieving mother, "Don't be so sentimental. Things explode every day."

Forgive me, but I'm about to be sentimental. Because books like this don't happen every day. At least not to me. And this book only exists because of the hard work and kind gestures of the following people:

The ridiculously savvy Michael Bourret, who is patient with my many wild ideas and fiercely supports my wildest ones. He believed in this book from the first mad scribblings.

The inimitably brilliant Julie Strauss-Gabel, who dug through a messy manuscript, discovered what my story was really about, and constantly encouraged me to make it better. It was an honor to work with her and learn from her.

Cover designer Theresa Evangelista and copy editor Anne Heausler, who got this thing all spiffy, beautiful, and readable.

The editorial, design, sales, and marketing teams at Dutton and Penguin Young Readers.

Dana Spector, who saw promise in a handful of pages and took a shot on me.

My cousin Alice Russell, who set me straight on a few things about high school seniors in 2016 (for instance: how the heck Snapchat works).

Mom, Dad, Toril, Tim, Dave, Jake, Will, Gwenn, Jim, and Pete, who appreciate my twisted sense of humor. Most of the time.

My extended family and my many friends who keep on buying and reading my books and showing up to events and tolerating my self-promotion.

Fayetteville Manlius High School's class of 1994. We made it. Now let's make it through a lot more.

Finally, Cate and Hannah, I love you. You are the ones from this book's dedication. You are the ones who comfort me. You are the ones who keep me together.

LOGAN

WE BURIED COLE WESTON LAST NIGHT, on the hundred acres behind Meeka's house.

"Are you sure you want him back here?" I asked her. "Where your parents might snowshoe over him, or something might dig him up? We could still use the firebox."

"This is my choice," Meeka said as she gazed into the waist-deep grave we'd dug on Friday night, out past the orchard and next to the mossy stone wall where Cole had threatened us. "I need to know exactly where he is. If it makes you feel better, you can bury him deeper."

It did make us feel better, and with four digging, we deepened the hole to our ears, very nearly the standard six feet under. Cole's body was encased in a Thule car top carrier. Big enough for an entire family's skis . . . or one teenager. We lifted the makeshift coffin from the tractor and set it next to the grave. I opened it a crack, barely enough to slip in the bag with our old phones, our only links to this, a failsafe if anyone considered betrayal. Then we pushed it into the ground, piled on the dirt and rocks until the hole was full and we could smack it flat with the backs of shovels and kick leaves over the surface.

In silence, with the rest of us standing and clinging to the tractor's frame, Meeka drove back through the mud and dark.

Outside the barn, we stripped off our coveralls and bagged them up with everything else that Grayson would throw in the firebox at his family's sugarhouse. Meeka had filled a pressure sprayer with water and a little bleach and we sprayed down the tractor, and then we all stripped naked and doused each other with the stuff. No one was embarrassed or confused. We were horrified, or at least I was, but not about the nakedness. We'd taken things as far as they could go.

There's a good chance we'll get away with this. A long, snowy winter would help. Plus some time to let it all sink in. It's crazy how fast it's gotten to this point. We're not even into November of our senior year. Up until the end of summer, Cole and Meeka were together. The rest of us were hanging out and hooking up, but they were *serious*. Plural. They spoke in the language of *we*, and about the future.

When we move in together. When we get married. When we have kids.

That third one nearly came true in July. Apparently, there was a broken condom that Cole neglected to mention. A scare. Crying. Arguments about money. And then, four days later than expected, blood. Relief.

By the end of August, the relationship was over. It happened in private. Only the two of them knew what was said, but it was enough to turn them against each other. And Meeka went from planning a future to regretting a past.

That's when Cole got dangerous.

"Are we evil?" Holly asked me last night as we drove away from the barn, the rocks from the dirt road dinging the underside of my Hyundai.

"No," I said. "He was the evil one. Would you have rather it been Meeka? Or us? Or other people?"

"Of course not. And I know, I know, I know we didn't have a choice."

"That's right."

"I know that."

"I doubt I'll sleep for days," I said, flipping on the high beams just as something skittered into the woods in front of us. "I'm not happy about any of this."

"Are you crying?" Holly asked.

"A little."

She was crying too. I could tell from the tremble in her voice. "This will always be a part of us," she said.

"But we'll get over it," I replied.

No one is going to miss Cole. We're counting on that. Sure, he used to have other friends, guys like Gus Drummond, but they don't hang out anymore. He used to have us.

He doesn't even have a family. Ever since his brother, Craig, took off to work the oil fields somewhere in the nowhere of Canada, Cole had been living alone in their trailer. No dad, no mom, no one.

Meeka says the last time Cole talked to his dad was in middle school, when the wispy-bearded guy passed through town on his way from Montreal to Florida. He was driving a pickup with who knows what stashed in the truck box, and he stopped by to tell his sons "not to fuck up your lives like certain people do."

It was a not-so-subtle dig on Cole's mom, Teri. A sweet woman who worked the register at Carlton's Bakery, Teri had struggled with addiction for years. Alcohol and painkillers at first, but by the time we were in high school and stuff like fentanyl was getting big around here, she dove in and never resurfaced. In the winter of our junior year, she passed away. Heart attack was what the obituary said, but we all knew it was the drugs that did her in. She had that bad skin, those mossy teeth, the dead eyes. It was inevitable.

Meeka worked at Carlton's on weekends and had known Teri. Teri had even revealed a secret to her. "*I had another kid*," she whispered early one Sunday morning as they crouched down to fill the display case with chocolate croissants. "When I was a teenager. I gave her up for adoption."

"Wow," Meeka replied. "That must've been . . . difficult."

Teri sat on the floor, stared at the wall, and said, "Tell me it was the right choice."

It was an awkward and unreasonable request, and Meeka was split between two decisions: push the woman away or hug her. She chose to hug, and as Teri wept in her arms, Meeka said, "It was the right choice. Kids like me have it way better than we would've otherwise."

When Teri died, Meeka told us she was surprised by how devastated she felt, so she wrapped her arms around Teri's son. Their grieving bound them together.

Meeka and Cole said they loved each other early and often, but when things got bad, Meeka knew it had never been true. They *needed* each other, maybe. They needed too much of each other, I think. But for different reasons, and that's what really broke them up.

After the breakup, Cole decided to not return to Plainview High for senior year. His grades were terrible, and college didn't seem like an option. He had a bit of money, though. Not from a job, but somehow he was paying for all the computers and gadgets he had stuffed in his trailer. He could afford takeout for almost every meal. Lots of Subway and pizza, but even that adds up after a while.

Cole wasn't dealing—I mean, he saw what drugs did to his mom—so Meeka suspected he was scamming old people out of their money. You know, like those con artists from Russia or Nigeria? Only Cole was smoother. He was fluent in both English and lies. Plus, he was from Vermont, and people naturally trust people from Vermont.

Whenever I was in Cole's trailer, there was this constant humming in the background and lights flickering on the switches of power strips, which were hung from hooks like flowers left to dry. The windows were covered in newspapers to keep the light out and there were always at least three screens glowing. Cole had mountains of tech. I don't know if he knew anything about coding. What he knew was how to find stuff.

He was always keyed into the latest viral video *before* it went viral. "Check this out," he'd say to me, and thrust a laptop in my face, and there would be some weird person yelling, or dancing, or, more often than not, getting hurt. His favorite was this video of a kid singing, "Walk like a man, talk like a man, walk like a man, my son," in the shrillest, most tone-deaf voice imaginable.

"Gets me every fucking time," he'd say, wiping tears from his eyes. It was a bit funny, I guess, but only the first time. After that, it seemed sad.

But it was infinitely better than most of the other things he'd watch. Disturbing stuff. With a few keystrokes, Cole could cue up a video with some shrouded guy chopping off another guy's head in the desert. Or worse, if you can imagine worse, and I hope you can't.

"Look at it, Logan," he'd squeal, chasing me around the trailer with a laptop. "You know you wanna see this shit. You know you want it to haunt your dreams."

I'd close my eyes and try to block out the images of death. My mind couldn't handle stuff like that. So it's fitting, in a way, that it's the image of Cole's dead body that I'll never have the luxury of blocking out. I'll be haunted, like he always wanted me to be. But trust me, I'd be more haunted if he had lived.